Readers love STOLEN FUTURES Past Rising:

"A page turner, the plot of this series just gets more and more interesting and extreme."
— Angus Stephens, Putney, England

"I enjoyed the third installment of *Stolen Futures*. It has so many twists and turns right up until the end; I couldn't put the book down. Great Sci-Fi read."
— Stéphane Fesnoux, Epsom, England

"An enthralling continuation of the Arkonauts' adventure as they resume their journey across space in search of a new hope - engaging from start to finish!"
— Beki Swinfield, Surrey, England

STOLEN FUTURES

PAST RISING

M. Drewery

edited by

NATE RAGOLIA

SPACEBOY BOOKS

Denver, Colorado

Published in the United States by:
Spaceboy Books LLC
1627 Vine Street
Denver, CO 80206
www.readspaceboy.com

Cover Art features Creative Commons Public Domain image by
Tithi Luadthong via Shutterstock | Twitter: @TLuadthong | Instagram:
grandfailure9 | https://tithi-luadthong.pixels.com/profiles/tithi-
luadthong

First printed October 2021

ISBN: 978-1-951393-12-0

To my family and friends who have encouraged me on my writing journey.

This book is also dedicated to Nic Bianchi, a good friend who helped with the edits and made this a better story

THE NEW FUTURE

Since awakening in the future, I had met only two humans. One stood beside me, the other was sealed in a cage before me, which I and the other aliens had hastily repaired. A creature from your worst nightmares once occupied it, so we were confident it would hold him, despite the crude welds.

His dark skin that we could see on his face, neck and upper arms was pockmarked with various ports, and in places bulging with technology just beneath the surface. His hair was short. His nose had been broken. There was a short, straight scar over the bridge. Something about him was very familiar.

Since this human had been helping the Thieves trying to recapture us, and take our Destroyer from us, we felt it prudent to keep him contained. Despite being, you know, a member of my species that I thought was all gone.

Human might not have been the right word for him though. His legs and lower torso were a tangled mess of tentacles—that's why we had thought he was a Thief of some kind. They were mostly giant octopuses or squid with cybernetics inserted into their bodies.

Ada and I stood together outside his cell peering in.

"Right, I have another theory," I declared.

"This should be good," Ada replied, rolling her eyes.

"The Thieves decided to clone humans, possibly from my DNA or yours," I suggested. "They were using them as cannon fodder."

Ada shook her head slightly.

1

"No?" I asked.

"Your attempts to come up with an alternative to reality are getting worse, more convoluted and sillier," she replied.

I sighed, so far she had objected to the following: 1. The Thief just really looked human, 2. Humans were actually not from Earth, but another planet in league with the Thieves and that Earth was an ancient colony of humans, and 3. The clone idea I had just pitched.

"Face it Callum, there can be only one reason we stand before another human. When you altered the past, you saved the crew. The Arkonauts then somehow encountered the Thieves and became a part of their society. This man is clearly one of their descendants. The Thieves must have discovered the Ark and the Arkonauts, and made humans part of their culture for whatever reason. The Arkonauts and Thieves must have chosen to put my pod in that museum sometime afterward."

"Why would they put you in a museum? You're a part of the crew too."

Ada squirmed a little and looked away from me. "Well not quite human," she replied. "Kind of like One."

"What happened to One? Why did the crew do this? Why would the Thieves do this?" I asked.

"When he wakes up we'll have to ask him," Ada said.

"Do you think he will tell us?" I asked.

The man's eyes then opened.

I realised something in that moment. My enhanced senses were picking up something from him. I could smell what my brain was telling me was fear, confusion. I could never do that before. I turned my head towards Ada and sniffed, nothing from her, she didn't seem to smell at all, except for a metallic tinge which I assumed was the gun she kept by her side.

Somehow, though, I could sense this man's emotions, wafting through the air as a smell. His heartbeat was quickening. My eyes were also lightly detecting traces of changes to his body heat. I wondered if I had to learn how to use my new body, maybe perfect its capabilities.

He was lying down on the floor of the cage and I noticed that he was trying to move, however we had removed all the power from his mechanical tentacles.

It did not stop him though.

Around where his arms and legs turned into multiple whip-like limbs the machines came apart, retracting, revealing the man's real arms and legs beneath. His limbs had not been replaced by the tentacles, just wrapped up in them.

His arms—indeed the rest of his body—was still heavily encrusted with cybernetic enhancements. Bits and pieces of metal poked out of his flesh, like he had been caught in an explosion at the electronics section of a Walmart.

He stood up, liberating himself from the tentacles that had formally been his arms and legs. He pulled wires free from his extremities to fully disconnect his body from the cybernetics.

He then stepped out and away from the body-horror suit he had been wearing and walked up to the edge of his cell.

I smelt that he was wary of us and his eyes appraised both me and Ada carefully. I heard the whirling of camera lenses; it was coming from his eyes. His teeth were all gold and his hair was actually fake fibre optic cables pulsating with multi-coloured lights.

His evaluation of us appeared to come to an end because he stood up straight, smiled warmly then said, "Hello, my name is Ogwambi. Thank you for freeing me."

My mouth dropped and I looked at Ada, and her left eyebrow raised.

She said, "Ok, maybe not descended from the Arkonauts, but I was still right."

THE PAST

1
LONG WAY DOWN

I lugged my hoover up to the top of the engine room, fresh from a shift of cleaning it for the last four hours.

It was not unpleasant work, despite its monotonous nature. Hoovering was one of those chores that was particularly pleasant as the results of your work were easily seen. I had often been given it as a task in my parent's home, to earn a little pocket money. Running our highly powerful Dyson over the carpet, hearing the little flecks of food get sucked up, or watching the dog hair disappear, was strangely satisfying.

And so it was with this job. Every day the engine accumulated particles on its surface, tiny crystals would grow everywhere and we had to make sure they did not build up. The engine hung from the ceiling like an upside-down skyscraper. Multi-coloured energy patterns toiled and shifted within and the light from that energy fractured into multi-coloured displays around the engine room. The hoover sucked up the crystals on the surface with ease and every day I ended my shift with feelings of a job well done.

Then, with the business of the day over, my mind would start thinking of the past again and my day would get worse.

I stowed the hoover in an alcove at the top of the engine and logged my activity with Moana who was running the engine room today.

"Thanks, Maiara," she said.

"No problem," I mumbled, not meeting her big, hazel eyes or returning her warm smile.

I backed away before she could say anything more, forcing her to move on to the next person in line behind me.

I strolled away along the gangplanks and lent on the handrail staring down at the engine.

My jaw clenched as I looked down and my stomach tightened. Down there was where Callum had died. Where my attempt to push him clear of a bullet had failed, where I had failed. That memory clawed at my brain like a spider striding around in my skull. I wanted to smash my head and pull it out and kill it.

Then as it always did, my thoughts of Callum's death moved onto more troubling memories. Of a screaming alien, of his fear and my guilt as my hand released his neck from my grip and he tumbled into the maw of a beast. From that, a new feeling, not clawing at my brain, but a pressure from my forehead boring into my mind and the feelings of glee...*NO!* I cursed my thoughts and buried them again, not wishing to feel what was so shameful.

But it was still there, the truth I had not shared that I dare not share, and not even voice to myself.

I needed to cleanse it from my mind.

I looked to my left. The hanging walkway I was on continued another ten feet and then stopped. It didn't lead anywhere; it had been hastily installed by humans and left incomplete. A single bar went across its width, preventing someone from walking off the end where they would fall fifty or so stories to the bottom of the engine.

All it would take is just to raise that bar, I thought.

"Hello Maiara," Ogwambi said, leaning down on the walkway next to me.

"Hello Ogwambi," I replied, although there was very little politeness in my tone.

He failed to pick up on it.

"The cinema is playing the thirty-fifth Marvel film tonight. You coming?"

"Thirty-fifth? Which one was that again?" I asked.

"*Avengers vs X-Men*," he replied.

I shrugged. "Why not. I always liked Hope Summers."

"Nerd," he said, after a little giggle.

I rolled my eyes, "Like you don't know all the characters," I replied.

"Moana does and she tells me even if I don't want to know."

"How are you two getting along?" I asked. "Has she finished her new room yet?"

Not that long ago the floor beneath mine and Moana's rooms collapsed—chalked up to bad welding when the Ark was rebuilt. We both lost our sanctums and had to relocate to new ones.

"We retrieved all her furniture and rebuilt most of it," Ogwambi said.

"With what?" I asked.

"We raided a supply of nails in the cargo bay."

"Nails? Dr. Ghost provided us with nails?"

"Yes, probably to help us build homes when we land on our new world. What about your replacement room?"

I went silent, picturing my domicile, which was blank and bare. The only things of mine were a potted plant, some clothes, and a vial of nanites.

"I'll decorate it when I'm ready," I said.

"Do you want a ha—?"

"When I'm ready," I repeated.

He smiled, nodded then walked off to help Moana.

No one else approached me. Maybe it was a **do not disturb field** I projected out from myself as I stared at the engine.

I sighed, loudly and purposefully, despite myself. I wanted people to hear, but at the same time I didn't want them to do anything about it. I think I just wanted them to know I was sad, that I was still being punished—For what though? The pain flared in my head again, as did the alien's scream, the chomp, the glee—*no keep it down Maiara. Don't acknowledge it.*

I went back to thinking of Callum. The sadness of his death was strangely comforting because it also triggered memories of love and affection, of his soft lips and his bravery. Not the firing a gun kind of bravery, the ability to face mistakes kind of bravery.

What would he have thought of me? I gasped and put my hand to my mouth in fear. The awful thought that he would be ashamed of me, tore at my heart. If he knew, if anyone knew what I had truly thought about Turso's death.

I had failed.

Failed to live up to everything my parents had taught me to be.

Failed to make the right choice even though I had screamed at myself to make it.

Failed to be a decent human being.

I was a murderer.

A failure.

I turned again towards the edge of the railing.

I walked down; behind me the voices of my friends didn't change they didn't call out to me.

With each step I told myself, *This is it. This is how you do it. It won't hurt too much.*

It's the right thing to do, the right punishment.

I reached the bar. It was not welded on, merely slotted in with a hinge at one end. Maybe it was supposed to be connected to another walkway, but someone never got around to doing it. For a moment I smiled to myself for caring about it, or even wondering why it was like this when it didn't matter. Finding a small moment of fun at my weird stupidity in this serious moment. Maybe it was an attempt to step back?

I lifted the bar and in front of me was a void, one more step and I would be free.

Finally, I would have paid the price, and everyone would know.

I closed my eyes. My right legs twitched; I couldn't will it to take the final step.

An updraft of air flooded my nose with particles from the engine, they stung my nostrils, I rocked back a little.

A sign to back away? But this is the only way. The only way.

I closed my tear-filled eyes, and my hands gripped the railing out of their own accord, a survival instinct kicking in.

Inside my chest I felt a growing desire to leap building, roaring within me.

I knew it was only a matter of time. At some point I would break and go and then it wouldn't matter. On my way down I might feel fear, and then maybe joy that I done what needed to be done to purge myself of my mistakes.

"Maiara?" Moana cried out.

I looked over my shoulder.

She and Ogwambi were standing there. Their muscles were tense yet they were standing in a relaxed pose. Ogwmabi had his hands loosely in his pockets. Moana's hands were on the rail like she was leaning on it casually, however her fingers didn't grip the metal bar—they were ready to move.

"Come on, the film starts in ten minutes," Ogwambi said.

I looked into his eyes. I could tell he knew what I intended.

My gaze flickered to the rest of the Arkonauts, standing behind the pair. All of them froze as they looked at me, their eyes wide, paused in their actions, their feet turning towards me slowly.

"Come on, Maiara," Moana said as cheerfully as she could sound.

My cheeks flushed red, embarrassment flooded over me. *What was everyone thinking? How were they judging me?*

"Come back. I mean... Come on, let's go see the film," Moana said.

I turned away from the chasm my, head bowed.

No. I needed to do this.

I wasn't worth saving.

I turned back to the void.

The walkway rattled as Ogwambi and Moana practically dived for me, and grabbed my arms then dragged me down onto the floor.

I tried to pull away, but I couldn't I closed my eyes and cried.

I hoped nobody would look at me. I hoped they would all walk away and leave me to wallow in this weirdly comforting sadness, this deserved sorrow.

Instead, Ogwambi and Moana gripped me tighter.

Another Arkonaut I couldn't see through the blurry haze of tears dropped the bar back into place.

I wouldn't be ending my life today. I wondered if it would be my last attempt. I glimpsed the sliver of red on my wrist, and quickly covered it with my sleeve.

Moana hugged me tight. Ogwambi rested a hand on my shoulder.

"Get One," I heard him whisper to another Arkonaut.

What could he do? I thought.

Nothing, I realised.

2

THE SHRINK

Humanity had made many robots before its homeworld was destroyed, and many of the different types ended up on the Ark. The robot sitting next to me right now was the only one of its kind on board.

The sofa I was sitting on was extremely comfortable, perhaps the most comfortable on the whole ship.

I told the robot sitting beside me exactly that.

I told it about the way my back was fully and gently supported by the foam stuffed into the cushions.

"Maiara, please," the robot said in Texas accent that was comforting and familiar. I wondered if it had put it on for me, or if it was because it had been built in the good old U. S. of A.

"Can I have this sofa for my room? It's not like there are any other Arkonauts who will need it," I replied.

"Maiara, this is not what I am here for," the robot repeated.

I sighed and just stared at the ceiling with my hands interlocked on my stomach.

"I cost one hundred thousand American dollars to build. I am top of the line. You can talk to me," the robot said.

I turned my head and looked the robot in the face. Like most robots it did not have a human face, mostly because the uncanny valley had never been scaled, and robot design was therefore geared to merely be functional. This robot had a smooth head and its only facial features were a pair of black, horn-rimmed glasses. There were no eyes behind the glasses.

Weirdly, I was comforted by that lack of a face, but I did wonder how it could see me.

"What do I call you again?" I asked.

"Doctor, will be fine or Doc," the Doctor replied.

One of its most distinguishing features was a red jewel on its chest.

"What's that for?" I asked.

The robot looked down, "That's my holographic projector, it allows me to change into the visage of another person." The jewel glowed red and the robot was replaced with a projection of a random woman that covered its body.

"Do you prefer this appearance?" it asked.

"No... That's weird."

The robot turned off its projector.

"What else can you do?" I asked.

"I have the latest nanite repair systems. They can rebuild me as long as they themselves are not destroyed. I could survive being hit by multiple bullets for example... Now, shall we talk about..."

"You have some packing material in your leg," I said, interrupting it and gesturing toward a piece of polystyrene in its leg joint, then I turned back to the ceiling.

I heard the polystyrene squeak as it was removed from the gap in the Doctor's joints.

"Perhaps now we could talk about your day yesterday?"

"Do you think there was maybe some sort of incident that triggered me?" I asked, through gritted teeth.

"No."

"Do you think I was having an old Vietnam War flashback?" I said, and chuckled.

"No," the doctor replied.

"Then why ask?"

"Why do you think?"

"I think you want me to talk about what I tried to do, without making me want to do it again."

"Exactly," the doctor replied. "I want you to be comfortable talking about the event without shame or embarrassment."

"Shame? Well, that's what I feel Doc. I've been granted a gift, one that billions didn't receive, something I squandered. Of course I feel a little shame."

"That's not wh—"

"Maybe you're right. Maybe the shame isn't that. Maybe it's because I know that Callum, my loving boyfriend from the future, chose to save us all and I'm throwing that away too by trying to kill myself."

"That's no—"

"Maybe you're right. Maybe the shame is because I tried to do something no one else is considering on this ship. I must stand out, therefore I must feel incredible amounts of shame at being so pathetic as to end my life, in front of a crowd... who would have been traumatised by the whole thing."

"That's—"

"Is that the shame you want me to talk about?" I asked.

"No," the doc said, and it tapped its notebook with its pen, a gesture I knew to be programmed... Or was it?

"What do you want to talk to me about?"

"I want you to talk about the bottom of the engine room," the doctor said.

"You mean where I would have landed if I did jump?" I asked.

"Maiara, I wasn't just pulled out of storage. You should know I was updated with reports from Two. I received an update before she was put into stasis to heal. I want you to tell me what happened at the base of the engine room."

I went silent. In my head I fought the desire to say anything, yet the crushing boredom of having those eyeless glasses staring at me was grating. If I waited this hour-long session would pass without another word, I could leave safe in the knowledge I had seen out my prescribed time.

Unfortunately, the doctor didn't have the patience to wait like I thought it did.

"Please tell me what happened at the base of the engine room?"

I glanced at the clock. I still had forty-five minutes left.

I shuffled on my bed and turned over facing the wall.

"I closed the hatch after getting rid of Turso," I said.

There was silence for a moment. "What does 'getting rid' of mean in this instance?"

I scrunched up my eyes as a pain started to build behind my forehead.

"You know, I think I'm getting a headache. I should go to the medical bay," I said.

"What does 'getting rid' of mean, Maiara?"

I rocked a little then said. "It means... murdered," I replied.

I then rolled back and sat up.

"I killed him," I said.

"You said 'murder' the first time," Doc said.

My eyes darted around as I replayed the previous conversation.

"I did," I said.

The robot didn't fill the silence.

"I did say I murdered him?"

"I thought that Turso had killed Callum?" the robot said.

"He did, not directly, but it was all because of him."

"Then surely it was a kind of justice," Doc said.

"I thought I had already dealt with this?" Maiara said.

"Dealt with what?"

"I spoke to Two after it happened. How I relinquished my hold on Turso..." I stretched out my arm and held it with my fist close. "I told her about it. I admitted my mistake."

"I know." Doc said.

I opened my hand.

"Surely, I should be over this? I know what I did. I accepted it, why does it still haunt me."

"Maybe that is not what bothers you."

"It must be," I lied, and lay down again.

"Did you discuss this with the other Arkonauts?" Doc asked.

I shook my head.

Doc paused for a moment, I heard the whirling of hard drives in its head and chest.

"I asked you for a medical history when you came in."

"I remember. I've got to say, reciting those things to a robot was much easier than to a human, since you don't feel anything."

"There was a question I neglected to ask. One ordered me to never pursue it. However, when it comes to the health of my patients that takes precedence. Tell me about your 18th memory."

"The 18th? What about it?" I asked.

"Did you have yours reactivated?"

I mused on the 18th for a moment. It was a secret injection of nanites, put in our minds by Dr. Ghost on top of the previous seventeen we had officially received. It was meant to keep us together, to give us a perspective that allowed us to get along, despite our huge differences. We had elected to switch it off when Callum told us about it, then I realised we needed it and implored the crew to reactivate it again.

"I did," I replied.

"Oh, sorry then it can't be—"

"But it didn't take," I cut in.

"It didn't take?"

"I felt it reactivate, then about an hour later it shut down again. I didn't tell One, but I snuck into the medical bay later that evening and asked a medical droid to tell me what happened. It said the nanite memory was degraded. I'm... no longer like the rest of the crew," I said.

"I'm sure you're not alone. Others would have chosen to reject the memory," the doctor said, taking its glasses off and wiping them with a handkerchief it pulled out of a compartment on its upper chest.

"No. You see, the device One used to reactivate the nanites was in the medical bay and it keeps a record of all the deactivations and reactivations it performs. I opened up its memory and took a look. They all reactivated their 18th. I'm the only one who didn't, I'm the only

Arkonaut that thinks like humanity used to think. I'm the only human left who can murder, who thinks of revenge. I'm no longer what an Arkonaut should be."

Silence fell on our little session.

"I see," Doc said. "Tell me, do you think of those things—murder, revenge—all the time?"

I rolled onto my side to look at the robot's blank face. "Of course not."

"So you're not obsessed with murder and revenge then?" it asked.

"No."

"Why then do you let these thoughts disturb you? You may not have this memory, but it doesn't define you, it never did before?"

"Of course not, but before I was just a normal teenage girl—a Texan who's also Apache—but just a girl."

"Then why dwell on what is in the past? Why did you keep coming back to it?"

"My mother used to tell me all about her tribe. She would have been mortified to forget about the past, of her family and their ancestors, especially when they had lost so much. Forgetting the past doesn't come easy to my family."

"That's history. Not feelings of revenge of hatred and anger... What are you angry about?" Doc asked.

I rolled away from the machine and faced the wall.

"Maiara?"

A thought tugged at my mind as the robot spoke. A feeling flooded through me every time I replayed the death of the alien that I had purposefully killed.

"I killed Turso. I purposefully made sure he would die. It was a line I never thought I would cross," I answered.

For a moment some pressure in my head was alleviated. I had admitted something and it was no longer a burden, but it was only the surface of the thought, a fraction of the burden.

"What line?"

I went no further. I kept the burden. I decided to start lying. I decided to not tell the whole truth, hoping that would be enough to exercise the thought I would not give voice to.

"Do you understand sin?" I asked the robot.

"A robot has no need for such things. Sin is a choice; robots are programmed?"

"Well sin is something all humans do. We always do bad stuff and usually when we are tempted to do a bad thing, doing it again is easier. I crossed the line for committing murder, the next time will be easier. Then again and again until maybe I'll just be able to kill with impunity. What if I can't stop? Then I have to face the fact that the Arkonauts are—in a way—without sin from now on. They have accepted something that will bind them together. I don't have that."

For a moment a memory flashed through my mind, the memory of letting Turso go, crossing that line. Like a dagger to my heart, there was something else—not just the guilt, not just the sin of choosing to drop him. Tears welled up in my eyes and I covered them with the palms of my hands.

"I wish I was dead. I am now the worst remaining human. I will always be like this. I see a dark future for myself. I failed."

"Failed? Failed whom?" Doc asked.

I said nothing for a moment. "Did you ever see the speech the Vice President gave?" I asked.

"He gave many speeches," the robot said.

"The one he gave when the Ark was raised."

"Why does it make you think you've failed?"

"Let me tell you about it."

THE SPEECH

At the time, I couldn't believe what I was seeing.

As the American representative, I flew with the Vice President's entourage to the launch. My parents came too. I sat on one of those lush helicopters the President flew in. But the President wasn't here, not that I cared. He was kind of a buffoon, keen to play golf rather than run the country. He called it projecting calmness, but it was really an excuse. So the Vice President was the one making this speech, a formality really, before the Ark was raised into orbit... before being used as a missile.

However, I knew different. The Ark was not going into orbit to be dropped onto the Destroyer. No it was being raised to get out of reach of those who might try to use it to escape the planet, to await my arrival and the others destined to be saved.

As sad and, I guess, despicable as that lie was, I didn't dwell on it and instead was amazed at the sight that greeted me as the helicopter landed on a platform attached to a mountain several miles from the Ark.

I am only one of two future crew members of the Ark to see this. The other would be the Icelandic representative, who must have seen this ship the day it landed on the horizon, as a boat took him away from his country.

The Ark sat like a dark pyramid surrounded by pools of lava. Its landing had cracked two tectonic plates brutally apart and magma had burst forth. The ship looked like the evil fortress of a dark wizard.

The helicopter's engines wound down and everyone began disembarking.

Some celebrities who had given money to the Vice President and President's campaign were present, along with other foreign dignitaries. I must have been the only one in clothing that cost less than a thousand dollars, more like fifty in my case, and these were my best clothes.

My parents ushered me away from the helipad. We walked across a gang way to a tiered seating platform facing the Ark, which dominated the horizon.

We joined a queue to take our seats. I stamped my feet to try and stay warm, and even rubbed my shoulders.

I stared at the ship that would soon be my home. I had mixed feelings, to say the least. The idea that soon I would be teleported aboard still failed to penetrate my mind. Sometimes it seemed laughable.

As my thoughts drifted away from the moment, I became aware that my family was being surrounded. Tall men in long dark coats circled them, looking outwards, studying everyone present.

The circle parted and entering this little isolated area was the Vice President himself.

I actually took a step back and bumped up against my parents, whose jaws dropped.

The real leader of our country—the one darting all around the U.S.A., holding everything together—was right before me. He was tall, with hair that said he was equally a working man, yet refined. He was young for a Vice President, only in his late-forties, still broad at the shoulders and thin around the waist.

"Mr. Vice President," my dad managed to blurt out.

The Vice President beamed at my father and reached out to shake his hand, timed and delivered to be forceful yet not dominating.

He stepped away and then looked down at me.

"Hello Maiara. How are you?"

It seemed like a genuine question, not a short conversation starter.

"Apprehensive," I managed to say.

"I'm glad you choose to come, and I wanted to meet you face-to-face and shake your hand."

He reached out with a giant hand, which I took, and he shook slowly, measured like he was savouring this moment, like I was the most important person in the country, which technically I was.

He then looked around, and then bent down a little.

"You will be the last American, Maiara. I wanted to meet you and pass on my thanks. I know you will do us all proud."

He gave me a slight smile twinned with a sad nod and walked away. His secret service detailed followed and he was joined by a blond, bored looking girl inspecting her fingernails.

I was suddenly overcome by the burden that had been put on my shoulders.

The last American, I thought.

My parents then ushered me into my seat. I got there almost on autopilot and sat down.

In front of the grandstand was a small podium and the Vice President took his place there.

Several cameras focused in on him. Big screens set off to the sides of the stage captured him on camera and perfectly framed him with the Ark in the background.

At the time I didn't realise that it was a useless speech, a sort of noble lie, I guess.

"People of the world," he began. "The time has come. Today we raise our hope into the heavens, to use a righteous spear into the Destroyer that steals away our very lives.

"Never before in human history has the combined efforts of so many worked to achieve a single moment. Resources from all over the world have built this ship back to working order. Workers from across the world have come to build our vengeance, and knowledge has been shared from around the world to make this a reality. If we had not come together we would be guaranteed a mutually assured destruction. But we were not selfish, and all this is only possible because of selfless sacrifice."

He paused and grabbed the podium in both hands, nodding at the crowd and to the whole planet.

"We thought we had lost this war. It almost seemed like our dream of a bright future for humanity had died. We worried we were unable to prevent the

Destroyer from its terrible work, but now we have a chance, and ironically, we are using the power of our enemy against them.

"This vessel," and he turned to gesture to the Ark. "Will be launched into orbit carefully. Then it will be used as a missile that will crack that thief wide open and restore to this planet to life.

"I am only one man out of billions, one human, one person, and I give you all my thanks for making this possible. You have sacrificed so much to save me and the life of my family in this moment."

He gestured to a woman and the blond girl who had been following him. His wife smiled and straightened up. The girl had to hastily put away the phone she was swiping through when the cameras turned to them.

I wondered if I was the only one who noticed this, but his smile looked amazingly genuine, no hint of a typical politician trying to trick the masses. I knew that he knew he was lying, that his family would not be going on the Ark. Yet here he was, projecting an air of dignity and faith in the Ark that was untrue.

I had to admire him because he held it together. He probably had convinced the whole world that he had no doubt the Ark would do its job. The people would believe him and that would allow me and hundreds like me to be saved. He was doing what needed to be done.

"We have all sacrificed and worked hard for each other to save all our families," he continued. "I think it goes without saying that when this great endeavour is done we will finally work together to end the conflicts that have separated us for so long. When we regain the water the Destroyer has stolen, we will give it back to world and rebuild after this awful calamity."

There were cheers in the crowd, I wondered if people were cheering in the homes of those watching.

"We are sending a message today that will show that these larcenous beings," he pointed at the Ark, "will not bring us down. We may fall, but we always rise again and again and again."

The cheer was louder than before.

The Vice President stepped a little to the side and raised a palm towards the Ark.

"And now we embark on our victory, victory over doubts, victory over despair, victory over our terror—however long and hard the road may be."

And then, timed beautifully, the Ark's engines came online.

They did not fully activate, for such a pulse of energy would surely cause all the volcanoes around the world to erupt as one. Instead the Ark rose slowly into the air. Magma slid off its sides as it rose. The mountain we were on vibrated as the engines blasted fire into the mantle. No doubt these earthquakes would cause problems, but not too many. It was the cost of getting our salvation into the sky.

Everyone in the crowd craned their necks upwards to watch the ship rise. It didn't take long for the base of the vessel, once embedded in our planet, to emerge shooting purple fire into the Earth like a slow rocket. Secondary thrusters on the upper pyramid kept the whole thing steady as it soared upwards.

People clapped and cheered. Others put their hands together and bowed in reverence.

I watched impassive, mulling on the words of the Vice President. I looked back at him, and he was staring at me.

He nodded of his head. He then stepped close to the podium; the roar of the Ark was lessening now as it soared miles into the sky.

"When this is done, we must stay together, and that will require sacrifice. It require us all to be better people than we were before," he said, his eyes lingering on me through the whole sentence.

He then addressed everyone. "For what is victory if it is not earned with grace and humility? Without those admirable traits, any win will be bitter, and we will question whether or not we deserved it at all. Do not let this go to waste."

The Vice President finished on those words, and then looked up as the Ark grew smaller and smaller, taking its place in orbit.

He meant those words for me. I was supposed to take those words—the substance of his speech—and live by them.

I felt I could, for to do otherwise would be a grave dishonour.

3

THE CHALLENGE

"Tell me why you think you've failed?" the doc asked again, once I had finished the story.

"I am no longer like the rest of the crew. I no longer have the 18th memory, the way forward for all of us. I am now so different, I cannot stand beside them."

"Maiara, you only have an experience they do not have, that doesn't make you less than them," the doc said.

"I killed because I wanted to," I said. "I let down the Vice President and all those people and my family... I—" I nearly continued, I nearly admitted more.

"You what?" Doc asked.

I rolled onto my side to face away from the robot. I felt the cold tears run down my face and darken the fabric I lay on.

There was a pause then the doc said, "Do you really want to die? Tell me right now. Do you want it to go dark?"

I rolled over again to face him, surprised by its bluntness.

"Dark?"

"Do you want to feel the agony of death? Do you want to become deaf and blind to the world as you slip into the next?"

I stared into space for a moment, imagining it all going dark, imagining the pain, the sense of my lungs crying for air that I couldn't draw into my body.

"No."

"Then I don't think you want to die. What you want is hope, hope that something will change," the doctor said. "Maiara, I want you to do something for me between now and our next session in a few days. I have an exercise for you."

I sniffed, "Ok."

"Every time there is a chance for fun, take it, take every offer from a crewmate to have fun and try to enjoy it. Try to focus on the feeling you have when you do, and when we see each other again tell me if you always want to feel that way. You get to choose how you feel, not the world around you."

"But I did something horrible," I whispered.

"You did. Yet you have to realise that what the Arkonauts are now is something you can be too. Death is not the answer for you, and you have to find out what is, by yourself.

"Please do this exercise over the next couple of days and come and back tell me how you feel."

I spun on the sofa and dangled my legs over the side, and nodded at the robot.

"Good. Thank you, Maiara, for attending this session."

Doc then reached around to the back of its neck and pressed something there, then instantly it powered down and fell silent. Even the motors in its limbs whirred to a stop.

I waved a hand in front of its face, then shrugged, and made for the door.

Before I left the room, I turned back and asked, "What do I do about —" but I would need to wait for my next appointment. So I left, heading for my room.

4
THE WORMHOLE

It was weird knowing that everyone was keeping an eye on me. Everywhere I went I got those looks, you know, where people are both happy to see you yet deeply concerned.

I felt their stares in the back of my head wherever I went.

I had been moved from working in the engine room back into the control centre. It was not fun being there. I had already had my fill of constant status checks and course checks and filing other Arkonauts' check reports.

I thought might kill myself out of sheer boredom. It's okay for me to joke about that. I am clinically depressed.

But at least one day spent in the control room was going to be fun, because today was the day we were finally entering the wormhole.

The wormhole had been discovered on the edge of the solar system around about the time we gained control of the Ark. We used the Ark's superior computer and sensor systems to scan the area of space around Earth.

Before the Destroyer, the Ark was going to tour the solar system, as part of an international scientific expedition. That never happened of course.

When Dr. Ghost realised that the Ark would instead have to be used as a city-sized life raft for some of the remaining people of Earth, he sent probes to the wormhole and discovered a habitable planet on the other side. And it was far closer than any the Ark could reach with its limited power, without the use of a tunnel through space.

It had been our goal since the beginning of this mission to reach it, and now, here we were a few minutes away.

It was, in many crew members' minds, the halfway point of our journey even though it was more like two thirds. Once we were through, it was only a short distance to the new homeworld.

I wondered what it would be like. Would it do weird things to our bodies? Would we get weird powers like the *Fantastic Four?* Who knows? No biological life had even entered the wormhole until now.

A stillness had fallen over the ship.

I was sitting at my station in the control centre. Through cameras around the ship, I could see that the theatre had a few people in it, as did the engine room. There were even a few in the water pumping station.

The engine room needed a full shift in case the wormhole did strange things to the power systems that needed to be corrected. The water pumping station needed to be manned in case any turbulence caused the pipework to become loose and we needed to plug any leaks. Arkonauts everywhere else got to watch our journey though the wormhole on screens.

I finished the last sensor sweep I had to do and decided to sit back and stare up at the dome above me. The entire ceiling of the control room was a giant screen and on it was the wormhole, a spherical ball of distorted light, like a pimple on the skin of the universe.

We were just a few minutes away, when One activated the intercom.

"Batten down the hatches everybody. The countdown to entry is five minutes away," he said, and his voice echoed in the corridors outside.

One then turned to us in the control centre. "I want you all scanning the wormhole as we go. Let me know of anything you see that is out of the ordinary. The 8th memory you received from the astrophysicist will tell you what to look out for."

"Are we going to be doing any course corrections while inside the wormhole?" Sanna asked.

"Hopefully not. In some sense we'll be along for the ride once we enter. On the other side we will have to fire the engines again," One said.

"Do we have the power for that?" I asked.

"We do, however, this will be the last time, which is why we will take a week to calculate it."

"A week?" Illarion asked.

"We have to be sure that the course is correct. Any remaining power will be used to slow us down when we reach the planet, and power the kinetic dampening field when we land on the new homeworld."

The kinetic dampening field was technically a shield that enveloped the Ark when it landed. It had the ability to absorb the energy of the giant ship impacting a planet. The ship did this to aid its landing, but also to prevent massive devastation on the world it was landing on. Since its function was to suck up water, the aliens who built it didn't want the vessel to impact Earth like a comet and flash boil all the water it was supposed to suck up. The dampening field prevented it.

"One minute left, One," Carlton said.

"Enjoy the ride everyone," One said, and he stood in the centre of the room, and looked up at the dome.

The wormhole now filled the giant viewscreen. In a few seconds we were going in.

Even though we were entering a phenomenon of extraordinary cosmic might and radiance, I felt nothing. I guess the moment had been sapped of its power and majesty.

The clock hit zero.

The sphere that was the entrance to the wormhole twisted and distorted as we entered and soon became a literal tunnel.

The sides rotated around us and were awash with nebula, stars and other space things I didn't know the names for.

"Do you feel that?" Sanna asked.

"What?"

"That vibration," she said. "I can feel it through my chair."

I stared into space and sure enough, through my butt, I could feel a low level vibration in the cushion covering my chair.

"That's nice," I joked.

"One, I'm feeling something through my chair," Sanna reported.

"Don't worry, this will be the extent of what we feel. The ship's so large and the hull is so thick we're barely impacted by the turbulence of the wormhole," One said.

"Hey look," Luciana said from her chair, and pointed ahead of the ship as it travelled through the wormhole.

Everyone in the room turned their heads toward where she was pointing. On the surface in the inside of the tunnel was another sphere much like the entrance to the wormhole.

"That's another wormhole," Illarion said.

"A wormhole inside a wormhole?" I exclaimed.

"That means this tunnel through space is connected to another tunnel through space," Sanna said.

"Like a highway! Is this wormhole part of a network?" Luciana replied.

"A fascinating possibility, however now is not the time for us to investigate," One reminded us.

"I guess we'll never know," Sanna said. "By the time humanity builds a space-faring civilisation again, we'll be long dead."

"Cheery," Luciana commented.

"I mean just think, we're seeing all this stuff, but we'll never know what it all is. This trip is giving us more questions than answers," Sanna added.

I pressed a few buttons on my console and the external cameras focused on the new wormhole as we passed by.

"Then get a good look now," I said.

We all watched the new spherical entrance to the wormhole as we passed by. It looked like a soap bubble alone on the surface of a pond.

Then, bursting out of the bubble, came several tentacles.

5
THE UNINVITED GUEST

"What in the fresh hell is that?" Luciana asked.

The tentacles writhed over one another piercing the skin of the bubble like a sea anemone tasting the water before fully emerging.

"Who knows," One replied.

I focused more cameras on the tentacles just in time to see a squid-like organism follow its tentacles out of the second wormhole and join ours. It was like a cuttle fish only it didn't have a fleshy exterior it was armoured and it had a row of eyes along its top and bottom.

It followed in the ship's wake. Cruising through the wormhole chasing us.

"That's a space-born lifeform," One said.

"A what?" Illarion asked.

"A creature that lives in space," One clarified.

"How big is it?" Illarion asked.

I keyed some commands into the computer and answered. "About the size of a small ferry."

"It must live in the wormhole," One said.

The creature picked up speed and started to catch up to us.

"If it lives in the wormhole, does that mean we're in its territory?" Sanna asked.

"You're saying it might see us as a threat?" Luciana asked.

"Either that or..." Sanna said, but trailed off, not wanting to voice the other possibility.

"Either way it's no threat to us, this ship is many times its size and inedible," One said. "Also, we're not that kind of vessel," he added to general laughter.

We watched the creature close in on us. It sped past the engines glowing at the bottom of the hull, and up the side of the lower section—a mere kilometre from the hull.

"Can you believe that there are creatures that live in space?" Luciana said.

"Amazing," Carlton added.

The creature continued to move up the hull, then suddenly it shot away then shot back in, its tentacles splaying wide as it struck the Ark.

The force of the impact rippled through the giant ship as it struck, there was a groan of metal.

"Report," One cried out, as even he had to put out his arms to balance himself.

"The creature has latched onto the hull," Illarion said.

I moved cameras on the outside of the ship around to show him.

"One, it's over an airlock on the south side of the Ark," Illarion added.

"Can we get rid of it?" I asked.

"The Ark has no means to remove it. We will exit the wormhole soon. Hopefully it will let go then," One said as calmly as he could, but I could see that he was sweating. No doubt Dr. Ghost had given him no nanite memories that could prepare him for this eventuality.

"One, the airlock is opening," Illarion reported.

"What?"

"It's opening. The creature is prying it open," Illarion clarified.

A computer console beeped and Luciana zoomed across on her wheely chair to stop it sounding. "Depressurisation warning."

One blinked. "Close all internal doors," he cried out.

Sanna and Luciana had control over those systems, and they started frantically pressing buttons.

"What's happening, One?" I asked.

"The Airlock has two doors—the inner and outer. If the creature is prying open the outer door it intends to do the same to the inner one. We have to maintain the air inside the ship."

"Engine room sealed," Sanna called out, her fingers dancing over the console.

"Cargo bay, robot storage, and internal doors, all sealed," Luciana said.

One ran to a console and activated the microphone. "Arkonauts, stay in whatever room you are in right now. The Ark is about to be breached. Stay put until you hear from me again."

"Observation room clear," Sanna said.

It was then the doors to the control centre started lowering from the ceiling.

"One, inner airlock door will be breached in three, two..." Illairon said.

"Grab onto something," One said. His hand gripped the console so tight the metal actually bent around his fingers.

Then the airlock blew.

On the camera, the creature had a tentacle inside the airlock and it was pulling the doors open with its suckers.

Then the seal broke.

Suddenly, any corridor linked to the airlock was depressurized, which included the corridors surrounding the control centre, which was not yet sealed.

A howling wind thundered down the corridors and into open space. The creature was momentarily blown back away from the ship.

Sanna and I did not have time to grab something.

The suction pulled us out into the corridor and I screamed, struck the door frame, and bounced off it. The corridor to the airlock from the control centre was a straight shot, and I saw the darkness of space at the end of the tunnel.

Following me as I flew down the corridor was Sanna, her Haji billowing around. Like me she was screaming, but I could not hear what with the howling wind.

Then suddenly the wind cut out and we both slammed into the ground as the air settled.

I gasped for air and found little to sate my exhaustion. It was like I had just run a marathon.

Sanna managed to pick herself up and came over to me.

"Maiara, what happened?" she said.

"Maybe the airlock resealed?" I said.

"We need to find something to hold onto in case it goes again," she said.

"I can barely breathe."

"This corridor and a few others are sealed and just lost a lot of air. It's like being up a mountain," Sanna answered.

One's voice came over the internal speakers.

"Sanna, Maiara, are you there?" he frantically said, which was unsettling to hear, he was normally so calm.

"We are," I managed to say.

I heard One sigh in relief.

"The creature reattached itself to the hull and created a temporary seal. Air is still leaking out, but slowly.

"We're coming back to the control centre," I said.

"You can't," One said.

"Why not?"

"The control centre has now sealed and since air is still escaping, a secondary protocol has kicked in preventing us from overriding the door controls."

"That's crazy! How is someone supposed to fix a leak if they are stuck away from it?" Sanna said.

"It's a mistake in the coding, we're working on bypassing it," One said.

"What about the creature?" I said.

One paused for a moment.

"What about the creature One?" I repeated.

"One of its tentacles has reached inside the vessel, it's—"

His voice scrambled and the lights starting flashing.

"Power is fluctuating," Sanna said. "It must have damaged the engine."

"The creature has found some of our energy conduits and is draining power from the ship," One said, his voice crackling back into life.

"We need to go stop that thing," I said.

"No, no!" One screamed at us. "Get back to the control centre. I want you here, ready to get inside."

"We don't have time. We need to get that thing off the ship," I called out.

"Maiara, do not disobey me. Return to the control centre now," One said and his voice was laced with anger for the first time since I had known him.

He was wrong. We didn't have time for this. We were out here, and we only had one chance.

"Maiara, we need to do something," Sanna said.

"Let's go get rid of this unwanted hitchhiker," I replied.

•

We ran down the corridor and made it to the airlock. The creature's tentacle had wormed its way from the airlock, past the storage area where the spacesuits were kept, down the corridor leading to the airlock and around the corner. The tentacle's tip was buried in a wall nearby. It pulsed with multicoloured light, and the light travelled down the limb and out the airlock.

"It's punctured the wall and has accessed one of the power conduits in this section," Sanna said.

I slowly walked up to the tentacle. It wasn't slimy or really that fleshy. The skin looked like rusty metal and a mercury-like liquid flowed through veins underneath.

"How do we get it off the hull?" I asked.

"Can we throw something explosive at it? Hurt it? Make it realise that we are not worth it?" Sanna said. "Or cut the tentacle off?"

"We don't have access to anything explosive or able to cut this," I said. "The cargo bay is sealed."

Sanna licked her lips and stared straight for a moment. "Okay, let's think about what we *do* have access too," she stated.

"It's just corridors. Maybe the antigravity room is open, but there is nothing in there that will help us. All we can get to is this corridor and that airlock where the spacesuits are kep—"

"Spacesuits," Sanna said, her eyes lighting up. "Jetpacks! There are jetpacks down there."

"They *are* explosive," I said.

"Let's go," Sanna said.

We entered the corridor leading to the airlock, pressing ourselves against the wall as we side-stepped down, passing the tentacle. We were afraid to touch it as who know what kind of shock it would give us with power running through it.

The Ark's lights flickered again.

"This thing is amazing," Sanna said.

"We need to stop it before we lose all our power," I said.

"Yeah I know but still—a space-born lifeform!" Sanna said.

We made it to the storage area. The airlock was surrounded by an open space and against the wall were various lockers holding a mishmash of various spacesuits, one for every Arkonaut.

"Find some that have jetpacks," I said.

I went to the other side of the room, limbering under the tentacle in order to the cross.

I opened lockers and checked the packs. The jetpacks were virtually empty, so I dumped all the ones with a modicum of fuel in a pile.

Sanna found more and slid them under the tentacle to me. Then she followed.

"These all have fuel in them, but how do we get them to blow up?" she asked.

"One of them blew up when we were on the outside of the ship when we—" and I trailed off because the memory brought back haunting visions of Callum trying to save Dehqan. Then of all of us flying through space, going into the belly of the Ark. Of Callum dying.

"How did that happen?" Sanna said, snapping me out of my nightmare.

"I have no idea. We always assumed it was just a fault."

"Wait! This jetpack has a cutting device on it," Sanna said

"Probably to do work on satellites or something," I said.

"Precisely."

"So if we point the cutter at a jetpack, it may explode, and the explosion might hurt this creature just enough to force it off the ship," I added. "But what do we do when we get it off the airlock? Won't it depressurise again?"

"Once the creature is free, One can activate emergency airlock controls from the control centre. If we can hang on for long enough we'll be fine."

"Let's do it," I said.

I grabbed a jetpack and brought it to the entrance of the airlock. The tentacle filled most of the narrow room. At the far end where the Ark stopped—and usually space began—was the mouth of the creature pressed up against the hull of the ship.

It had no teeth, but it was no less scary. I placed the jetpack on the floor and went back for another one.

As I retrieved a second, Sanna went down the airlock to place another.

We leap frogged over one another, piling up the jetpacks.

I picked up the final jetpack just as Sanna went with her last one. I looked at the cutting device on the one I held; the controls were simple enough. I assumed it would take some time for the cutting device to penetrate the tank maybe a few seconds; enough to grab onto something.

Suddenly Sanna screamed.

There was a flash of light from the corridor.

I dropped the jetpack and looked down the airlock.

Sanna was on the ground smouldering. Her clothing was singed. There were burns on her face.

I went down the airlock and dragged her out, getting small burns on my hands where her clothing was still burning.

She was out cold. If the airlock blew, she was unable to hold onto anything. She would get sucked out of the ship.

I dragged her to one of the lockers and placed her at the bottom curled up, and groaning in pain.

I then shut the locker and bent the handle so it wouldn't open easily. I figured One could get her out when this was all over.

I picked up the last remaining jetpack and took it down the airlock, being even more careful not to touch the tentacle.

I placed the jetpack down and pressed the cutting tool against the nearest tank.

All I had to do was activate it.

I looked up into the maw of the creature. I looked the other way down the corridor.

You could, you know, just not hold onto anything, my mind told me.

There it was again. The thought of death. But why?

This would be heroic, my mind told me again. *It would pay for your sins.*

"I did what I had to do. I've already faced my sins," I told myself.

But not everything. Not the darker secret you've hidden about Turso.

My mind went blank and I reached down for the cutting torch. There was no objection from anywhere in my mind.

Just push the button and pay. Die heroically. No one will ever know the truth then, my mind told me. *Who cares about the pain. It will be over quickly.*

"Maiara, Maiara, are you there?" One called over the internal speakers.

I blinked and sort of awoke even though I wasn't asleep.

"We're losing power," One said.

I shook my head. What was I thinking? Dying this way wasn't heroic! I pressed the button on the jetpack and darted for the airlock door. I heard the cutting tool whiz as its powerful beam started burning away the fuel tank of the other jetpack.

"One, get ready to seal the airlock," I cried out.

I ran for a locker of my own and jumped inside, pulling it shut. There were no locks. Just the handle and latch, I hoped it would resist the decompression.

The door had a window in it, and I looked out.

The jetpack must have ignited because suddenly there was an explosion of fire from the airlock, then the tentacle exploded too.

I tried to cringe away from the flames that filled the area and rushed down the corridor as the whole tentacle disappeared—as it exploded from within—but I could not go anywhere.

Then the fire suddenly got sucked away.

It had worked. The explosion had forced the creature off of the hull.

Pressure rushed from the surrounding corridors and took the fire with it.

The locker rattled as the airflow was like a tornado.

I thought it would end only when all the air would disappear. That Sanna and I would die from asphyxiation.

The air then settled. The airlock closed itself, and the pressure died down.

I tumbled out of the locker and gasped for air.

Almost all of it had been sucked from the corridors. I hoped One would be able to open all the doors and restore the air flow.

I lay down, and my vision blurred as my lungs seem to burn me from within, begging for oxygen.

Then I blacked out.

6
HEALING

When I opened my eyes again I was in the medical bay.

I was lying on my side, and across from me was Sanna, also lying on her side as a robot worked on her right arm, replacing bandages laid over nasty burns.

Sanna was awake and smiling.

"Maiara, these pain killers are amazing," she managed to stay.

"I'll have some," I said, but my voice was muffled, and I realised an oxygen mask covered my mouth.

I pulled it down and repeated. "I'll have some then."

Sanna smiled again.

"Please put your mask back on," the medical robot said.

I obeyed and replaced the mask, and took the deepest breath I ever had and loved it. The pure oxygen I received was like a boost to my system and I rolled over onto my back.

I then pulled it down again. "Hey Sanna, how are you feeling?"

"I have burns to sixty percent of my body, but don't worry, they will heal with few scars. At the moment there's no signs of infection," she reported. "You?"

"A touch out of breath and very achy," I replied.

"What happened after I was knocked out?"

"I shoved you in one of the lockers and went through with our plan," I said.

"You shoved me in a locker? Like a school bully?" Sanna replied with a giggle.

"How many pain killers have you had?" I said with a smile. "That joke was not funny at all."

"It's my first time needing such high-strength painkillers," Sanna said in bliss.

We both laughed. "I think there is some nitrous oxide in my oxygen," I said, in fits of laughter.

"There is no nitrous oxide in—" the robot began to say, but was cut off by One entering the medical bay.

My laughter stopped when I saw him.

His jaw was clenched. He was glaring at the two of us.

He drew a deep breath and said, "How are you both?" through gritted teeth.

"I'm fine," I said sheepishly.

"Fine," Sanna said, with a wave of her hand. She looked almost ready to drift off to sleep.

"Good. Never ever do that again," he said raising his voice. "You could have killed yourselves. It is not your place to risk your lives. Do you understand me?" He practically yelled the last part.

I sat up a little, and pulled my mask from my face again.

He pointed a finger at me before I could speak.

"No Maiara, I don't want to hear it. You are the designated survivors on this ship. It is up to me, or the robots, to handle situations that are that dangerous. My life is forfeit for one of yours. I told you not to resolve this situation. I don't care if you have something to prove or a belief that you can play hero. No."

He stared at us and I sat back down, gazing at the ceiling. "What happened after the explosion?" I asked.

One bit his lip and looked down at the floor. After a second of composing himself, he replied.

"The explosion and decompression forced the creature to let go of the ship minus a limb, Once free of the airlock, we closed the door and left the creature in our wake. We're out of the wormhole now. We made it through."

"What was that thing?" Sanna managed to ask.

"We found a database in the Ark's computer. Apparently the Ark and ships sent by the aliens who built it, know about these creatures. They are like barnacles on a ship's hull. Apparently the wormhole isn't unique. It's connected to a large network, and those creatures attach themselves to the hulls of ships travelling through them, slowing them down."

"At least we saved the ship," I blurted out.

"I don't care, Maiara," One shot back, his fist balled for a brief moment. "I can't protect you if you do something stupid like that." Then he came in close and leaned over me. "Especially someone so willing to cast their life away."

I glared at him for saying such a thing. Then he stepped back and looked embarrassed for the first time since I had known him.

"Get better. Tomorrow there will be a report on the ship's condition in the theatre. You need to be there."

After he had gone I huffed. "Little hard on us don't you think?" I said to Sanna.

"He just feels like a failure," she said bluntly.

"What?" I replied.

"Think about it, Maiara. He's lost Mathieu, Nuan and Callum. And with Callum, he was the one who pulled the trigger."

Her mention of Callum's name made my chest tighten.

"He's getting worried that more of us will die and it will be his fault," she added.

I didn't respond to that. Then I realised that if I died during the explosion—if I had let it take me then—how would that affect One? I hadn't considered it before.

That thought stayed with me as I stared into space.

•

My second session with the shrink happened in the medical bay. The robot leaned over me as I lay on my bed. Sanna was out of her bed, so we had some privacy.

"I thought you were doing better," Doc asked.

Tears filled my eyes and streamed down either side of my face. The pillows on the bed were damp with the endless streams of water.

"I thought so too," I said.

"So, you tried the exercises I suggested?" Doc said.

"It was hard to do them. My depression is like gravity. It pulls at you, like a black hole, sucking in everything and never letting it out, despite any small desire to be free of it."

"Why not be free of it?" Doc asked.

I wiped my face and breathed in deeply.

"Because it would feel like a lie." I answered.

"A lie?"

"I don't think I should be happy, Doc. I should be depressed. It feels like pretending to put on a smile and trying to have fun. That's fake. I'm sad all the time because I'm no longer the person I thought I was. I thought I was a good person. I thought being an Arkonaut made me feel like a good person."

"How so?"

"Because it was a fresh start, unlike any other. No one here on this ship knew my past. No one I knew from Earth is around to judge me. From the day I arrived it was a clean slate. Now I've sullied it again. I don't deserve to be happy. How can I live like that?"

Doc once again took its glasses off and rubbed them, then placed them back on its face, where I assumed a magnet kept them stuck there since it had no ears.

"Tell me what you were feeling when you considered taking your life in the airlock?" it asked.

Images in my mind flashed of me staring at the open doorway on the ship hull. A small portal set in metres of metal. I remember peering through the portal out into the maw of the creature, knowing beyond was the uninhabitable wormhole.

"It was beautiful," I said.

The robot didn't reply.

"It more peaceful than when I thought about chucking myself from the top of the engine room."

"Why."

"Because it was more like sacrifice. I would be killing myself for a good cause. I had to stay and die to make sure the explosion worked."

"Did you not think of how painful it would be?" Doc asked.

"I did not. I told myself it would be painless and of course I believed myself. I would walk through the portal and die instantly and be free."

"But you didn't?" Doc asked.

"No."

"What stopped you?"

"One spoke to me over the speaker. It snapped me out of my thoughts. It felt like someone was a witness to my lie."

Doc paused for a few seconds and I realised that unlike a human the pause would have been calculated to the millisecond as its programming figured out how long to give before responding.

"What is this lie you refer to this time?"

"You know, that it would have been sacrificial to stay with the jetpacks. That's a lie because I could have got to safety."

"Is that the real lie you are talking about?" Doc asked.

I looked into the robot's eyes, wondering if it was capable of being that deductive, or if it was clever programming that made it ask such a question—a question that made me angry, sad and guilty all at once.

"No," I replied.

"I want you to keep going over the exercise we talked about. That will make you feel better, and when we meet again we'll talk about your progress."

"I know what I need to do to feel better," I said.

"What is that?"

"Pay for my crimes," I said.

"Maiara, why do you really want to pay for your crimes?" it asked.

I didn't reply. I merely turned away from the robot, clever programming or not it would never understand the truth.

7

THE DROUGHT

Me and Sanna walked into the theatre together, feeling much better and relatively healed by the medical robot.

We were greeted with applause when we entered. Everyone was cheering and there was whoop whoops from people, as well as clapping.

"Three cheers!" Koyla called out

I had to endure three hip-hip-hoorays.

Sanna waved merrily while I managed a half-hearted one.

"Okay. Settle down," One said sternly from the stage.

The adoration ended, and Sanna and I took two empty seats, receiving some slaps on the back and high fives as we sat down.

One let the mood subside, then he spoke again. He stood with his arms behind his back, slumping in to his chest, his gaze sometimes far away.

"I have bad news," he began.

Every smile in the room instantly disappeared.

"As you know, after passing through the wormhole the plan was that we would then fire the engines to put us on course to our new homeworld. This takes a huge amount of power. Also, to land our ship on the surface of our new world, we need to raise the ship's kinetic shield to prevent the ship from exploding on contact with the ground. Unfortunately, the creature we encountered drained energy when it latched onto the ship and it drained so much that our projected energy reserves will not allow us to do both. We can fire the engine, but we can't land. We can land, but we can't fire the engines to get to a homeworld."

"What do we do?" Koyla asked.

"From this point forward, we are going to conserve as much energy as we can. That means lighting will be turned down to a minimum. Robots will also not be allowed to re-charge themselves. We're going to have perform extra tasks ourselves, including preparing meals. The heating will be turned down, so wear warm clothes. The anti-gravity room will be shut down. We will do everything and anything to conserve power. It's possible we could figure out a way to conserve enough to make up the difference."

"But if we can't get to the world and we can't land on it aren't we all as good as dead? We can't survive on this ship indefinitely," Illarion said.

"No, we cannot. I must also tell you that when the creature was knocked off the ship, it took with it a section of pipework that fed a reservoir of water. We discovered that the pipe leaked a substantial amount of water. Water we could not afford to lose."

"So, we're going to die of thirst?" Luciana asked.

"It will take a while, but eventually our recycling plant will no longer be able to filter the water we use. The reservoir was supposed to supplement us until we reached our new planet. Now we no longer have it. In the future we will be drinking contaminated water, which further tests our survival."

One hung his head after delivering this news.

Murmurs spread through the theatre. Scenarios were jumping back and forth.

"We need to get to that planet," Sanna said to Ogwambi, next to her.

"I say we at least try to get there," he replied. "Maybe the calculations are wrong, and when we make it the ship can survive the impact after all."

"We can't stay here," I said. "We're in the middle of nowhere."

One patted the air and everyone settled down. "It's time for us to start thinking about solutions to our problems. Everyone has had the same training and experience by now. You've all worked in the different departments on the ship. We're going to spend the next several days figuring out solutions to our problems. Get together with each other, discuss ideas, then bring them to me. We need to figure out a way to get more power out of the engines and supplement our water supply.

"We can do this Arkonauts. We are the remnants of humanity and we will not end it all drifting in space. Let's get to work."

•

Getting to work was easier said than done. The last three days were a nightmare for most of us. We washed less to conserve water and people started to smell, and their hair looked lank and unwashed. The air had become staler, the days colder. However, I can say that I enjoyed those days. I spent more time with the Arkonauts preparing our food. One had formed us into teams that prepared all the meals, saving the robots from doing it, and using our power. I always liked cooking and now I had a chance to do it again, which I thought would be years away. However, the edge was taken off slightly when I had to cook for two hundred fifty people, which became very samey.

What really challenged me was the task of finding a solution to the problems our recent disaster had forced upon us, such as no water.

I was trying to solve that problem as I sat around a table in the cafeteria with Illarion, Gerlinde, Sanna, Ogwambi, Moana and Koyla. We had been the cafeteria staff for the day and were left with the clearing up to do. In the kitchen area above us were a mountain of plates and trays that we would have to take care of. For now, we sat and ate our own meals. Those who cooked were always the last to eat.

Tonight's dinner was spag bol and we slurped down the spaghetti and tomato sauce with relish after a hard night's cooking. We also had a single piece of garlic bread, which we slowly nibbled at.

There wasn't much talk, we were all so tired. I had been on my feet for four hours and they felt ready to snap off.

"How long until we have to do this again?" Koyla asked.

"At least a month," Illarion said.

"Thank goodness. Remind me never to volunteer for this work when we finally get to our new homeworld," Koyla said.

"*If* we get to our new homeworld," I said.

I received frowns from everyone. Then their faces suddenly softened. I realised why, for a moment, they were angry at me for such a bleak suggestion. Then remembered I was suicidal, which meant they had to bite their tongues.

"We need to resolve the water situation," Sanna said. "Everyone stinks," she said. Changing the subject.

Koyla leaned across at Sanna and sniffed theatrically.

"Some more than others," he said, then shoved a fork full of spaghetti into his mouth.

"Hey," Sanna said, to general sniggers. "You're no bunch of roses either, you know. In fact, have you showered at all since coming on board?" she added, to even more fits of laughter.

I even managed a smile.

"Not really no. Ever since the Destroyer arrived I must have had—" and he looked up as he counted in his head. "Five, five showers. Kind of got used to not having one."

Sanna rolled her eyes. "Eww," she mouthed, and made a face like she was throwing up.

"Did you have showers?" Illarion asked.

"Not exactly," she answered. "In the last days of Earth, as the Saudi Arabian representative, I was secluded in one of the royal family's palaces, deep in the desert. It was built over a natural spring, with water inside that the Destroyer could not reach. I had baths every day."

"Nice for some," Moana said. "I washed myself with wet wipes. I smelled of disinfectant for weeks," she said. "I didn't like the smell. It burned my nostrils, but I needed to stay clean. Infection was rife.

"I would have killed myself if I didn't have a shower. I love to feel clean," Ogwambi said.

I froze. I saw eyes darting at me and then away. The silence was palpable.

Ogwambi felt the change in mood instantly, then his eyes widened. "Oh, look guys I didn't mean it."

"It's alright guys," I said raising my voice slightly. "No need to feel horrible or awkward. It is what it is," I said.

"I once tried to kill myself," Moana suddenly said.

More silence, and this time I felt awkward and embarrassed. Then, like someone had driven a baseball into my chest, my heart ached a little. I had a sudden epiphany that was both a revelation and a reproach. All this time I thought I was special and alone, that I was the only one suffering with these feelings.

"Moana?" Ogwambi said, putting his plate down and sitting up.

"It was years ago now," Moana said. "And now I just feel stupid that I tried. I am so much better now."

She looked at me and said. "I don't mean that you're stupid Maiara. I mean that when you're in a good place again you will feel the same way."

I didn't reply.

"What did you do?" Koyla said, ever the blunt one.

No one rebuked him for his comment. Of course it seemed like the natural question to ask.

"I tried to drown myself," Moana said.

"Where did you ever find the water?" Koyla asked, and that got him shushed by everyone else.

"It was right after the Destroyer landed on my home. When the ship was coming in, the islands got the order to evacuate. We projected its landing site when we first spotted it. I was on a cruise ship standing at the bow as it sailed away from the islands. At the time, the islands could not be seen. That's how far away we had moved. I watched the Destroyer come in and strike the Earth like a god was driving a tent peg into the sand. If it hadn't been for its shield, there was no doubt in my mind that even at that distance I was from the impact, the explosion would have vaporised me. Thankfully, there was a small explosion and although there was a tidal wave our ship's captain was able to get us through it without too many issues. Although we got thrown about a bit.

"That was when I realised that Hawaii was gone. Completely obliterated. The Destroyer was as large as the archipelago itself. It sat right where the islands were supposed to be, displacing miles of ocean and land.

"My home was gone and there was no hope of returning to it. I was only twelve—thirteen I think, I forget the date really—and I had just watched everything I had known disappear. I had never left the area before. Where the ship was sailing to seemed so alien to me. So I climbed the railing and jumped off, right into the churning water around the ship's propeller. I remember thinking that doing it this way would be less dishonourable. People would think I was tossed off the ship when the wave stuck, an unfortunate casualty. Then I wouldn't have to worry about people wondering why I had done it. Silly really.

"My father dived in after me. He was a good swimmer and made sure I returned to the surface, and he kept me above the water. There were so many ships around in the evacuation that we were picked up quickly."

"My family never spoke to me about it, I guess they thought I really did accidentally go over the side, or maybe they didn't want to face what I had done," Moana finished and she looked down at her dish and picked at it.

After a brief moment of silence, people turned to me but I kept my head down.

I shovelled on last spoonful of spaghetti into my mouth and slurped it down. I felt a little happy at hearing her story. She had come through. She had people to help her. Maybe I did too.

"Well, if we want to shower again properly, we need more water. Has anyone heard any good ideas?" Sanna said, changing the subject again.

Out of the corner of my eye, I saw them all look at the floor in sadness. Koyla shook his head a little.

"Come on. How do we purify the tainted water from the pipe leak?" I said.

Sanna said, "We can't purify it. This was toxicity the planners didn't account for. We don't have enough cleaning resources to remove these toxicities and continue normal operations."

"We need more water," Koyla. "We have to replace what's unusable."

"Yeah, but we can't get more water," Moana said.

Gerlinde, Ogwambi, Illarion and I suddenly straightened, all having the same thought at the same time.

It was Gerlinde who voiced the thought first. "I know where there is water."

"Where?" Sanna said.

"Below us! Me, Maiara, Illarion, Ogwambi and—We all saw it!" she said.

Sanna slapped her head theatrically, "Of course!"

"Yeah! Of course! The water," Koyla bluffed.

"How do we purify it though? It's still salt water, isn't it?" Koyla said.

"We must be able to rig up a distillery," Gerlinde suggested.

"There is one more thing," I said.

"Kraken!" Illarion uttered.

"That guy is not going to let us have his water. I don't think he's in the best of moods after what One did to him."

"Then there is only one option," Koyla said. "We need to do a deal with the croco-devil."

8

SUMMONING THE BEAST

One opened the hatch at the base of the engine room. He held it open at a ninety-degree angle, and then threw it to the ground, where it struck the floor like a gong that echoed up the engine room.

I looked up at the walkways above me. Everyone who had a free shift was there peering at us, some holding their heads to one side to listen in.

One and I peered over the edge of the hatch and down the shaft leading to the lower section of the Ark.

One then took out a grenade, pulled the pin, and threw it down the shaft.

It had a long fuse, and about half way down it exploded, creating a louder sound than the hatch, like a cannon blast from an ancient warship.

"Just in case he didn't hear the hatch open," he said.

We waited for a few minutes. For all we knew Kraken was sleeping. In all honesty he could be miles away, cocooned in water, or could have mistaken the blast for any of the myriad sounds that would occur below.

"We could go down and get his attention from the walkway," I suggested.

"That would give him the metaphorical high ground," One said. "No. If it comes to it, I'll go down there and take care of him." He pulled out from a case a grenade launcher.

"Do you think you can kill him?" I asked.

"I can. However the issue is: do I break my father's agreement with him?"

"He tried to eat us all," I pointed out.

"He is the last of his kind, and my father made him a bargain. Technically he has not broken it. However, he didn't make that deal with me."

Another minute passed and One checked his launcher.

He then took out another device and placed it on his upper chest. He pressed a button on it, and suddenly—projected around him—a new set of clothing appeared. But it wasn't clothing. It was made of light. It looked like a Mountie's uniform, but there was no insignia, or epaulettes. It was more conservative, and looked more like armour.

"This is a portable kinetic shield," he explained.

"Where did you get it?" I asked.

"We reverse-engineered it from studying the Ark. When the ship impacts a planet it raises around itself a kinetic shield that absorbs the impact energy. Upon study, our engineers found a way to make a shield that could protect humans."

"Why does it look like the Mounties?" I asked.

One shrugged. "My father was Canadian," he answered. "Plus the projection of the shield can be tailored, so he went with this. The shield can mitigate limited damage and protect its wearer, hopefully it will keep me alive even if I am swallowed," he said.

"Swallowed?"

"Don't worry. If he does that I'll cut him to pieces from the inside," One said, and he strapped a short sword to his back.

He then lifted a leg over the hatch to start his descent into the bowels of the ship, but he stopped.

I looked down and—at the base of the shaft—four yellow eyes stared at us.

One stepped out of the hatch and switched his shield off.

"Kraken, my name is One. We have met before."

Kraken didn't respond.

"I have news for you and I wish to make a deal. Come up to us."

I heard a low growl from the base of the shaft, like a crocodile clearing its throat.

"Why don't you come down here?" Kraken replied.

"We make the deal from up here," One said.

"It sounds like you need my help more than I need yours. Come down here or there is no deal."

"If there is no deal then I will be forced to come down there and take what I want by force," One said.

Kraken growled again and I saw two of the eyes on the right side of his head sort of flicker, like a nervous twitch.

"Fine."

Kraken pulled himself up the shaft until it shrank to a point too narrow for his gigantic body.

He stopped a couple of hundred yards down and he looked like a gecko trapped in a toilet roll.

"Speak," he said.

"No doubt you have sensed a problem with the ship," One began. "Our power has been greatly reduced." He then pointed at a power line running down the shaft to the engines at the base of the vessel. It was very dim, barely illuminating Kraken's many white teeth as he spoke.

"It is getting darker in my domain," he agreed.

"The ship has encountered a problem. We have lost a lot of water. We need some of yours," One said.

"Why is that my problem?" he asked.

"Because without water my people die and without us, the ship can't make it to its destination. You will spend the rest of your life down there contained in your cage. Once we go, the power goes. When the power goes the ship will lose its heat. Without heat, everything on board will freeze and so will you."

Kraken twisted in the shaft.

I wondered if maybe he was preparing to leap up at us. If he breathed in he might just be thin enough to make a lunge.

"I see," Kraken said. "Well then, if you're taking some of my water perhaps you can give me something in return."

"We don't have food to spare," One said.

"I don't want food."

"It's the only other thing you could possibly need," One shot back.

"Not entirely. There is one more thing I need: assurance."

"Assurance?" I said.

"You're asking me to give you some of my water, but I see you came prepared to take it. I have to wonder if you're here to bargain from a place of honesty."

"I have kept the agreement you made with my father," One said.

"Yes... that I made with your father, but not you."

"Fine. I promise not to harm you or take the water. You freely offer it," One said. "Do we have an arrangement?"

"No, I need more assurances than your words. I want your crew."

I looked up at One and saw that his jaw had clenched. His fingers also gripped the grenade launcher a little tightly."

"You want me to give you some of my crew. To eat?"

Kraken bared his teeth, "Did I not say I do not need food? No. they stay with me and I promise I won't eat them. You can have my water. When we get to this new world, I give you back your crew members when you let me out of this ship."

"I can't—" One began.

"Excuse us," I said, and I motioned for One to step away from the hatch.

"We should take his deal," I said to One.

"Maiara, we can't give him some of our people to remain down there for the rest of the trip. We can't trust him."

I licked my lips and looked away for a second.

"Maybe we meet him half way? What if one of us goes down there and every day we swap out an Arkonaut? Every day a new hostage? He gets what he wants, but we don't have to risk a large group of Arkonauts.

We make a sacrifice, but now so does he. Plus, we're taking his water, which risks his environment down there."

"I can't put any Arkonaut at risk. My conditioning... my orders don't allow me too."

"This is what we have to do. You *could* fight him, but we're not sure you would win and who knows what damage a fight could do to the ship. You're going to have to choose new orders now—your own orders—for the best possible outcome."

One now looked away and bit his bottom lip.

"This is not what I'm meant for," he muttered. "This does not feel like a safe and certain path for the future."

"Coming to agreement rarely feels that way, but he knows that if he kills one of his hostages it's over between us and him. We won't betray him if he has just one hostage. Both sides are making sacrifices, any betrayal is mutually assured destruction," I said.

One looked confused, "Are those your words?"

"No, I borrowed them from the Vice President of the U.S.," I said.

"Then we will try it," One said.

"I'll be the first one down into the depths," Maiara said.

One didn't object. I guess he knew it didn't matter who went first and in his eyes we were all equal.

We stepped back to the hatch and looked down.

Kraken was yawning, showing us his forked tongue and gullet like a railway tunnel entrance.

"We have a deal. However, one Arkonaut will stay with you and each day a new one will swap out with the old," One said.

Kraken looked away and his tongue flicked out for a few seconds.

"As long the as the transfers happens down there, not up here."

"Fine," One said. "Please vacate the shaft. The first Arkonaut and the pumping equipment will be down in a moment."

Kraken nodded and squirmed his way down the shaft and then turned around when it was wide enough to head down.

One gestured to the Arkonauts above and they started lowering the cobbled together pipework. He stopped it as the mouth of the pipe reached the hatch.

"Put these on," he said, giving me his pair of magnetic boots. "When you're down below, I'll drop the hatch twice. Have Kraken respond with three taps of his own, so I know you made it there safety."

He then offered a hand and I stepped up onto the pipe and hung onto the sides.

One then offered me a small bag. "Water and some food. I assumed I would be down there for a while hunting him. This time tomorrow we'll pick you up and have the next person in line."

"I understand," I said.

I then gestured to those lowering the pipe and it descended.

Once beyond the hatch, the zero gravity kicked in, and I clung to the pipe to stop myself from drifting away.

It descended deeper down the shaft and in five minutes the mouth of the pipe entered the bottom of the Ark, where a beast the size of a jumbo jet was waiting for me.

9
THE BEAST BELOW

I looked around. The shaft's ladder was wrecked at the bottom. There was no way to use it to get back to the top. I remembered when Kraken had destroyed it in an effort to reach us.

"Come over to here," he said, and a large claw tapped the walkway beyond the mangled shaft. If I made that leap, I would be stuck down here. While I could jump up the shaft in zero gravity, I would not be able to ascend fast enough to escape Kraken.

I bunched my legs and leapt across, landing awkwardly, and attached myself to the metal deck plates with the magnetic boots I wore.

I looked back at the pipe. It descended further—searching for a water source—controlled by the Arkonauts above.

Then I heard the hatch slam down twice.

I looked at Kraken, floating nearby, and said, "Can you make the same sound three times, please."

Kraken reached out with a claw and tapped the metal wall of the shaft three times.

I walked to the edge of the walkway and looked out across the bottom section of the Ark.

I then looked at Kraken.

"What do we do now?" I asked.

He looked taken aback.

"In all honesty I didn't think your captain would allow this situation."

"We needed the water and you needed assurances. It made sense. Thank you for accepting our extra terms. Just so we're clear, you're not going to eat me right?" I asked.

"Only if One tries to take you away once you have got all the water you need," Kraken said. "From now until this ship lands, one of you will always be down here. I know now that I will finally be free of this place."

"I'm going for a walk to Turso's home," I said. It was the only place I really knew down here that was theoretically safe from Kraken should the beast change his mind about eating me. I mean, as a giant crocodile, you can't trust him not to eat you.

I started down the walkway partially covered with metal bars.

Kraken followed me. As there was no water up here he had to use girders and support beams to move along. My walk was punctuated by his claws scraping on metal as he pushed himself off.

Eventually the sound got so bad I just had to say something.

"Don't you have better things to do?" I asked him.

"Oh yes. I guess I can do my laundry or accounting?" Kraken shot back, as he floated next to me.

I stopped and turned to him. "How do you know words like laundry and accounting?" I asked him. "You don't have clothes and you don't have money."

Kraken tapped his head, "a human by the name of Ghost gave me all sorts of words to communicate with. I know what these words mean even if I didn't have equivalents."

I walked forward to the railing of the walkway and looked out at the beast, who drifted closer, and set one of his eyes directly opposite me.

"How did he get you to talk?" I asked.

"He sent down a black and white creature. It mooed and I ate it. Afterwards, I could speak your words," Kraken answered.

"No offense, but I'm surprised he didn't try to poison you."

Kraken chuckled, "He did. That was not the first creature he sent down. The first two he sent down tasted weird, however human poisons had no effect on me. In the end like your captain, he had to bargain."

"So, when we get to our new homeworld, what happens then?"

"Your One opens up the doors and I crawl over land to get to the sea. Then I spend my days swimming in new oceans." Kraken floated away and curled his body, smiling and closing his eyes.

"It will be wonderful to swim an ocean again, to feel all that water. Not like the meagre lakes in here. To eat new beasts. To see new volcanoes. To bask in the sun."

"Or get eaten," I suggested.

Kraken opened his eyes. "What?"

"You're assuming that you will be the largest predator in the sea. On the new planet there might be creatures as big as you."

Kraken stared off into space. "I hadn't thought of that," he said, and grasped a support beam to steady himself.

"My race was the largest species to ply the waters of my world, but now," and I heard the fear in his voice. "Maybe I'll be the hunted."

Kraken swallowed.

"I'm sure you'll be the biggest," I said, trying to calm him down. It was tempting to make him go over the edge.

I looked past Kraken and out over the top of the Ark.

I deactivated my boots and leapt off.

Kraken eyed me in curiosity and twirled his body as I floated past.

"What are you doing?" he asked, and as he spoke his tongue whipped out near me.

"Getting a better view," I said. When I reached the nearest support pillar I reactivated my boots, stood on the pillar, and looked down towards the bottom of the inside of the Ark.

The coils feeding power to the engines below were dimmer than they had been last time I was here; no doubt the engines were off since we were trying to preserve power. But they were glowing just enough for me to see the swirling currents and wrecks of ships drifting around.

"There is not much to see," Kraken said, drifting next to me.

"You've been looking at this for...for how long?"

"Dr. Ghost told me thirty of your years."

"Thirty years?" I replied.

"Yes. Ever since I was taken from my home planet."

"Well in thirty years the view is going to get boring. I, on the other hand, have only seen this once before. And how often do I spend time in a place like this?" I replied.

Kraken made a noise that sounded like a snort of derision, but he floated nearby, watching me look over the space down here.

I looked around and just so happened to look at the right angle to see all the way to one of the corners to the ship—the one where Turso had made his home.

"Kraken, can you take me somewhere?" I asked.

He grabbed a pillar to steady himself and moved around to face me. "Where?"

"Turso's home," I said tentatively.

I half expected him to fly into a rage at the thought of visiting the home of his nemesis, but he merely growled.

He then moved around and showed me his back.

"Climb on," he said.

I deactivated my boots and leapt onto his scaly back. I made my way to the ridges and spikes running down his spine and held on for dear life.

"Are you secure?" he asked.

"I am."

He then took off and I screamed. Riding on his back as he leapt from pillar to pillar was terrifying, like a roller coaster where your seat belt had suddenly broken and the greasy teenager running the ride hadn't noticed.

Then I realised I should probably do my part for the dignity of the human race and calmed down.

We reached the far corner of the Ark in minutes, and without warning Kraken came to a complete stop, knocking the wind out of me as my body was slammed into the spike I was holding onto.

"We're here, human," Kraken said.

"Maiara," I managed to splutter.

"Maiara, we are here," Kraken replied.

The house was not as I remembered. Before, water had bunched up around this part of the ship and the house had been protected by a razor sharp labyrinth of coral. Now the water had receded, and the coral seemed to have melted away, revealing the house.

"It's different than I remember," I said.

"With Turso gone the coral stopped growing. I pushed the water away to get to his house," Kraken replied.

"Why did you want to get to his house?"

"Curiousity."

I stood on his back while I looked at the house. It almost seemed haunted.

"Why did you hate him so much?" I asked Kraken.

"He took my leg. He was the first creature to ever harm me in such a way. And he took something very special from me—" and he drifted off.

"What was it?"

Kraken raised a leg up and held it flat, inviting me to step onto it. I held onto one of his claws to steady myself as he brought me round and placed me on a nearby beam.

He breathed in deep and looked away from me.

"When I was brought into this place, it wasn't just me. This beast of metal also took in a clutch of eggs."

He breathed in deep again.

"Turso ate them. I don't know why really. There were plenty of other things to eat down here. Maybe he didn't want the competition," he said.

I felt my heart break at his story. He didn't well up. I suppose he couldn't cry. Not all animals do. He just went silent.

"That's where my revenge really came from. Taking a leg was just a reminder as to why I hated him."

"How did it feel when you finally got your revenge?" I asked.

Kraken smiled and turned back to me. "It didn't bring anything I had lost back, but at the same time, it felt like justice."

He then leaned in closer.

"Is that what you felt?" he asked.

I looked into Kraken's eyes then I turned away from him. I leapt over to the house and landed right by Turso's front door.

Kraken poked his head through the gap in the remaining coral to watch me. He looked like a big dog trying to peek through a cat flap.

I went inside the house, not really knowing why I had decided to come here.

Maybe I thought that I would find Turso here alive and well, and while I hated him for killing Callum, at least he would not be dead by my hands.

But, he was a killer. A selfish one, killing only to favour himself.

The house was empty, devoid of life, even the seaweed had dried and shrivelled up. Kraken hadn't done too much damage.

On a desk in the corner of the room was something I hadn't expected to see. It was a piece of rectangular coral and it had carvings and raised sections on it. I recognised Turso's face carved into the coral, and behind him, two other members of his race. It was like a photograph, just like the one I had of my parents.

I threw it against the wall and it shattered.

He had parents. I killed someone with a family. I seethed at him for cursing me from beyond the grave.

Then I laughed. I was so stupid. His parents were long dead. They weren't sitting at home somewhere wondering where their dear son was. No. They had died.

I let myself drop to the floor. My hair, lank from a couple of missed showers, flopped over my face.

I was such a mess.

These were the consequences of my actions.

Through my locks, I spied a coral knife on the floor. I picked it up and held it in both hands, blade turned towards my heart.

All it would take, I said to myself.

I slowly brought the blade closer to me, feeling it poke at, but not through, my Arkonaut hoodie. I pressed the tip into my chest and a small bite of pain flared right above my heart.

I stopped. The pain was awful, and my mind was telling me it was about to get worse. Survival instincts reminded me that dying was the worst thing imaginable. Even if it seemed like the only way out.

Suddenly, something crossed my mind.

Kraken.

He was waiting for me outside to come out. If I was dead, what would happen. One would think that he had killed me, and then One would kill Kraken. I had no doubt he would do it.

I let the knife drop.

My life held another's in the balance. I couldn't do it. Then I realised my death would hurt One, hurt the others. Sanna's warning in the medical bay had finally sunk in. Moana's own experience crystallised with the fact that people did care for me and I cared for them.

I threw the knife away and stood up. Then I wiped my face and tied back my hair.

This must be what an epiphany feels like. I'm certain this was the first I had ever had. It was like I had paused myself and the world. As if my brain absorbed a new reality, and an update had downloaded to affect the code of my brain.

It felt good.

Suddenly all those suicidal thoughts were gone. It wasn't the way. I had people to help, people who loved me, people who relied on me.

I looked down at the thin, white scar on my wrist. It didn't make me want to repeat the action. The desire was gone. At last.

My heart seemed to tense again though. My pain was disappearing. Like a desktop on a computer, all the windows that had been opened and demanded attention were closing down. But one more window remained, refusing to close, frozen, the X in the top corner didn't work.

I still had to face one last slither of guilt.

But not right now.

Instead, on that desktop in my mind, I minimised the window.

A wave of euphoria swept over me. For the first time in a long time I had a clear head.

I walked out of the house, and Kraken actually smiled.

I looked beyond him to the underbelly of the Ark and saw the water, the light from the power lines, and the old ships.

A thought crossed my mind.

"Kraken, do you want to go treasure hunting?"

He looked confused.

10

SHIPWRECK AND RETURNING HOME

I screamed—mostly in joy, but a little from fear—as I rode on Kraken's back across the Ark. When I spotted, out of the corner of my eye, exactly what I was looking for I shouted: "Stop!"

Kraken came to a halt, which was accompanied by the sound of loud shrieks as his claws dug into the metal of a nearby pillar to slow himself.

"To your left," I said, and Kraken turned right. "No, the human left," I said, and he turned back.

We were now looking at an old sunken galleon, or what remained of one. There were no sails or rigging, just a rotten hull.

Kraken moved closer to it and then I jumped over to the galleon. I managed to land on the hull, grabbing pits of broken planks to steady myself.

"Let's see how lucky we get," I said.

I moved through the ship and found various rooms, and floating within them were whatever the vessel was carrying when it was sunk.

"What are you looking for, Maiara?" Kraken asked.

"You'll see," I said.

Eventually I found what was probably a cargo bay at the very bottom, and inside was a chest.

I didn't open it. Instead I took it up top and brought it to Kraken, who leaned in closer.

"This what I was looking for," I said. "Hopefully, a treasure chest."

"Treasure?" Kraken asked.

"Well, if we are lucky," I said. I clasped the padlock on the chest. It was rusted and no doubt useless, but the wood of the chest had severely deteriorated after years at the bottom of the sea. I simply pulled the lock off the chest.

I licked my lips and lifted the lid. Inside was exactly what I was hoping to find.

I dug my hands in and threw a bunch of gold coins into the air.

"We're rich," I said to Kraken.

"What?" the beast said. "What is this?"

"Centuries ago, humans used to travel the oceans in ships like this one, and some of them used to carry treasure: precious metals and stones that human valued for some reason."

I saw a ring with an emerald in it among the coins. I plucked it out and put it on my finger. It looked good.

Kraken came in close. His nose nuzzled the chest and more coins spilled out in the zero gravity. "Your people collected this?"

"We used it to trade for goods and services," I replied. I dug down deep in the chest and my hand found something circular.

I pulled it out and saw it was a golden cornet encrusted with diamonds.

"Give me your hand," I said to Kraken.

Although he looked dubious he extended his nearest limb.

He had four claws and, like humans, the one at the end was the thinnest.

I bent the coronet a little bit and managed to widened it. Then I put it over his tinniest claw like a ring.

"How does that feel?" I asked him.

65

Kraken held up his hand to his face and looked at the coronet, which was inlaid with large colourful jewels.

"I like how it shines," he said.

"That, Kraken, is treasure hunting," I said.

I dug around in the chest some more and pulled out handfuls of coins and gems and pocketed them. Then I closed the chest and pushed it through the air towards Kraken. "I've taken my cut; the rest is yours."

Kraken grasped the chest.

"I'll guess I'll buy myself something nice," he said.

•

My time in the underbelly of the Ark was not as bad as I thought it would be. I slept in Turso's house and after a day Kraken took me back to the shaft leading up to the top of the Ark.

One was already waiting for us and I got to surprise him when I turned up riding Kraken, wearing a pearl necklace and several rubies and sapphires on my fingers.

Kraken moved close to what remained of the walkway and I leapt across landing next to One and Gerlinde, who was going to take my place.

I turned back to Kraken who stared at me down his long snout.

"It's been great, Kraken. I'll see you again when it's my time to be back down here," I said to him.

"Thank you for the coronet," he replied and wiggled his new bling in front of me, much to Gerlinde's and One's confusion.

I stepped up to Gerlinde and whispered her ear, "Don't worry he's a teddy bear. Really."

I then stepped up to the ladder, waved one last time at Kraken, and ascended. As I climbed, I heard Kraken ask Gerlinde, "Do you like treasure hunting?"

•

As I ascended the gangplanks and walkways to the top of the engine room I was accosted by other Arkonauts who wanted to know where my jewels had come from. I told them about our treasure hunt and gave a few Spanish doubloons away.

It was only when I reached the top of the engine room that I realised that I hadn't even noticed that I wasn't triggered by the hatch. It hadn't upset me like before. I smiled. This was great. Maybe I was finally getting over it.

I walked back to my room elated. I was due a shift in the control centre, however I assumed that staying down below meant I was entitled take a shift off.

Once in my room—which had clothes and furniture strewn about because I hadn't bothered to tidy up in weeks—I dumped all the coins and jewels on my bedside table.

I looked around and started folding clothes and moving furniture.

In an hour I had my room how I wanted, and it was tidier than it had been for ages.

Then I took a very short shower and emerged feeling happier.

I fell into bed in my pyjamas, and relaxed in the soft bedding.

The only thing that troubled me was a tiny, niggling thought in my brain: *You still don't deserve to be this happy. There is still one thing you haven't admitted to yourself.*

I fell asleep, trying to ignore it.

11

STRANGE ORBIT

It was my turn to woman the control centre as the crew slept and One—I don't know—went to his cupboard and stared at the wall. It was hard to imagine One going to sleep.

I pushed off from one side of the room and my chair zoomed across to the other side.

I then repeated the process.

Normally, it would not be so boring. Normally, the Ark would be careering through space and there would be lots to do. However, everything was on minimal power. The lights were off and the only illumination were the dome above and TV screen-like floor, both of which showed the wormhole behind us glowing faintly, and the stars all around.

My eyes had adjusted hours ago.

There was not much to do except ensure the air and minimal heating were working.

I stopped at one console and tried to find our new homeworld.

The computer was tracking the planets within its solar system and managed to show me some sensor details, but not much. The image on the screen was extremely faint and blurry. It looked like Earth—mostly blue with some green land.

Yet we might never reach it, not without One coming up with a plan.

I pushed my chair away again, although weakly, and ended up in the centre of the room. I flipped the paddle under the seat, the chair slumped back, and I stared up at the dome.

I couldn't really understand why the aliens who had built this thing had put their computer screen above them like that. I mean, you had to lie down to comfortably look up at it. Maybe they had eyes on top of their heads or something.

As I stared at the stars on the viewscreen, I wondered if another was close enough to get to. Maybe we could fire the engines once, just, enough, and calculate the right path?

Seemed hopeful.

As I stared at the stars I thought about that one remaining thought in my head. It felt like an infection already spreading tendrils into the good vibes I discovered while down below.

I needed a way to take care of it.

I needed to do something that would finally balance it out.

It had to be a big thing. My secret—that I dare not admit to myself—demanded as much.

I noticed something strange as I looked at the stars. One had brought the ship to a complete stop. Well, not a complete stop, of course. That's impossible in space. But it appeared the ship was moving faster than I thought.

I pushed myself back to another console and reactivated the sensors, just in case we were drifting somewhere we didn't want to be. Like back into the wormhole.

The sensors told me that the ship was indeed drifting and I plotted the course of the drift. If we were heading out into clear space, then I would not bother One with it.

The computer did a projection. A curved red line from the ship out into space showed me that the Ark was actually going to move in a circle around the wormhole. In orbit around it, in fact.

The anomaly seemed to have hold of us, and was going to force us into circling around it for the rest of our lives.

This might be a problem. After all, if we got stuck in its gravity we might not be able to get away, even if we had enough power.

At least the computer told me that the orbit would take ten years to complete, meaning it was weak.

Not that we could get away right now anyway.

I watched the computer complete the orbital path and at one point a gap appeared and then the red line continued. I frowned at the gap. Why did it do that?

I zoomed in and enlarged the image, seeing something within the gap.

I enlarged it again and focused.

Whatever it was was too far away to visually bring into sharp focus., so, I switched to heat sensors.

My jaw almost hit the console when a shape appeared. In fact, there were multiple shapes.

Each one of them were diamonds with a squat top section and elongated bottom shape like an old fashioned kite.

I did a quick size comparison.

I was right. I knew what they were.

I pushed myself across to the other side of the room, and activated the comm. "One, come to the command centre now. I have something to show you."

I let go and turned back to the images in front of me.

Suddenly I had energy in my body again. I paced the room, waiting for One to arrive.

Then I realised I was happy. My discovery meant something. Then the dark thoughts tried to rise in my brain, seeking to suck away the joy. I pushed them down and closed my heart to them. I felt happy again, and like Doc had suggested, I let the happiness in.

I clenched my first and closed my eyes.

"This is good," I said to myself. "I want to feel happy."

For a moment the turmoil of my despair and hope toiled in my gut. Then One stepped into the control centre.

"What is it, Maiara?" he asked.

I ushered him to the screen showing the important information.

He looked down at the data, then bent forward to get a closer look.

"There are more Arks out there," he finally said.

"Not only that," I replied, and tapped a button that revealed more information. "They are giving off heat, which means—"

"They have power," One said.

12

THE PLAN

I perched on the edge of my seat in the front row of the theatre.

Other Arkonauts were streaming in from behind me. I heard the squeak of the old cinema chairs being folded down as they took their seats.

I was joined by Sanna, Koyla, Ogwambi and Gerlinde in the front row.

"What's this about, Maiara?" Sanna asked, smoothing down her long flowing dress as she sat.

"I discovered something," I said quickly. "It will solve our problems," I added nodding my head.

"What is it?" Koyla asked.

I pointed at the screen currently showing sensor details from the control room.

One was standing there, breathing deeply, and counting heads as the theatre filled.

The second the last Arkonaut was inside, he started, "Crew, I think we have a way to resolve our power issues."

One gestured to the screen and it showed the Ark on the far right hand side and a red line leading from our ship around the wormhole. The red line traced a narrowing circular path and showed the Ark hugging close to the wormhole, being thrown away, and then arcing back in again.

"This is our projected course for the next decade. The Ark is caught in the gravitational field of the wormhole and in that time the ship will take up a place in orbit of the wormhole. Kind of like how the moon became a satellite of the Earth.

"It seems that we are not the only vessel to do this, however." He directed our attention back at the screen again and this time it traced the same path until it reached what I had found.

"While Maiara was in the control centre last night she discovered that there are other vessels in orbit of the wormhole. It's possible that these other spaceships have travelled through this wormhole in the past and, like us, burned up too much power, resulting in their drifting into the wormhole's orbit.

"The history of these vessels is not important to us. What is, is that one of them has power."

The screen zoomed to show the vessels in more detail. Overlaid on top of that image was a thermo scan, and one ship was still warm. The heat pattern showed everyone the shape of a vessel we were all familiar with.

"That's an Ark!" Koyla blurted out.

"Indeed, it's a little smaller than ours and missing a piece of its lower hull, but it is an Ark type vessel.

"What's it doing here?" Sanna asked.

"We don't know, maybe who ever built the Arks sent out multiple vessels and when they made their passage through the wormhole they were drained of power and could not return to the place from where they came. We all saw that inside the wormhole are other paths. There is a network out there of sorts. It could have come from anywhere in the galaxy.

"What's important is that there is power for us to replenish our own stores. Yes, these ships have less power, but they have just enough for our needs."

"So we just wait for the Ark to drift close enough?" Gerlinde asked.

"That will take too long," One said.

The image on the screen shifted again, and in place of the star-filled sky was a diagram, a technical readout for a spaceship of some kind.

It looked like a slimmed down more angular space shuttle, with a cluster of engines on the back, white panelling on its top and a skin of black heat shield on its belly. It had various NASA, European and Indian space program insignias on it.

"This is the Endeavour A. It was built from spare parts from other shuttles and technology gleaned from the Ark. It was a prototype, mankind's first inter-solar system craft, capable of great speed and atmospheric entry. It was named for the Endeavour space shuttle of the 1990s, which was also built from spare parts.

"Since mankind could not make use of it as a lifeboat due to its limited amenities, it was allocated to the Ark. My father presumed it would be a great tool when we reached our new homeworld."

"I've never come across this before," Ogwmabi said.

"It's parked in a concealed hanger," One explained.

"I will fly it to the other Ark and attempt to guide it to us. Maybe then we can siphon the power from it into our own engine and use an engine burst to break free of the wormhole's orbit."

Gerlinde raised a hand.

"Yes, Gerlinde."

"You're going to go by yourself?" Gerlinde asked.

"No. I will take some of the robots with me, but I will be the only crew member going."

"And what if something happens to you?" Koyla said.

"If I should not make it back, you'll have to wait until Two recovers. That could take a year. I'm sure that in the meantime you can fend for yourselves. Two will then come up with a plan, I'm sure."

"In a year's time you said we'll barely have power! What could she do?" I asked.

One patted the air as murmuring started amongst the crew.

"This is what needs to be done. I can't risk your lives. I can only risk my own."

74

"You're our captain. Captains don't do this," I said. The others grumbled their agreement.

One answered, but for a brief moment his loud voice came through gritted teeth. "I will not lose another crew member. It's bad enough that one of you has to spend time with the beast below. No one else! I leave in two hours, once the shuttle is loaded."

He scowled at us all, walked off the stage and down the centre aisle.

No one spoke up against his decision.

I huffed and followed him.

13
MY OPPORTUNITY

One walked really fast and I could barely keep up with him as he descended the main flight of steps down to the cargo bay.

I knew he knew I was following him, but he didn't slow.

"One, One!" I called out after him.

The cargo bay door took a bit of time to open, so I finally caught up.

"You can't go. You're supposed to be the one who protects the Arkonauts," I said.

"Sorry, Maiara. It has to be me. I'm the one who has to make sacrifices, and put my life on the line for my people," One replied.

The cargo bay door rolled open and he walked inside.

For a moment I was lost for words.

A shelf right by the entrance was packed with weapons taken from the invaders of the Ark. One ignored them, and instead went to another crate.

He lifted the lid off and inside was a foam package, and in pre-cut indentations, were several discs—kinetic shields.

"Let me go in your place," I said.

One stopped what he was doing and looked at me.

"Maiara, it has to be me who goes."

"No you're the captain, our leader! You need to stay behind and lead."

"This is leadership," He said.

"No it's not. Leaders have to make the tough decisions sometimes. They need to send others in their place. If you fail in this mission, we won't have a leader anymore. We won't be able to fend for ourselves without you."

One paused as he put on the extra gear.

"Maiara, I can't put your lives at risk. This is a dangerous mission."

"So is staying on a giant alien trashcan with no power. Let me go. I can do it," I said.

I pushed down the shame from lying to him. "Don't forget, I got rid of Turso. I am capable of leading a team of robots."

One shook his head. "It has to be me."

"But why?" I asked.

"I don't have to explain myself to you," he said coldly. "It's my duty to take on the most dangerous assignments." He fumbled with an ammo clip as he added it to his gear.

I was taken aback by his response.

"One, you have to stay here," I said.

"NO. I DON'T," he shouted at me.

He didn't apologise, but he looked down at his shoes like a child that overstepped the line. He then shook his head, moved over to another crate and continued to pick through it.

I turned away and started out of the cargo bay, then stopped.

"Please don't go, One." I said to him. I turned to face him. "Callum would want you to stay."

He froze, an arm outstretched for another piece of equipment. There were tears in his eyes.

"Did you ever speak to Doc?" I asked him.

"Doc?" He asked blinking, which caused those tears to fall down his cheeks.

"The shrink robot. The one I've been speaking to."

"No," he replied, staring off into space.

"Have you spoken to anyone regarding what happened on the day Callum died?" I asked.

He finally picked up the piece of equipment his hand was reaching for, held it in his hand, and looked down. "I would have talked to Two instead. She was better prepared to understand me than that robot."

"But, she's not here, unfortunately," I said.

"No. She's not."

"I never once blamed you for Callum's death," I said.

"I know. That's what made it harder," he replied. "I know I didn't shoot him. I was never under control of my actions when that happened. But when that starfish thing attached itself to my head, I didn't stop it from taking control. There was a moment—like driving a car and being so tired at the same time. Turso's tech was telling me to go to sleep, but I knew that if I did, that metaphorical car would crash. It kept telling me : Go to sleep. Get your rest. And do you know what I did?"

I didn't reply.

"The tiredness crushed me, and I let myself go to sleep," he said, starting to shake. His fist clenched around a device he held and it shattered. "I went to sleep and the car went off the road... and Callum died."

He released his hand and the remains of the device fell.

"So you see, Maiara, I don't really want to put anyone else at risk," he said.

"You want to put yourself on the line, to sacrifice your life, because you think it's a just punishment? But in doing so you're dooming us all. We need you here. Someone else needs to take this risk. You can't let the crew die to punish yourself."

"I also can't let you take the risk."

"Yes you can," I said.

"Why? Why you?" He asked.

"You're not guilty. You don't need redemption, One. You did nothing wrong. You weren't weak. A piece of technology took you over and no one could fight it. But I do need redemption. I made a real choice. Stop trying to punish yourself for something you didn't do, and let me find a way to redeem myself.

"I'm not like the other Arkonauts now, One. I'm not special. I'm not the saviour. I'm no longer like them. I know that they all took the 18th memory back, but mine didn't take. It hasn't been working since that day. I'm not capable of being like them anymore and that's fine. I'm like you and Two now. I'm not here to be saved anymore. I'm here to help."

He looked away then wiped his eyes.

"I don't know if I want to send someone who's suicidal on this mission," he finally said, with a little smile.

I smiled back and took a deep breath. "I don't feel that way anymore. I promise," I replied. "I had a moment, down in the belly of the Ark. I finally understood what the Doc, and everyone else had been encouraging me to think. That I can move on from Callum's death and from Turso's. Me doing this is a way to move on."

"And me?" he asked.

"Don't forget, you are still human. You can't let what happened cause you to make another mistake. Instead, let the mistake teach," I said. "Stay here. Be our captain. Let me do this. I can. Besides, you have to let us do some dangerous things. You won't be around forever.

He closed his eyes, deep in thought, then he opened them and took the kinetic shield off his jumpsuit and handed it to me. "It has a limited charge and protects you for only so long. Follow me to the medical bay. You're going to need some training," he added.

He started taking off the gear he wouldn't need, but placed it in a bag instead.

I stepped back and looked at the shield.

It had to be me who goes on this mission.

I knew deep down, this was my way to cleanse myself of the lingering thoughts that remained.

This would absolve me, even if I died.

14
MY TEAM

The training was quick and involved short stabbing pains in my arm. One gave me a series of injections. The first gave me the skills to fly the Endeavour. The second was a series of tactical awareness training designed to allow me to assess situations critically.

One then gave me everything I would need for the journey. More kinetic shields as back up. Some weapons, scanning devices and supplies.

"The medical robot will just scan you and make sure the new nanites are working."

He paused as he placed the syringe back in its drawer.

"Head to the launch bay and take off when you see fit. The robots I assigned to this mission should already be there waiting for you."

I nodded and stood straight, breathing deeply.

"I can still go, Maiara," One said.

"No. It's fine. It has to be me," I replied. "I can do this. You need to stay here and project the crew. If I fail, find a new way to survive." I said. I couldn't lead like One does, or figure out new solutions. But I could put my life on the line for the crew and maybe make up for my mistakes.

One nodded, gave me a pat on my shoulder, and left. As he entered the corridor he breathed out deeply, straightened up, and walked off with more spring in his step.

I made my way to a section of the corridor right up against the hull of the ship. I pushed a button on the wall, cunningly concealed as part of the ordinary wall panels. It then slid apart slowly on rails.

The doorway they revealed was wide enough for the whole crew to walk through all at once, and it opened out into a hangar bay. Parked in the centre was a spaceship.

Although I had seen the ship in One's presentation earlier, seeing it up close gave me a little thrill.

It was slick and shiny, fresh out of the box.

NASA, European and Indian space agency logos adorned the surface; a collaborative effort. Mankind's first and only interplanetary craft. It must have been built when the Ark was going to be used as a vessel of exploration—which never happened once the Destroyer landed.

As I passed under the hull, making my way to the back, I reached up and brushed my hands on the belly of the craft. The heat shield material was rough and cold. The vessel was propped up on four sets of wheels.

The ramp up into the ship was already open, and I climbed up into the craft. A long, wide central corridor ran the length of the vessel towards the command centre. On either side were two rooms, each with seats in them like an airliner.

My new nanite injections told me these seating areas were actually meant for the whole crew. If the Ark needed to be abandoned this ship would serve as a life raft. Of course it wouldn't last long. Just a last ditch effort.

When I reached the bridge of the ship, the corridor split into four smaller hatchways that I knew led to an engineering section, and small cargo bay, as well as four gun turret emplacements.

Human spacecraft were not known for having weapons emplacements, but since it was clear that hostile alien races existed in the galaxy, the designers had seen fit to upgrade this one.

As I walked through the ship I felt a mixture of excitement and apprehension. The ship was new, fully fueled and ready to go. And I was going to fly it. I was going to be in complete control. But everywhere I looked I saw wires, pipes, computers and equipment. The ship was massively complicated and I still didn't understand it all. What if something were to go wrong? Could I fix it? I didn't know.

Luckily, I had some help from a motley crew and now I was going to meet them.

I opened the door to the bridge of the ship, a triangular room with seats facing forward towards a viewscreen.

Sitting in each chair except for the pilot's, was a robot.

One robot I instantly recognised.

The Doc. It was slumped in its chair, powered down like it always was when not in use. I had no idea why it was here. It was a shrink, but it was also the most advanced robot on the ship. Maybe it could be helpful.

The robot nearest to me turned its head to me, which was just an orb. I don't know why it turned to me. It had no eyes. Those sensors were underneath the surface.

It had a humanoid body, but six fingers on each limb.

It didn't say anything.

The third robot was a mass of tentacle like limbs that writhed around its body atop four separate caterpillar tracks. I had seen these before at restaurants. They were cooking robots that could keep track of ten meals at once. I realised that this one must have been one of the robots who cooked our meals for us. Strangely it had a large number of scuff marks, scratches, and—I'm positive—a bullet hole. I gave it a polite nod.

The fourth and last robot was the biggest and had two fork lift like hands and four legs that ended in caterpillar tracks. It turned two large lenses towards me, and they focused and refocused as I made my way through the room. It was painted in a desert camouflage pattern and had British army designations on its right and left shoulder. It even had a medal, which was really a coin glued to a strip of ribbon pinned to its chest.

I sat down in the pilot's chair and started the ship up. Everything was like second nature due to the nanites I had received.

As the ship powered up, I turned to face the robots.

I leaned over and tapped the Doc, who immediately activated and sat up straight.

"Hello, Maiara," it said. "I'm sorry but I am going on a mission with Captain One right now and cannot provide a session until we return."

"I'm not here for a session Doc. I'm going on this mission instead of One," I replied.

All the robots stood still as they processed this information. The robot with an orb for a head and no eyes displayed a swirling circle on its face as if it was stuck and trying to load new information.

"Hi. I'm Heston. Can I cook something for you?" the cooking robot said, extending all its arms out for a handshake. I leaned away from all the hands, reached slowly for one of them and shook it. "How about a sandwich?" I said.

The giant robot leaned down and stared at me through its giant optics. "Captain One was designated to lead this mission," it said in a deep electronic voice.

"Well, the plan has changed," I said, leaning away from the robotic space invader.

I then looked at the robot with an orb for a head and saw the circles still swirling, so no help there.

"Do you have written permission from One?" the giant said.

"Not with me," I replied.

"Have you led or taken part in such a mission before?" The giant said.

"No."

"Have you worked with a G5 heavy lifter before?" the giant asked.

"No."

The robot stood up straighter. "I do not believe you should be leading this mission."

"Look I—" I began, and suddenly a plate was thrust into my face with a neatly sliced ham sandwich on it.

"Your sandwich," Heston said.

I took it and set the plate down on a console.

"Err, thank you. Do you have any chips?" I asked as an after thought.

Heston produced a packet of salted chips.

"Thanks. Can't have a sandwich without chips, I always say," I added. "Now look. I'm in charge and as I understand it all robots on this ship must obey all humans correct?"

"Affirmative," doc said.

"We must," the giant said, as if it was gritting its teeth as it spoke.

"Would you like dessert?" Heston said, which I took to be a yes.

The robot with no face displayed a *no* on its face.

"No?" I said to it.

The no disappeared and was replaced with, "Sorry. Yes."

"Good. Well, let's get going. The faster we do this, the safer everyone will be."

I activated the controls, opened the bay doors, and took the ship out into space.

I didn't know if I would return, but I knew I wouldn't fail either.

15

THE ARK CLUSTER

The shuttle handled like it was a ship in a computer game. The controls were very easy to use and it responded to my guidance without difficulty. Unlike earlier human spacecraft, this one didn't need complicated calculations and thruster burns. It had powerful engines—fully fueled--and a guidance system that was the best humanity could create.

I used the new nanite memories I had been given to set a course for the cluster of ships we knew to be similar Ark vessels. I had to take into account the gravity pull from the wormhole, but that was all. This area of space was mostly devoid of things that could get in the way.

The computer was also capable of acting on automatic pilot, so I simply set the course, and off we went.

I turned in my seat to face the robots who were—I guess—my team.

Doc had switched itself off again, Heston was probably in some sort of sleep mode, as his arms keep swirling around in a repeating pattern.

The giant forklift robot was staring at me, and as I moved in my seat he constantly followed me.

"Do you have to do that?" I asked him.

"Do what?" The robot replied.

"Look at me all the time."

"I await your orders," he said. "I have to keep an eye on you and listen out for the commands."

"Like some sort of Terminator-Siri," I said. "Do you have a name?"

"My designation is G5 Heavy First Class," the robot replied.

"I'll call you G5. It's shorter," I said.

"My designation is G5 Heavy First Class," the robot repeated.

"That's too long."

"My designation is..."

"Wait. Am I allowed to change your designation?" I asked.

The robot went silent for a moment. "Yes."

"Your new designation is G5," I announced.

"You will need to type in your operator password—"

"For crying out loud," I shouted at the robot. "Your designation is G5, and that's an order."

The robot went silent again and I wondered if it was sulking.

I then turned to the robot with a blank orb for a head.

"What is your designation?"

On the robot's face appeared a name: Toby.

"You're called Toby?" I asked.

On its... face, I guess, more words appeared: "I was owned by a deaf family and they called me Toby."

"Is that why you don't speak?" I asked.

"Yes. There was no need, but the talk function can be switched on," the Robot displayed.

"We'll do that later," I said.

I looked around again and wondered if I should give some sort of pep talk, but then what was the point? Robots didn't need one.

I went back to looking at the ship's systems.

"Maiara?" came a voice from behind me, a human voice.

I turned slowly in my seat. I was in space, thousands of miles from the Ark. Who the hell was on my ship?

Standing in the doorway to the bridge were Gerlinde, Moana, Ogwambi and Illarion.

My mouth dropped open and they said together, "Hi."

•

The first thing I did was turn to the robots one by one. "Why didn't you tell me there were Arkonauts on this ship?"

G5 shrugged, Heston got out four extra sandwiches, Toby was displaying a question mark, and the Doc was still in sleep mode.

"Useless," I said to them. "Why are you guys here?"

"We heard that you were taking One's place and we decided to go with you. You might need some help," Moana said.

"Yes. We can't let you do this by yourself," Ogwambi said.

Gerlinde and Illarion said together, "Exactly."

"We have to turn back," I said immediately.

The others objected.

I definitely didn't want them here; this was my mission now. "One did not intend for all of you to risk your lives," I said. "We're going back."

"Ill advised," G5 said. "This ship has only so much fuel and while you have enough to go to the Ark and back several times, wasting it on an unnecessary journey is squandering resources."

"This isn't wasteful," I said through gritted teeth.

"You must conserve fuel on this ship and not engage in misuse," G5 said.

I paused. I hated to admit it but the annoying robot was right. The entire mission, the Ark, the Arkonauts all relied on scrimping and saving energy, food and water. I couldn't waste it.

"Fine," I said. "But on this mission I am One. I am in command," I said.

"No problem," Ogwambi said. "So, captain, what can we do?" he asked.

I smiled slightly. He had just given me an idea of how to keep them out of my hair. "There are some jobs for you to do," I said. "Moana, Ogwambi, go clean the phase inducers. Gerlinde and Illarion, please inventory the cargo bay," I said.

"Me and my fellow robot's ca—" G5 began

"Quiet G5. Those are my orders," I said, partially drunk with power.

The robot made some clicks and beeps, which almost sounded like it was purposively bleeping out some swear words.

"Go get started," I said.

Enthusiastically, the others left the room to perform their tasks. I knew that enthusiasm would disappear with the tasks I gave them. Hopefully, they would think this mission too boring and leave me alone.

•

Two hours later and we were coming up on the Ark-like ships.

Moana and Illarion had tried popping into the bridge to start a conversation with me, but I managed to ward off such discussions by giving them more work to do. If I told them their work was important, which it was not, they seemed to believe that it was important—more important to talking to me anyway.

Now that we had reached our destination, they all came up to the bridge.

"Can I have your seat please?" Ogwambi said to Toby.

The robot didn't reply until Ogwambi tapped its head, and Toby slowly got up to allow Ogwambi to sit.

"Ahem," Moana said to him.

"What? We'll swap in a few minutes," Ogwambi said.

Gerlinde and Illarion found empty seats of their own.

"What's going on Maiara?" Illairon asked.

"We've reached the remains of those Ark-like ships," I said. "Now, we just need to locate one with power that we can take back."

"Do you know what we are looking for?" Moana asked, shoving Ogwambi aside a bit in his seat so she could share it.

Toby stood behind them, some of his lights were going red.

I stared out of the main viewer trying to gauge which ship seemed like the best choice.

Their orbits of the wormhole had formed them into a stream of debris. The biggest pieces—which I hoped were whole versions of former Arks—were clustered near the middle of the stream, orbiting each other.

I kept my distance. My ship had its own kinetic shields, but they could be overwhelmed by bigger pieces.

Since I wanted to do this as quickly as possible, I focused on the cluster of bigger ships first.

I passed the debris field at a distance and started scanning.

Much of what I saw were simply hull fragments. Over the years the remnants of the ships must have banged together and broke apart further.

"I wonder how long these pieces have been here," Gerlinde said.

"The Thieves had obviously sent these ships out at one point, and presumably they had travelled through the wormhole. Yet, for some reason, they had left the wormhole and gone no further. Since they are all Ark sized we can assume that they are the same age, meaning they've been here a few centuries."

"Maybe that creature who had drained some of our power had done the same thing to these ships? When these had left the wormhole they were so drained of power they could not continue? So, they fell into the wormholes orbit and stayed here," Moana suggested.

I wondered why the Thieves had not come back for them. Not my problem, I guess.

I checked the sensor data again.

"How do we get these back to the Ark?" Ogwambi asked. "This ship can't pull them across space."

"One said that we could use these ships' engines to get it to the Ark," I responded.

"So, one of these has to work, or we are completely out of luck?" Gerlinde said.

"It will be fine," Illairon said, sitting back and slouching in his chair.

Everyone fell silent as I moved our ship closer. There appeared to be a dozen vessels here, some broken up, others largely intact. Three looked promising. They were giving off heat that could indicate that they still had power. I discounted two of them immediately. Because while they were giving off heat, they were also split open from top to bottom. Their engines were ruined, and there was no way to get them back to the Ark.

I was looking for a ship that still had working engines—engines that I could fire—so I could get it the short distance to the Ark, and maybe we could rig a power transfer.

That left only one ship.

It was exactly like the Ark, except the lower section was skeletal. It had no outer hull, which revealed the central, glowing power lines, and a network of support pillars surrounding it, like a splayed open rib cage. Ice had formed around some of the pillars, so that meant this Ark had scoured a planet of water at one time.

"How did this ship survive?" Ogwambi asked. "The engine is exposed to space! If one of these pieces of debris struck the power lines the whole thing could explode."

"Only if there is enough power," Illarion said. "These conduits don't seem to be fully active."

"Plus, the conduits have a self-repair mechanism, kind of like forming a scab. If a conduit is breached, it lets out the energised plasma from within, but a secondary element inside the conduit immediately starts to form a seal. Only a truly giant break in a conduit would cause a massive explosion," Gerlinde said.

"Bigger pieces can't get through that maze of support pillars," Moana added.

"This bottom section looks intact. Energized plasma could be inside. I'm detecting heat. Let's check the top half of this Ark," I said.

I raised the shuttle upwards. The top section of the smaller, squat pyramid was intact, and hopefully air tight.

There was only one way to find out.

I woke up Doc by tapping its head.

"Yes, Maiara, would you like to talk?" Doc asked.

"No. Look, why did One put you on this mission?" I asked.

"I am the second most sophisticated robot on the Ark. although I am a programed psychologist. I also am programmed with technical skills and information. Dr Ghost was not going to let my abilities go to waste."

"What does the red jewel on your chest do, Doc?" Illarion asked.

"It allows me to project a holographic image around my body so people can feel they are talking to a real human."

"Cool! Can you change into Koyla?" he asked.

Doc obliged, and suddenly Koyla was sitting in his place.

"Can you do his Australian accent?"

"Ok. That's enough," I interjected, and Doc returned to his normal form. "Doc, I need you to use your console to calculate the trajectories of all the debris. Plot their orbits so we can navigate around them."

"Very well, Maiara," the robot replied and went to work.

I turned to the big robot. "Now G5, why did One bring you on this mission?"

"He didn't. You did," the robot answered.

I sighed. G5 was going to be like snarky child. "Never mind. Why are you here?" I asked.

"Heavy lifting. And I have a variety of tools," the robot replied, and a number of hatches opened, and arms extended with various implements.

"I see," I replied. "Why are you so snarky? I thought robots didn't talk back to humans?"

"All robots can learn from the humans around them. I was stationed at an army base, and I learned from the soldiers around me."

My gaze once again went to the medal on its chest, I wondered if it was a joke by a soldier. In my mind, like all Arkonaut minds, were the memories of a soldier from their armed forces. My memory was from an Air Force colonel. His memories of battlefield humour permeated my mind, and something told me that it wasn't a joke, but maybe a sign of respect.

I turned to Heston. "Heston," I said, bringing the robot out of sleep mode.

The robot rose a little on its tracks and opened a compartment on its belly. "Would you like that dessert now?" it asked.

"No, I'm fine," I replied.

"I'll take that," Illarion said, and Heston handed him the dessert, which was a Black Forest gateau. He also handed over two forks and Illarion and Gerlinde started picking at it.

"Heston, why are you on this mission?"

"I provide refreshment," it said simply.

The robot offered no more info and I assumed that One must have brought him aboard to provide the food and drink he needed. But that sounded wrong, One could take care of himself. Maybe Heston had another function.

I turned towards the eyeless robot, but then turned back to Heston briefly.

"Heston, why do you have a bullet hole in your chassis?"

"I was shot at," the robot replied.

I realised that Heston had only basic interaction programming and interrogating him was not going to reveal a whole lot.

So I turned to Toby, who, as soon as I stared at it, displayed the word "What?" on its face.

"Rude," I said. "Toby, why are you here?" I asked.

"Communications expert," Toby replied.

"Why did One need a communications expert?" I asked.

"To talk to the computer of the Ark we maybe boarding," Toby replied.

"That does make sense," I said.

"I know it does," Toby displayed, and I frowned.

"Doc, can you tell me if this ship is air tight?" I said, pointing at the one on the screen.

Doc turned to a computer and started typing activating sensors and reading the information quickly.

"It is. There are several airlocks and a ship bay."

"Can we access the airlock or the bay?" I asked.

"Yes. When the Ark was captured over a decade ago, we obtained the standard codes for accessing these ships. We could try them on this version," Doc replied.

"Which one of you can do that?" I asked.

Toby raised a hand and set to work sending the signals to the Ark.

I took the ship closer and the giant vessel loomed in the viewscreen.

As we approached near the peak of the top pyramid, a small opening appeared. I say small, but the doors were roughly the size of two football pitches—small compared to the overall size of this vessel.

I slowed the ship down, then switched on the forward-facing search lights.

The lights swept the inside of the bay and revealed nothing.

The bay was in its original state, untouched by any hands other than the aliens who built it themselves—if they even had hands.

I turned to the robots and the other Arkonauts.

"Prepare for landing. Let's hope this goes well."

16
ALONE?

I landed the ship very carefully. I remembered being told once that landing a plane was more difficult than taking off. For the sake of my dignity, I also didn't want to muck it up in front of the others and the robots.

The ship landed gently on its struts and rocked as it settled on the floor of the bay.

I sent the close signal to the bay doors and they responded, sealing us in.

"Can one of you check to see if the bay is airtight, please?" I asked.

I heard Toby tap at some controls, and his console responded with an all clear.

I turned and his face was displaying a thumbs up symbol.

"Right, the ship was scanned for life forms and found none. Me and all the robots, except G5, will go and find the command centre. Everyone else stays here," I ordered.

Before the Arkonauts could say anything G5 piped up. "Why do I have to stay here?"

"You served in the armed forces. I want you to protect my friends," I said.

"But why do *we* have to stay here?" Ogwambi said. "Maiara, we're here to help you."

"Yes, you are not here to do this alone," Moana said, and she stood up and crossed her arms, staring me down.

"We've all seen the films. It's an alien ship, adrift. Who knows what's out there? Stay on board and if you don't hear from me in an hour, do not follow me. Leave. When they tell stories about us in the future I want our descendants to recognise that we were smart. No looking into strange alien eggs, no activating the ancient technology of a lost civilisation without knowing what it does. Do you understand? I don't want that embarrassment," I explained. "Stay here. If I need you I will call."

I left the room. I was followed by Toby, Heston and Doc.

I diverted to the cargo bay and grabbed what I thought would be helpful, including the personal kinetic force field One had supplied.

I put it on my upper chest and activated it.

The shield formed around me—a second skin shining a centimetre off my body. It was still set to One's Mountie uniform. I activated the list of present designs and found one I liked. A mixture of midnight blue armour that also projected a tattered cape around my body. I liked it. I wondered if some nerd had programmed it in. It had an anime vibe to the design.

I went to the doorway and opened the hatch, providing me with a ramp out of the ship. I heard a crunch as it fully opened and I hoped I hadn't scratch it or damaged the hull. I should have checked to see how low it needed to be let down.

I looked over my shoulder the others were gathered in the doorway.

"I'll be back soon," I said.

The robots followed me out and then shut the hatch behind me.

The landing bay in this derelict Ark was cold. The only illumination in the whole bay was provided by the ship's lights.

"Do any of you have torches?" I asked the robots.

Toby responded by lighting up sections of his body with white light.

This bathed a small section of the bay, and showed me that it was virtually empty.

The only thing around was something about five feet away.

It jumped back as the light played over It. It had four legs, two arms and a head as far as I could tell.

The robots remained where they were, and all turned to the figure on the ground.

"What is that?" I asked.

"Unknown," Doc replied.

"Is it alive?"

"No biological readings," Doc answered.

I moved closer. Every step slow and hesitant. I was ready to bolt the other way if this thing started moving.

It never moved. It just lay there. As I got closer I realised why it had no life readings. It was a robot. But not like any robot I had ever seen. It had a smoother design than Earth robots with stranger materials on its surface.

I beckoned Toby closer. As the lights from his body illuminated the area a little better, I saw that this robot had been shot. Its body was riddled with holes—not from bullets, as the edges were melted. This had been some sort of energy weapon.

"Heston," I said, and the robot rolled over and looked at me. "Prod that for me."

I stepped back as the cooking robot poked the thing with a tentacle.

The figure didn't respond.

Heston rolled back away from it.

Despite what I had said earlier, I crouched down next to the destroyed robot and turned it over. It was surprisingly light, even though it was my height. In fact, I wasn't sure it was made of metal at all. It splayed out on its back and the holes showed me whatever had struck it had gone right through. I felt its various extremities. It was stone cold. No energy inside.

I realised that I had no idea what to do next. What was this thing? Why was it on this vessel? Were these the aliens that had sent the Ark in the first place, somehow stranded on their own vessel after leaving the wormhole? So many questions and so few answers.

I heard a hiss from behind me. it was the hydraulic arms on the ship's ramp activating.

I spun around and saw the others walking down, exiting the ship. They were all wearing kinetic shields from the case One had me take on board the ship, but they had not selected a design, so it was just the default blue shield.

My fear of the creature disappeared. "What are you doing?" I yelled at them, my voice echoing around the bay.

Ogwambi reached the base of the ramp first, he carried some equipment as did the others.

"We're here to help you Maiara, and we're not sitting on the side lines while you purposefully risk your life," he said.

I gritted my teeth and stamped over, followed by the robots.

"I am not risking my life on purpose. You weren't supposed to be here," I said.

G5 rolled out of the ship after Illarion, who then retracted the ramp.

"Get back inside," I said.

"We're staying, Maiara," Moana said forcefully.

A high pitched screech suddenly filled the air, and sparks flew. As the ramp rose to seal the ship, it revealed underneath another robot.

It was crawling towards my friends, screeching like a car being crushed and rent apart. It shot sparks from its mouth.

It reached out for Gerlinde.

17

ACCIDENTALLY PICKING SIDES

The group backed away, shouting in surprise.

G5 calmly reached out with an arm and four fingers, and activated the ramp again.

It came down on top of the robot and pinned it to the floor of the cargo bay.

It kept trying to reach for Gerlinde, who was closest, but it could not pry itself free from the ramp.

I moved around to stand between the robot and the others.

The creature screeched again.

The others gathered behind me.

"It's a... robot?" Ogwambi said.

"Like none I've ever seen," Illarion said.

"It's not a human robot," G5 said.

"So it's an alien robot?" Gerlinde said.

"What's it doing here?"

The robot stopped screaming then slumped forward, throwing a few more sparks out.

Then it went limp.

"We killed it," Ogwambi said.

"G5 is it... dead?"

G5 rolled forward suddenly and scattered us out of the way. Its large caterpillar track crunched the robot's head.

"Now it is," G5 said and rolled back.

"No energy signs," Doc said. "It is indeed, no longer functional."

"Can you scan for signs of mechanical life?" I asked G5.

The giant moved away from us, then twirled around like a ballet dancer.

"There are several signs of mechanical life. Heat signatures moving about, sounds of machinery in the distance," the robot reported.

"We're not alone on this ship," Moana said.

"But who are they?" Gerlinde asked. "Are these the things that built the Ark?"

"I don't think so. When humanity took our Ark, they didn't find such things on board."

"The real question is do we go out there and find out? That robot over there," I said pointing at the shot up robot, "had been attacked and destroyed on purpose."

"We need the energy on this vessel or we're all dead," Illarion stated.

"Guys, get back on the ship," I said. "Only one of us should go check it out."

"No, Maiara, enough of this," Moana said sharply. "I know you're not trying to be a hero; you're not trying to prove yourself. We all know why you're doing this—"

"You think you know why I'm doing this?" I asked.

"It's obvious to all of us, and we're not letting you do it."

I stared into her eyes hoping she would blink first, but she didn't. "What am I trying to do, Moana?" I asked.

"Be a Martyr."

I didn't deny or agree, because she was only half right. I just stared into her eyes for a moment. Then I blinked and turned away.

"We go slowly and quietly. Maybe in the control centre we can get a grip on what's going on here," I said. "Close the ramp into the ship. I don't want something getting in."

G5 closed the ship.

We stepped away from the vessel and into the rest of the ship.

●

"These kinetic shields are cool," Ogwambi said. He tapped at the one on his left pec, scrolling through options, and he started changing the colour scheme, giving the basic holographic shape of his shield a yellow and red tinge.

Illarion was doing the same, "So these are like the shields on the Ark. They absorb energy. Though they are called kinetic shields they absorb all energy types. Problem is, the internal power systems can't absorb too much or they explode."

"I thought the Ark uses its kinetic shields to partially recharge its engines every time it crashes into a planet?" Gerlinde said.

"It does, but its power systems can absorb that much. These ones are reversed engineered by humans. They are a little primitive by comparison."

"Interesting. It turns out that while the shield can take only so many hits, releasing the energy it absorbs gives the shield a slightly longer life," Illarion explained.

"Release it how?"

"A concussive beam from the right arm," Illarion said.

"Do not test that," I said sternly.

"I'm having fun with the visual settings," Gerlinde said. She changed the holographic display on the shield to give herself armour like mine, except hers was more medieval and silvery.

The others immediately starting playing around with theirs. Illarion settled on some very heavy armour. Moana went with a clothing option of light looking fabrics flowing off her body. Although they looked unimpressive armour wise, the shield was just as powerful as the armour that mine was projecting around my body.

"You should conserve their power," G5 said.

I tapped the shield generator on my upper chest and the shield retracted back into it. The others did the same, sighing.

Toby, who was leading the way, turned to us. A question mark displayed on his face.

"What is it?" I asked.

His face showed us a top down map of the area. Toby must have been capable of scanning an area and forming a bird's-eye-view. Considering he worked with deaf people it made sense. He could show on a map where to go when giving directions.

I saw the landing bay we had just come from. A big wide open space. Several corridors branched off it. Then I saw an area that might be the control centre. However, beyond the control centre was nothing, just more empty space.

"What's there?" I asked Toby.

"Unknown."

The others gathered around me and peered into Toby's face.

"It looks like there's a gigantic area is beyond the control centre," Gerlinde said.

"Does anyone know what the Ark looked like before humans modified it?" I said.

They all shook their heads.

"As far as we know this was how it was, and humans added the other floors and rooms."

"That is the control centre though. The corridor configuration is the same around it," Ogwambi said.

"Let's keep going, but silently until we reach it," I said.

The others nodded, and we kept following Toby.

It didn't take long to reach the command centre. This Ark was pretty much the same as ours, but there were not additions to the ship—no decoration or influence of another race.

I kept my eyes wide and my body tensed, peering carefully into every shadow, just in case. So far it seemed like this ship was under the complete control of the aliens who had built it. That meant those four legged robots had been members of the race who had killed mine.

Suddenly feelings of rage welled up inside of me. This was a chance for me to get revenge. I started imagining the possibility of finding one and destroying it. I wouldn't need to feel guilty because it was a robot.

Not like Turso.

Before feelings of guilt could overwhelm me, I shook them off, and we reached the control centre.

Like the one on our Ark, it had a dome with a screen on the floor. The controls lined the edge of the room. There were two entrances opposite each other. The other entrance was dark.

The screens were switched on and currently displayed a rendering of the debris field this Ark was floating in. The controls were lit, but dimly.

"This looks like ours," Ogwambi said.

"No added controls though," Gerlinde pointed out.

"What's that?" Moana said, and she pointed down at one control panel.

Toby shifted his body and illuminated a wire, which had pierced the underside of a console, and ran across the room and out the other exit.

"Check that out. I'm going to see what the status of the ship is," I said.

The others nodded and slowly made their way across the room.

I walked up to the console and started bringing up information on the ship. The top section was airtight and sealed off, which was good. Power was at 30% of normal operating capacity. If we could transfer even half of that to our Ark's energy reserves, it would be enough for an engine burn, and powering the kinetic shield on re-entry.

Now we just had to move it to the Ark.

I heard Ogwambi say "Wow!" from the other side of the room, and ignored him for the moment.

I checked the engines. I didn't want to use the main ones. I only wanted to use the lateral thrusters—a line of small motors where the two sections of the Ark met. They would be enough to get it to the Ark. And half of them were functioning, spread around the circumference of the ship.

"Doc, can you do complex calculations?" I asked.

Doc didn't reply.

"Doc," I repeated.

The robot had gone into sleep mode again, so I tapped on the red jewel embedded in its chest.

"Yes, Maiara, would you like to talk?"

"No, Doc. Can you do complex physics calculations?" I asked.

"Yes. They were added to my programming," it replied.

"I need you to look at these power levels and calculate how much would be used up if we engage these thrusters to take this ship to ours."

"Give me a few moments," the Doc said, looking at the info. Then it turned back to me. "While my system is computing, are you sure you would not like to talk?"

"Doc, I appreciate it, but this isn't the place."

"You were very harsh with your friends earlier," it said.

Well, what do you expect? They weren't meant to be here. This was supposed to be just me," I said.

"You think they are getting in the way?"

I looked at the group across the room, then leaned closer to it and whispered. "Doc, I'm angry they are here on what was supposed to be my mission. I was the only one in danger."

"You've put yourself in danger on purpose. Why Maiara?"

"Look, let's be clear. This isn't an attempt at suicide, or anything like that. This will solve everything for me."

"Solve what?"

I bit my bottom lip and stared off into space for a moment. *Maybe just tell the Doc a little,* my brain said.

"There's something I haven't told you, Doc. A lingering truth. It still haunts me. I can't just erase it by killing myself. I have pay it back," I said.

"Pay it back? What do you owe?

"Maiara! This is not like our Ark. There is no corridor on this side of the room," Moana interrupted and beckoned me over.

I walked away from the Doc immediately, grateful for any distraction.

I stepped up to Moana who was holding onto the door frame poking her head out.

"What's here?" I said, easing to the edge of the room.

Heston grabbed my loose clothing with his arms.

"Careful customer," he said, pulling me back slightly.

I looked down and saw that there was no floor past the door way. instead the room opened out into a large space that even Toby's lights failed to illuminate.

"Thank you, Heston," I said.

I had no idea how far the space went on for. "Toby, can you make your light more intense, maybe a beam?" I asked.

A thumbs up appeared on Toby's face, and a high powered beam of light lanced out into the gloom.

The light faded into the darkness at what must have been hundreds of metres away, showing nothing.

"This space must be huge," Illation said.

"That cable from the console goes out into the space," Moana said.

Toby bent over, lit up the cable, and followed it out into the darkness. Several hundred meters out the beam revealed that the wire connected to a building.

"What is that?" Gerlinde asked.

"This space is meant to store the chimney's the Ark used to suck water out of the air. Maybe it's a left over one?"

"Then what's the wire for?"

"Maiara, my calculations are finished," Doc said.

We all returned to the main console.

"We would lose 4.3 percent of energy reserves on this ship to move this Ark to within range of ours," Doc said.

"How do we transfer the power?" Moana asked.

I searched the new memories One had given me. They contained more knowledge on the Ark than I had originally been given by Dr. Ghost.

"The Ark has a charging point on the equator. Power can be transferred wirelessly if we're in range. Our scientists theorised that when the Ark returns to where it comes from, it is drained of water then recharged for its next mission," I said.

"Shall we start moving?" Moana asked.

"We still don't know if there are more of those things out there or not, and what they are doing on board," I said.

"Let's check the sensors," Ogwambi said.

He crossed the room again and looked at the info from another console.

He stepped back from the console for a moment. "This console has been altered... and the one next to it."

"Altered how?" Moana asked.

"It's been taken off the wall and re-attached. I can see the seams are a little bit off." He then activated the sensors. "There is movement inside the ship. No life signs. Just more robots."

"So, there is something here," Gerlinde said. "We should leave."

"I agree. We'll get back to the ship and study one of those other robots there. If we can determine what is and how many there are, we will know what we are dealing with," I said.

"Guys, something is happening," Moana said.

"What?" we all replied.

"Can't you feel the vibration through your feet?"

Moana was wearing thin-soled slippers. I had on combat boots. I crouched down and felt the floor. "There *is* a vibration. What is it?"

"That's the engines powering up," Moana said.

"Something is bringing all the systems back to full power," Illarion said from a console.

A sound from the corridor made my blood run cold. It was the skittering of metal feet.

All the lights suddenly started coming on. The corridor we had used to get to this room was bathed in light. The control room lit up proper, and through the other doorway the entire cavernous room started to come to life.

I looked down and saw that, beneath the control centre—which sat at the top of the Ark's top pyramid—was a city.

Skyscrapers that easily fit into the miles-high ship stretched out beneath me. There were roads, houses. Some buildings were made from the chimneys of the Ark themselves.

There was a whole civilisation here.

Lights then began ascending up to me.

Someone was on their way here.

"We need to go. Now," I said.

"Maiara, we're all detecting multiple creatures all around us," Doc said, as the robots turned this way and that.

We made for the doorway we had entered, but that suddenly filled. Several new robots, just like the ones we had seen in the landing bay, were huddled in the doorway. They stood on their four legs, looking at all of us with three eyes that rotated around their faces.

More skittering behind us announced the arrival of similar robots using some sort of jetpacks to fly up to the doorway. These had red lights beneath their chassis. The other group had darker blue.

Were we looking at two factions?

I backed the others up against one side of the control room.

"Get ready to activate your shields," I said. "We make a run for it. G5 clear a path. Heston, Doc and Toby will cover our rears."

"Maiara, they can hear you," Moana said.

"There is no way they can understand our language," I said.

Two robots from each side took one step into the room. The one glowing blue was much larger and walked on only two legs.

They started talking to one another. At least I assumed they were talking to one another. Their language sounded like an old modem connecting to the internet.

"Doc, please tell me you can understand what they are saying," I asked.

"I cannot," it stated.

The two robots reached the end of their conversation, then raised two hands, pointing them at Toby.

Simultaneously the hands shot towards Toby and each finger pierced his body.

We all gasped as Toby was held aloft between the robots, shaking and sparking.

Then the two robots let go, and Toby fell to the floor burnt, charred and throwing random sparks.

"Toby," I called out.

The robot didn't move.

Then the two lead robots turned to us, and spoke in perfect English together. "What kind of lifeforms are you?"

18

THE TRUCE

"You speak our language," Gerlinde blurted out.

"We do. We took the knowledge from this thing," the red robot said, pointing at Toby's carcass.

"Who are you?" the blue robot asked.

"This person speaks for us," G5 said, pointing at me.

I scowled at G5, but then realised that, yes, I did speak for everyone. Heston actually pushed me forward, smiling.

I stood up straight like One did, with my hands behind my back.

"My name is Maiara. Erm, my race is Human."

"You are a biological lifeform," the red robot asked.

"I am. We all are," I said gesturing to the others.

The blue robot looked at G5. "You have our components, but are not one of us."

"I was built by humans and I serve them," G5 replied. "I am a robot. What are you?"

"We are the Ammon," the red robot said. "We are artificial lifeforms, as you understand the word."

"What are you doing here?" the blue robot asked.

I paused, wondering how much I should tell them. What did these robots want? Would they help us? Maybe they were the ones who destroyed Earth and built the Ark. I still didn't know. What would One do? He would destroy anyone who wasn't an Arkonaut and call it a day, I guess? No. One could also negotiate, and be patient, and he never seemed to lie.

I needed to know if they were the enemy of my enemy, or at least a potential friend.

"We are here to explore your ship. We thought it was deserted," I said, a suitably vague answer.

"We live here," the red Ammon stated.

"We know that now. Sorry for intruding. Would you like us to leave?" I asked.

The red and blue robots looked at each other and started speaking in their language again.

I turned to the others and, in Spanish, said, "We need to know if they built the Ark, or found it like we did." I hoped the robots did not assimilate the other languages we spoke from Toby.

"If they are those Thieves who stole our water, we can't let them know we have an Ark. They might try to take it back," Moana said.

"Even if they aren't the Thieves, they may try to take it anyway," Ogwambi added.

"Maiara, ask them this question," Illarion began. "Where is your homeworld?"

"Why?"

"Because if they, like us, made the Ark their own when it came to their planet that means it was probably destroyed."

I turned back to the robots and interrupted them, hoping I wasn't going to cause a diplomatic incident. "Excuse me. We would like to know something. Where is your homeworld?" I asked in English.

The robots stopped speaking, and the red one said, "Our homeworld was destroyed by a vessel just like this one, only larger. We captured this one and moved our whole civilisation aboard."

We now had a common enemy.

"We live on a ship just like this one. It, too, tried to destroy our world, but we captured it. A larger ship... destroyed our world," I said.

The two robots turned to face us.

"You have another vessel just like ours?" they both said together.

"We do," I said.

The red and blue stepped away from each other a little bit.

"Did you come through the wormhole?" I asked.

"We did," the red robot said.

"Guys, these robots are not one race. They are two. Two factions," Gerlinde said in Spanish.

"Que?" I replied.

"This Ark is not run by one group. There are two."

The red and blue robots inched further apart, raising their hands. I remembered the robot which had been shot up in the landing bay. A sign of a battle.

We were about to be caught in the middle of it.

19

THE WAR

I stepped between the two robots and held up my hands.

"Hold on. Do not do anything! We are here to help you both," I said.

The red and blue Ammon lowered their hands.

"Help?" the blue Ammon said.

"Yes. I can see that you both represent two groups. Is that correct?"

The red and blue robot looked at each other.

"There is a difference of opinion," the red Ammon said.

"This room is neutral ground. That is why it remains untouched and pristine," the blue robot said.

Ogwambi opened his mouth to say something, but then closed it again and shrugged.

"What are you arguing about?" Moana asked.

"We have calculated that staying here is the best course of action."

"We have calculated that firing our engines and trying to a reach a new world is a better idea," the blue Ammon said.

"So you're fighting over who does what with the ship?" I asked.

"Yes," the blue robot said.

"How can you help us?" the red Ammon asked.

I had no idea.

"Could you both leave the room for a moment? I need to talk to my advisors," I said.

The red a blue robot nodded at each other and backed out of the room.

G5 and Doc stood between us and the red Ammon, while Heston stood between us and the blue Ammon.

We gathered in a circle. "What do we do, Maiara?" Moana said.

"We need their power and we need them to trust us," I said.

"We can't spare power," Ogwambi said. "And they need it too."

"Can't we just take the power?" Gerlinde said, and we looked at her. "It's an option. It's them or us," she said. "Besides if we took their power they don't die. They just shut down. We could always come back with power one day."

"They probably won't go for that," I said.

"What if we allowed them to join us?" Moana said.

"Join us?" I said.

"Yeah. We take this Ark to ours, we transfer the power, then we take them aboard our ship," Moana said.

"What, and we share our new homeworld?" Ogwambi said. "I'm not sure that would work."

"I can't see another option," I said. "We can't take over their ship. They are another species. I'm not going to harm them. We need to negotiate."

"One more question. Which one do we negotiate with?" Ogwambi asked.

I looked over my shoulder at the red and blue Ammon.

"Both. Our solution solves both their problems," I said.

"Ok. Let's do this," Illarion said.

Everyone nodded to me. I suddenly felt a tremendous weight off my shoulders, and for once I was glad they were here to help me.

I turned around to face the robots.

"We have a plan. You will fly this ship to ours. We will transfer all the power from this ship to ours, then your civilisation comes aboard our vessel." I paused as my mind gave me one more option. "To conserve power, your race will shut themselves down. And when we get to a new planet we transfer you off."

The red and blue Ammon looked at each other—a brief exchange in their language then they said together, "We require that we are allowed on your ship before the shut down."

"Half of you may board our ship before the transfer," I threw back.

Another brief talk.

"Very well," they both said.

"I require that the leadership of both the Ammon give their consent. In person," the blue Ammon said.

The red Ammon paused. "That is not necessary. You know they can see all from where they are."

"In person. I need to see that their command protocols are still in effect. They still lead you," the blue Ammon said.

"Very well," the red Ammon replied.

"What is happening?" I asked.

"Our race... races are led by command protocols—what you might call passwords. They reside with members of our race and they can dictate our actions. An Ammon can speak for the whole, but only does so in concert with those who possess the protocols."

"Where are your leaders?" Ogwambi said to the blue robot.

"I am the last of my kind to possess command protocols," it replied.

"Just one of you?" I asked.

"There used to be more, however command protocols can be stolen," the blue Ammon said, and for the first time there was a sign of emotion in its voice.

"During our conflict we managed to steal command protocols from their side," the red Ammon said.

"And when they had them, my Ammon followed their leaders."

"The leaders are on the way," the red Ammon said. "Send your warriors away and we will do the same."

The blue Ammon motioned behind it, and I heard all the robots scuttle away.

"G5?" I asked.

"All robots on that side of the ship have backed off by one hundred metres, as have all the robots on that side," G5 reported.

Now only the red and blue Ammon we had been talking with remained.

I heard a whine coming from the big open space where the city was, and then landing on the edge of the doorway were four robots. They were larger than the ones we had been talking with, and walked on two legs.

They stepped into the room and the red Ammon we had been speaking with backed away and left.

"We are the leaders of the Ammon," the new arrivals said in unison.

I heard the grinding of gears from the blue Ammon left in the room.

"We are here. You can see that the command protocols lie with us," the five said.

"Two used to be on our side," the blue Ammon said.

"When the Calculated Divide occurred, we went to war. These command protocols switched sides appropriately," the four red robots said. They turned to me. "We speak for our faction and agree to your terms. We can also guarantee that we will not need to share your world. We are heading to a planet in the nearest solar system, but probably not the one you are heading for. We will be sharing a solar system, but not the same world."

I felt a little relieved at this news. Sharing a world might not be a problem for a little while, but knowing the history of humanity, when two sides needed resources war was usually to follow. Being on different planets would help.

"Acceptable," I said.

"We can also reveal that it will not be necessary for us to move onto your ship." The four robots gestured to the dome screen above us and a diagram of this Ark we were on was displayed, and it showed one half of the top pyramid separate from the rest of the ship. "We have converted our vessel to detach from the main structure."

The blue Ammon seethed.

"Why have you done this? This ship is shared!" it said, the volume of its speakers increasing.

"It was our compromise," the four robots said. "Our side wanted to stay here and conserve power. Your side wanted to continue on even though it was calculated that we do not have enough power."

"Those calculations were wrong," the blue Ammon said.

"So, our solution was to shed the weight of the ship. With less mass, and barring any unforeseen obstacles, we could have enough power to get to the planet. Fortunately, we no longer have to take that risk," said the four robots, who then gestured to us.

"Ok. So we're all clear... We'll take this ship to ours. We transfer the power. Your part of this ship breaks away, latches on to ours, and we both go together to the new solar system?"

"That is correct," the four robots said.

"That is a solution," the blue robot said in a quiet voice.

"So I guess there is no need for these factions now?" Illarion said.

"The human is right. Our war is over. Join your command protocols with ours," the four red robots said.

"No. We have been separated for too long. There are now too many code diversions. We will stay separate and live our ways."

"Ammon, that will not work. Your split will cause more splits and then more. When we fled our world on this vessel, we agreed on no more diversions, lest we be doomed to repeat the miscalculations of the past."

Moana went to say something, but I stopped her. This was not for us. We had our agreement. Let's not get involved.

"That is a shame," the blue Ammon said, who then turned to us. "Our agreement stands," it said. "But I am leaving and my people will stay separate."

"No, Ammon," the four said.

The blue robot issued a shriek, and I heard its friends scuttle back to the room.

Illarion leant over to me. "Maiara, the blues are betraying the reds."

"No they're not," Ogwambi said, and he pointed the consoles across the room—the one he'd mentioned had been moved and replaced. The console broke apart, and robots, glowing red, erupted from within. A trap!

The blue robot howled and backed away as the robots came for it.

"Your people will join us again," the red robots said.

The blue Ammon suddenly threw out an arm; a wire shot out and stabbed G5 in its torso."

"Our agreement is void unless you keep my people separate," the robot said.

Then the new red robots descended on it and started tearing it to pieces, cutting the wire that led to G5. G5 stumbled back across the room.

I gestured for my group to follow G5. We clustered near the entrance where we came in.

The rest of the blue robots gathered at the door, surrounding G5. Then they started flashing their blue lights going on and off.

"What's going on?" I shouted at the red leaders.

"We are taking the command protocols. Then we will lead all of Ammon. Our agreement is set."

As the blue leader was stripped apart into junk, the red robots that had attacked him looked to their leaders. Then looked at G5.

"The command protocols have been downloaded into me," G5 said. "I now lead this blue faction."

"What?" I said.

"They do not belong to you," the four robots said.

"G5, give those protocols to them," I ordered.

"No, Maiara. The commands have overridden some of the human programming. I must stand by these people."

The red robots gestured and, from behind them, lights floated up in the command centre.

"Shields up," I said, activating my kinetic shield.

Red Ammon swarmed the control centre, and G5 commanded his new pals to enter the room.

Then everything went crazy.

20
LEAK

Both groups of robots went at each other in the middle of the room. They did not fire any weapons at each other, even though they could. They probably wanted to avoid damage to the equipment in the room.

"We need to get out of here," I said.

Doc and Heston backed up. Although they were robots, they were not a part of this fight.

The Ammon robots clawed at each other with sharp blades, or used hydraulic arms to crush each other's heads and wrench limbs free.

The four leaders of the red Ammon backed out of the room, letting their soldiers fight for them.

G5 was waving its arms forward, gesturing for its soldiers to fight.

Doc stood over Illarion and pushed at him.

"Time to go, children."

We avoided the odd robot that was cast aside, and nearly hit us, as we made for the exit.

I reached the doorway first and pushed through the approaching throng of robots and out into the corridor.

The others piled out after me. We all backed against the wall, and shuffled down as the robots moved past.

Eventually we reached a section of empty corridor, although, in the background, I heard the screeching of metal and explosions.

"What-just-happened?" Gerlinde said between breaths.

"We're in the middle of a Civil War," Ogwambi answered.

"What do we do now?" Illarion asked.

"We don't have to do anything. They're fighting each other, and you heard them both. They agree to our demands. We just have to wait for them to fight it out, and when there is a winner, we do the same deal with them," I said.

"We can't let them fight it out!" Moana said.

"We have to. We can't risk getting involved," I said.

"Maiara is right," the Doc said. "Your first goal should be to protect yourselves."

"Heston, can I have a drink of water, please?" Illarion said.

The robot produced a bottle.

Illarion took a swig and passed it round.

"Let's get to the ship," I said.

We made our way through the corridors. We passed various robots as we went. Each off to join the battle, no doubt. We reached the landing bay without getting harmed, and the ship was where we left it.

I opened the ramp and was ready to usher everyone inside, but there was a sudden rumble from deep inside the ship.

"What is that?" Ogwambi said, pointing down the corridor we had just come from.

I looked and saw a glow in distance. It was moving towards us. The light pushed dancing shadows ahead of it, and I felt a rush of hot air.

"Fire! Get inside," I said.

Everyone rushed up the ramp and inside. I was the last in and closed the ramp.

The fire belched into the landing bay, searing its way towards the ship.

The ramp shut, cutting off a slither of flame that made it through. The ship rocked as the explosion tore through the landing bay, then dissipated.

"One of those factions must have detonated a bomb," Moana commented.

"Who knows what damage that's done?" Gerlinde said.

I pushed past the group to the control room and started scanning.

Now that this ship was active—and crawling with Ammon—I had a better picture of the interior.

The landing pads and the corridors surrounding it occupied a small portion of the upper Ark, reaching across the cavernous space in the interior like a twisted finger. The control centre was at the tip of the finger, and beneath it was the wide open space. It was usually meant for the Ark's chimneys, but now hosted a city the Ammon robots had built before their split.

I could tell from the data that a large explosion had happened in that space. The others followed me into the control room.

"What's going on?" Moana asked.

"An explosion has occurred. It's one of the power conduits," I said.

"Has it affected the engine?" Ogwambi said.

"No, but there is another problem. The larger conduits transfer power using highly energised plasma," I said.

"We've all worked in the engine room Maiara," Gerlinde said.

"Sorry. Well, as you know, if a conduit breaks the plasma can ignite causing that explosion we saw. The network has closed valves to stop leaks, but some of the plasma was ignited. It's melting sections of the interior structure, and if it continues down to the engine room it will be critically damaged."

"Without the engine we can't transfer the power," Ogwambi concluded.

"We need to save this ship from being destroyed."

"While robots are fighting one another," Illarion finished.

"And in one hour," I added. "That's how long we've got until the plasma reaches the engine room."

21

THE NEW LEADER

"Won't the robots fix it?" Ogwambi said.

"They might be too busy. Or they might not know. Not if the command centre is in dispute."

A bang resounded through the shuttle.

"What was that?" I asked.

The bang happened again, twice, then repeated a third time.

"Maiara, someone is knocking on the ship's hull," Doc said.

I stood up and tried to calm myself. I went to the back of the ship and opened the door.

Standing a few metres from the bottom of the ramp was G5 and behind it was hundreds of blue robots. They were all charred or blackened after being baptised in the fire.

I walked halfway down the ramp and said. "Please tell me you have won."

"We have not. The battle continues, but we need your help," G5 said and I noticed its voice had changed. It was quicker, sharper.

"Our help? G5, turn those command protocols over to the red Ammon. End this so we can get out of here and save the Ark. That is your priority."

G5 rumbled forward a fraction and I backed up the ramp a little. "Those protocols are no longer active. I am now the leader of these

Ammon and we must win this war. The red Ammon have calculated that they must betray us to win. Our calculations say differently. You will help us win."

"You think me and the others are going to fight? No way," I declared.

"You will or we will destroy you," G5 said.

"If you destroy us then One will never let you join with the Ark. You will be stranded."

"I will not kill all of you. Just a few. The rest will be taken as hostages," G5 said. "Either way. As long as we win. As long as our calculations succeed."

"Our calculations? You're robots! All your calculations should be the same," I said.

G5 ignored my comment and said, "Help us or become hostages."

I looked back at the others waiting for me to make a decision I didn't want to make. This was not how it was meant to be. I was supposed to be here alone, risking my life to absolve myself of my final sin. And yet I was about to help eliminate another group.

"What do we do?" I asked.

"The red Ammon are launching units across the hull. They are heading for this landing bay. They intend to open it and fight us from behind. Take the ship and intercept them."

"Alright everyone we're going to help G5," I said.

"Maiara—" Moana began, shaking her head.

I glared at her and pressed a finger to my lips.

I started to shut the door, but G5 lumbered forward, stuck his arms in the ramp and kept it from closing. "Two of you will stay behind, while the remaining three do what I have asked."

I gritted my teeth. This robot was smarter than I thought.

"Moana, Ogwambi stay behind," I ordered.

"Maiara, no," Moana said.

"I'm in command here. Please do what I have asked," I said.

Moana and Ogwambi looked at each other, then reluctantly stepped down the ramp and left the ship.

"Heston, stay with Moana and Ogwambi," I ordered.

The catering robot happily left the ship and even gave Moana and Ogwambi sweets.

G5 let the ramp close, sealing me, Gerlinde and Illarion in the shuttle.

"Are we really doing this?" Gerlinde asked.

"We have to," I said.

"This is taking sides," Illarion said. "If we do this and the blue side doesn't win we don't know if the red robots will help us," he said.

"We have no choice," I said. "Both of you, go operate the external weapons. They are fairly intuitive. There are two on the top and two on the bottom of the ship. Go activate the bottom ones. We'll strafe the robots from above like bombers. I'll do the flying."

Gerlinde opened her mouth.

"Now, Gelrinde," I said, stalking off to the bridge, followed by Doc.

On the bridge, I started activating the ship.

"Maiara, now might be a good time to talk," Doc said.

I didn't reply.

"How are you feeling?"

"I feel like I'm either going to make a big mistake or solve this situation," I said.

I powered up the ship fully and lifted it off the bay. G5, his new friends, and my friends had already vacated the bay, so I opened the doors and took the ship out into space.

I put a headset on, connecting me with Gerlinde and Illarion.

"Our ship will be faster and better armed their theirs, but I'm detecting fifty robots heading our way from the other side of the Ark. I'll fly fast, strafing runs. Do what you can to take them out," I ordered.

"I've never used these before, Maiara," Gerlinde said.

"We'll get used to them. Ogwambi and Moana need us to win this," I went silent, and let that sink into their heads.

I throttled up as the landing bay closed behind me.

Onscreen, I had a wire frame display of the Ammon Ark. Fifty robots were orbiting the vessel in a close knit group. I wondered if they would suspect us.

I brought the shuttle up one side of the Ammon Ark, keeping the giant vessel between us and fleet of robots for as long as possible.

"Get ready," I said to the others.

I powered the shuttle to maximum and swept over the corners of the top pyramid, approaching the fleet from above.

"Fire when in range," I said.

Gerlinde and Illarion opened fire. On top and below the shuttle were two revolving turrets with three cannons. They fired bolts of green energy across space.

Some of the shots found a target and several of the robots erupted in green flame. The robots looked like ordinary Ammon, however they had large jetpack attachments on their shoulders.

As we passed overhead the small fleet immediately split up, breaking into several squares. One continued on to the landing bay while the others came at the shuttle from different angles.

"Gerlinde, abandon the turret you are in and operate one of the ones on top of the shuttle. We're going to get attacked from multiple angles," I said.

Behind me I heard Gerlinde run from one part of the ship to the other.

In a moment, weapons fire was about to assault the ship from all sides. The kinetic shield was up, but who knew how long it would survive. I needed to take each square on one at a time.

So I swung the shuttle right and headed into a nearby debris field.

Small bits of wreckage struck the shield, which flared. The pieces did no damage, but each flare weakened the shield by minor percentage points. I dodged behind a giant section of hull plating, once part of a giant vessel floating in the debris field.

The squares behind ducked away from the ship.

We passed behind the fragment and were heading straight at one group.

"Fire," I ordered.

Green blasts flew from the front of the shuttle and the robots fired back.

Red energy bolts hit the shield and it flared brighter than before. I checked the status and saw the percentage points dropping fast.

Our pass totally decimated the small group. One didn't get out of the way fast enough and the shuttle's flat wings sliced it in half, and the two pieces tumbled off the shield.

Then the remaining squares were on us, approaching from all sides.

The shield absorbed multiple impacts.

I took the shuttle down, passing underneath the Ammon Ark's equator.

The lower section had no hull and was only the crisscrossed structures of support columns, some covered in ice. I took the shuttle through the very middle, dodging the columns with ease. Whatever pilot's memories I had been given were amazing. But the robots behind me kept pace, easily dogging the columns, blasting the tail end of the shuttle. Gerlinde and Illarion fired backwards at the robots, nailing one or two here and there.

One shot from a robot made it through the shield and struck an engine.

"Fire in engine three," Doc said.

"Fire suppressing systems," I ordered.

The robot lumbered across the bridge to a new station and obeyed the order. The red alarms stopped sounding.

"Engine broken. We've lost a quarter of our thrust," the robot said.

"Maiara, we can't get away from them," Gerlinde said.

"I need ideas," I said.

"The ice. Gerlinde, shoot the ice," Illarion said.

"What? why?" I asked.

"We break it up then fly though the field of frozen water. The robots following us will be struck by the fragments. We'll survive, but they won't."

"It's a plan," I said and aimed the shuttle at an outcropping of ice around one column.

Both turrets—manned by Gerlinde and Illarion—rotated forward and started firing.

Each blast penetrated the ice at first, then exploded. After a few shots the whole block of ice shattered.

I took the ship straight through it.

Little pieces hit the shield, but melted with each flare.

One broke through though and stuck the forward window, leaving a small ding.

I stared at it. My blood turning cold at the thought of the explosive decompression I almost experienced.

"Are we ok?" Illarion asked.

"Yes, fine," I said, and wiped my brow.

We had passed through the ice field and now the robots were about to follow.

Half the robots disappeared as the ice shattered them into pieces. The whole group split off again, disappearing into the network of columns.

"I've lost track of them," I said.

It was then that one robot, perhaps lost or maybe on a suicide run, came out of nowhere and impacted the ship right on top of a turret, breaking through the shield and exploding right on the hull.

22

SACRIFICE

"Gerlinde," I cried out.

Suddenly air starting rushing from the shuttle.

Thankfully, I was strapped in my seat, but my hair flew backwards being sucked to the hull breach.

"Doc, the hull is compromised," I managed to say, although rushing air tore at my face.

The Doc reached out and pressed a button.

The shuttle had the ability to isolate small hull breaches with small kinetic shields. It was useless for keeping us safe from weapons, but strong enough to provide a temporary skin on the vessel.

The air became still.

I breathed in deeply, the second time in two weeks I had experienced decompression, which terrified me to my core.

I tapped the headset. "Gerlinde, respond," I shouted.

"Gerlinde," Illarion cried out.

Then I heard her ragged breaths over the com.

She coughed, and I smiled and sighed in relief.

"Sorry. The decompression almost made me pass out. I'm in the other turret," she said.

I couldn't celebrate, as twelve remaining robots converged on the shuttle from all sides.

I took the ship upwards, between the columns.

"Guys, we need a new plan. I don't think they will fall for the ice trick again."

I twirled the ship around the centre power conduit of the Ammon Ark. It was a giant, thick cable running down the length of the vessel from their engine room. It was now lit up, glowing with energy. The robots above had brought their ship fully online.

It was then I noticed the scabs on the ship. Ogwambi had been right. The ship had been struck down here by debris. The conduit had been punctured, and also healed itself.

"Illarion, Gerlinde, I have a plan. I need to corral those robots. Shoot around them force them closer and closer together behind us."

They both rotated their turrets back and fired.

The robots dodged the blasts, and as Illarion and Gerlinde fired, they brought the blasts closer to together in a curtain of green energy.

The robots clumped together and started firing back.

The combined weapons fire was bringing the shield's power down. It had thirty percent left.

I stopped dodging the ships and aligned the bottom of the hull to face the conduit.

"Illarion, fire at the conduit now," I said.

"You want me to do what?"

"Please, Illarion," I said.

"Ok," he said, and for a moment my heart skipped a beat.

They trusted me.

Illarion fired, and at that moment, I powered the remaining engines to full.

His blasts struck the conduit and burst it open, creating several holes. The conduits belched a stream of energised plasma into space.

The small fleet of robots tore right through it. The plasma instantly melted them and they all crashed into pillars. The firestorm of highly energised material streamed out like a geyser, then was attenuated as the holes closed themselves up.

"That was nuts," Illarion said.

"It worked though. Get ready! We have one last batch of robots to deal with."

I took the shuttle upwards to the top section of the Ammon Ark, right to the landing bay.

Seven robots were outside, shooting at the landing bay doors.

On one pass we obliterated them.

I swung the ship back around, opened the bay doors and took the shuttle in.

G5 was not waiting for us.

"Where is everyone?" Gerlinde said.

"Maiara, I've just checked out that plasma leak. It's still heading for the engine," Doc said.

"Why haven't the robots tried to fix it yet?" I asked.

"Maybe they don't know about it. Detecting issues with the ship is done in the control centre. They are currently fighting over the control centre, so they probably haven't seen the damage that has been done," Gerlinde suggested.

"Grab tools. We need to fix it or we'll lose this ship, and our only way to a new home," I said.

•

Five minutes later, I opened the ramp. I had a bandolier of tools wrapped around my chest—my bag containing everything One had given me. Gerlinde carried a big bag of materials and Illarion was hefting a large welder.

In the distance I heard laser blasts and the screeching of metal.

"Where do you think Ogwambi and Moana are?" I asked.

"With G5 as hostages, hopefully."

"I can't believe that robot disobeyed us. If the Earth wasn't destroyed I would complain to customer service," Illarion joked.

"How do we get through the war that's happening right now?" Gerlinde asked.

"Our shields will protect us and, presumably, the blue Ammon will not bother us at all. But the red Ammon might see us as enemies right now," I replied.

"Let's go and fix this ship," Illarion said.

We headed out of the landing bay. Doc was still with us. I had a device in my hand tracking the source of the plasma leak. We found it a level down—at what on our ship was the cargo bay level, but on this vessel was a viewing balcony of sorts. The balcony was circular and set right where the entrance to the cargo bay would be. It gave a fantastic view of the city the Ammon had built in the giant cavernous space at the top of their Ark.

We paused to look out over the balcony.

"To think they built a whole city in here," Gerlinde said.

"They saved millions more of themselves than we could," Illarion said.

"I guess they don't have to worry about water, or air, or food... only energy," I said.

"Plus, they could switch themselves off to conserve it. We can't do that," Illarion muttered.

We went down the next flight of steps and found not only the source of the leak, but the source of the explosion too. The stairwell used to be enclosed, but a gaping hole had been rent open thanks to an explosion in the city on the other side of the wall. A major conduit had been torn open and the usual self-repair was not enough. The conduit had a long gash across it and plasma was leaking out.

My mouth suddenly stung as we approached, and I held my hands out to hold the others back.

"The plasma is evaporating," I said.

Gerlinde dug around in the bag she held. "Gas masks," she said, and handed three out to us and we put them on.

As I studied the leak my skin started to itch. "It's an irritant," I said and held up my red arm.

"We need to patch the conduit," Illarion said.

He and Gerlinde bent down and rifled through the bag Gerlinde had. They pulled out more welding equipment and a fire extinguisher-like device.

Illarion set up the welder and stood away from the plasma streaming out of the pipe. He then nodded to Gerlinde.

Gerlinde sprayed black oozy substance from the extinguisher onto a small part of the gash in the conduits. The streaming plasmas stopped bubbling up under the ooze, which stuck to the conduit like tar.

Illarion came as close as he dared, his gas mask fogging up, and started to weld over the black ooze. He then stepped away when done and the weld held.

I watched them repeat the process, moving along the gash, but it would take them several minutes to fix it and I was no help.

I looked up the stairwell. Gerlinde and Illarion would be fine here. I knew where I needed to be.

"Guys, I'm going to look for Ogwambi and Moana," I said.

"What?" Illarion said, his voice muffled by the mask.

"I need to make sure they are alright. Finish here then get back to the shuttle."

I ran off before they could stop me. I made it to the balcony before I heard footsteps behind, and I turned to berate them for following me. However, it was Doc, not the others.

"Doc, stay with them and protect them."

"They will be ok. I need to stay with you," Doc said.

"I am ordering you—" I said.

"Human orders are overridden when a patient is endangering their own life," Doc said.

I stopped. "What do you mean 'endangering their own life?'"

"You are not in the right frame of mind. Yes, you need to save Ogwambi and Moana, but not like this. I can't let you go when all you see at the end of this is death."

"I'm trying to save my friends," I shot back.

"Don't do it like this. I calculate that if you continue in this frame of mind you will fail."

"I don't care about your calculations. Calculations can be wrong. Besides, I need to do something." And I stepped away.

Doc followed. "Why? So you can die trying?" the robot said, its voice rising.

I spun around. "Don't talk like that to me, robot. What I do with my life is my choice, even if I want to sacrifice it," I blurted out.

"Sacrifice it, why?" Doc asked. "Maiara, you've been better since returning from the underside of the Ark, but there is still something you've not told me."

"It's so I can earn back my—" I trailed off. My anger and rage had boiled over I had lost control.

"Earn back what, Maiara?" Doc said. "I thought we had discussed this. Yes, you were overcome with feelings of vengeance and, yes, you killed Turso, but there is nothing you can do if you truly feel sorry for his death. You may not want to kill yourself, but getting yourself killed in an attempt to right a wrong you can't undo, solves nothing."

"It's not just about the fact that I killed him," I said, tears in my eyes, and I bowed my head to hide them.

"Then what is it?" Doc asked.

My mind wanted to say it. The words were being fed into my mouth. I almost mimed them with no sound, but I held them back. I didn't want to say the words. I still didn't want to admit—

I looked up, but Doc had disappeared, and standing before me was myself. Doc was using his holographic display. It wasn't perfect. The image was a little distorted, but it was me.

I was looking at myself.

"Admit it to me. Admit to yourself," Doc said in my voice.

I turned away and wiped my eyes.

"You don't know me, Doc. You don't know how I feel," I said.

Doc, wearing my face, paused. "You know that phrase when someone says 'I know you better than you know yourself?'"

I scoffed. "What you think, you can reveal a surprise to me?" I said, laughing in derision though my tears.

Doc switched off the projection and became himself again. "Of course not. It's a lie, always has been. The only person who knows you best is yourself. The problem is humans lie to themselves."

I froze, because yeah he didn't know me, but he knew I was lying.

I looked at the robot again, and he was me once more.

The person I hated most in the world.

Doc had planted an idea in my head. Let it out. This is ok.

"I hate you," I said to me, and only me, not Doc.

My doppelgänger said nothing.

I stepped forward and pushed myself, and I staggered back.

"You let me down. You sinned. You broke a promise," with every statement more pushes.

"You were weak," I shouted into my face.

The projection looked down in sadness.

"When you killed Turso, you were glad. You liked it."

My doppelgänger looked away.

I grabbed my chin and pulled my face back to meet me eye to eye.

"No, you did that. You threw Turso down the hatch and you liked it. For a brief moment you enjoyed that power... that feeling."

I gasped.

I had said the words, out loud.

The truth... I was more monstrous than I would ever admit to myself.

I suddenly felt limp and broken. I had said the words. I had admitted that for a moment I had reveled in the death of Turso. I had let myself feel things no one should ever feel.

I barely registered the pain in my knees as I fell to the floor and stayed there.

"Tell me more. Don't lie," my doppelgänger said.

I looked up into my own eyes and said. "I failed. Do you remember the Vice President's speech? That one that was for you, to give you hope. You let your people down. You became the worst kind of person. You're a failure." I then buried my head in my hands.

Doc bent down to my level. "Maiara, why do you want to die... not by your own hand but in their conflict?" the robot asked.

"Because I need to regain my purity."

"Purity?"

"I was perfect when I came to the Ark. I was the hope of a nation. I was moving forward. Then Callum died I was filled with rage and I enjoyed killing someone, I should not have killed. I feel tainted.

"This mission was my way to un-taint myself. If I suffered if I died solving this problem then at least I would have paid, and earned back that position I had fallen so hard from."

"This whole time you've raged against your weakness and your failure, wishing that it wasn't true. You've been lying to yourself this whole time. You wanted to die because you thought it would cleanse you, that somehow you could earn back this righteous you lost, the righteousness you thought a speech gave to you.

"But Maiara, Turso is not coming back. Your death will not change things. If the ghost of Turso were here he would no doubt berate you and wish you dead. But you don't need his forgiveness or his blessing. You are alive and you have to keep living. You have to face this side of you that you hoped you would never face, and you have to move on. Your death will be a waste, a waste of everything your mother and father and your people represented that is now in you.

"You can't earn back your righteousness Maiara. You crossed a line, and you can't go back. You let yourself down. This will not change that. Turso will still be dead. However, you can learn from it. You can grow and be stronger."

"I was glad I killed him, Doc," I whispered.

The robot hugged me.

"Accept it. Don't bury it again. You can't be perfect, Maiara. No human can. You can't pay it back. You can only accept that you still need to live and still need to learn and grow. Do that for the people who love you more than they could ever hate you, no matter the things you've done."

I sniffed again and stood up.

I slicked my hair back and wiped my eyes.

My heart felt lighter. I felt much better. The secret was out. Suddenly, my desire to sacrifice myself was gone. I wanted to live. I wanted to try and do better.

"Thank you, Doc," I said.

"Happy to help," Doc said.

It then reached to the back of its head, said, "Returning to sleep mode" and shut itself down, going limp.

I sighed and tapped the robot and it woke up.

"Yes, Maiara. How can I help?"

"Where are Ogwambi and Moana?" I asked.

The robot looked around.

"I sense them in that city," Doc said, pointing at the city within the Ammon Ark.

"Then that's where we are going," I said.

23

BATTLE

The city was exactly how I expected a robot built city to look. It was ordered, layered, efficient, and dull.

Yeah I said it. Dull.

There were differently designed buildings, and it was lit like a cyberpunk cityscape, but it was still boring. Mostly because I could see the mind of a robot working out where everything should be. The buildings were different only because they were to function differently. Five built in a row were clearly just improvements on the previous design, as opposed to different architecture.

It was impressive because it was a city inside an alien spaceship. Humanity had only built far simpler structures.

It was also a mess.

This civil war amongst the Ammon had spilled out of the Ark corridors and into their city.

"Maiara, something big is approaching."

Crashing through a building came a large robot glowing red. I recognised it as one of the ones we had talked to in the command centre.

I raised my kinetic shield, but stayed still, trying to appear non-threatening. I relaxed a little. This was one of our allies, technically.

The robot turned toward me its eyes blazing an orange light.

I took a step back.

"You fired on our ships. You took a side," the robot said. "I must destroy you."

The robot raised a fist.

"Wait, I can change sides again," I said.

The robot paused.

"Calculations predict that you are either lying, or since you are changing sides now, you can change sides again and again."

The fist continued down, and I leapt to one side.

"Doc, back away," I shouted.

The Ammon ignored Doc and came for me.

I was not scared. I felt no need to cower. I let new memories One had given me take over. Military training. Tactical awareness training.

However, I was not as quick as One.

The robot's fist came at me again and I failed to leap aside quick enough. The first hit me and my shield flared as it absorbed the impact. I was forced backward a little. Though the shield absorbed most of the energy, it did not take all of it in.

The holographic display showed that the shield was overloading. It absorbed way too much energy for its storage systems to handle.

The robot's fist then broke apart into four fists, and it raised its limb again to strike.

I dodged aside, just in time, as the robot's multi-attack crashed through the wall of a nearby building.

I rolled amongst the rubble and got to my feet and started running.

I couldn't take any more hits.

I darted down a deserted side street.

Then I remembered Ogwambi said that the shields could vent the excess energy as a beam of concussive force.

I quickly tapped at the shield generator on my upper chest and flicked through the options. I found the release option and activated it. My left arm started to glow red, as the shield dumped its excess energy there. If I was remembering the instruction correctly, simply forming a gun shape with my hand would activate the beam. Clearly the inventor had a sense of humour.

The Ammon rounded the corner of the side street and came straight for me.

Just as it swiped with its fists—a hit that would have surely broken the shield and killed me—I leapt, spun in the air, and pointed my fingers like a gun barrel.

The fists missed me, and I missed with my shot.

The beam of red light grazed the right shoulder of the robot. It didn't burn or melt the robot. It simply shattered the metal on its right shoulder, then carved a line in the building behind it.

The robot groaned and stumbled backwards.

"Recalculating," it said to itself.

I raised my arm and tried to fire again, but I had depleted the excess energy the shield had absorbed, so I started again.

I darted around another corner.

The robot came careening through the building instead of going around it.

Fragments of stone assailed my shield. One struck my side, getting through the projection. It was like a taking a punch from a world class boxer, with cement in her gloves. I grasped my side and gasped as I tried to keep running, but my body was having none of it.

I checked the shield. It had absorbed enough energy for another blast, but I only had one shot.

Then all four fists of the Ammon grabbed my legs and wrapped around my hands, splaying them out like I was tied to a cross beam.

It lifted me up to its face.

I flexed my left fist trying to force my fingers into the right position.

"Calculations complete," the robot declared. "You will die and your death will be used to prove our resolve. We will force your leaders to take us with you, and they will know what we are prepared to do."

"You forgot to carry the one," I grunted.

I managed to form my left hand into the right shape.

The shield released the excess energy it had absorbed.

The force beam shattered the robot's fist from within and before the beam could fade, I swung my now free arm round right into the robot's face, hoping that these robots kept their brains in their heads.

The beam tore the robot's head apart, and it immediately collapsed.

The hands holding me relaxed, and I dropped to the ground. Pain flared up my legs as I tried to land properly, and failed.

"Doc," I shouted. I hoped the robot had some medical knowledge beside being a Psychiatrist.

I heard the clatter of the Doc's legs from down a street. It was on its way.

The Ammon then rose, sparks flying from its ruined neck.

"Rerouting complete," it said. "Secondary processor online. Recalculating."

A blade shot out of one arm that came at me. My shield didn't have the strength to repel it.

Then a hole suddenly appeared in the Ammon's chest.

A laser blast had plowed right through it.

The Ammon tumbled forward, and Doc quickly stepped up to me, pushing the giant robot aside.

Doc had a gun in its hand, which it then placed in a small compartment in its left thigh.

I stared at Doc, in a state of shock.

"My creator was a fan of an old film called *Robocop*," Doc explained.

"You have a gun?" I exclaimed.

"One told me to take it."

Doc knelt down and started scanning me.

"A cracked rib, Maiara," it stated.

"Do you have anything for the pain?" I asked.

Out of its other hip, the robot pulled a syringe, "This should do." Doc held the needle over my arm and I nodded.

There was a small jab. I felt pressure in my arm, and after a few seconds the pain in my side was gone.

"Let's get going. Ogwambi and Moana need our help."

24

REVOLUTION

Whatever battle had taken place here in the city, it seemed to be over.

Doc and I walked over the broken remains of many Ammon, red and blue.

The city opened out in a giant plaza in the centre, and there I found a small group of red Ammon, surrounded by blue.

"Maiara, Ogwambi, and Moana are in the centre of that group," Doc said.

"Are they unharmed?" I asked.

"They are."

They don't seem to be fighting," I said.

"I detect no weapons fire," Doc said.

"Then it's time to renegotiate."

I stepped out into the plaza, and made my way to the edge of the group of blue Ammon. The robots at the edge parted to make way for me and the Doc.

I was assuming that G5 had led his side to near victory in this short civil war. And my friends were probably still being held by G5.

As the final row of robots parted, I saw G5 in the centre of this mass of robots. It was standing over a red Ammon that was being picked apart by lesser blue robots.

Ogwambi, Moana and Heston were behind G5, watching with fear, and a little bit of revulsion, as the red Ammon was picked clean.

G5 extended a wire and one of his robotic servants took it and plugged into an adapter, which was then plugged into the defeated red Ammon.

G5 buzzed as it downloaded something.

The small group of red Ammon watched as G5 took their last remaining leader's command codes into its circuitry.

G5 then turned to face me.

"Hello, Maiara. I have now taken over the Ammon. This race is united once more."

The remaining red Ammon suddenly flashed blue, and the crowd melded with the other blues.

I wasn't sure how I felt about this. I mean, they are just robots following programming. They had no emotion. I wasn't even sure if they were alive in the technical sense.

But we needed their power for the Ark, so I had no choice.

I walked to Moana and Ogwambi. I pushed a plate of food that Heston tried to offer me to one side, and he replaced it in his chest cavity.

"Have you guys been ok?" I asked.

"We're fine. What's happening with the ship?" Ogwambi asked.

"Gerlinde and Illarion are fixing the leak," I said.

"What now?" Moana asked.

I turned to G5. "Your predecessor said that our agreement will stand. Are you going to honour it?" I asked G5.

The robot blinked for a few seconds.

"We require a new arrangement," he said.

I stiffened. The old agreement was just right.

I hoped that maybe G5 still had to obey me. "You will honour the agreement G5," I said.

The robot blinked again.

"Do you know what I have that these robots don't?" the robot said.

The training One had given me told me to keep him talking while I figured a way out of this.

"I do not," I said.

Ok he's a robot. He's gone all crazy because that blue Ammon gave him the command codes. If he didn't have them anymore then maybe a robot who calculated a little differently would be nicer.

"It's because I know all about humans. How you don't calculate. That you can't. That you do things by trial and error. We can't trust you. You do not see things all the way to the right conclusion. When I fought by the side of soldiers, I saw how they were illogical. I had to do ridiculous things in combat that did not make sense."

How do I get the codes to a new robot? I wondered.

"Our new arrangement will be that One will allow us to latch onto the Ark. We will share power, but the Ammon will take control of the Ark. We will not leave it in the hands of humans," G5 said.

"One will not accept that," I said, which I knew to be true since I was thinking like him right now.

"He will. I have five Arkonauts who can die to show him we are serious," G5 said. "I liked One. He used to think like a robot, but now he worries about all of you. There are more than enough humans. He can sacrifice a few."

Could Doc attack G5? Would he even win? Could I attack him?

"And we'll start with Ogwambi and Moana," G5 turned to them. "Better they die because One will trust you—the leader of this group."

G5 rumbled to Ogwambi and Moana. They were so shocked they had forgotten about their shields.

But that wouldn't protect them for long anyway.

Then I noticed Heston, sitting by them idly. The most useless robot, unless a chocolate cake could gum up G5. Then I noticed the bullet hole in his chassis.

One would never had enlisted the help of a useless robot.

"Heston, protect Ogwambi and Moana," I said.

The robot looked at me.

Heston opened his compartment. I sighed. He was going to offer food... Instead, the short cheerful-looking robot brought out several guns in his tentacle like arms, and a couple of knives.

His body extended upwards on its small tracks, and his eyes turned red. He went for G5.

The two tentacles holding knives speared G5 in his torso and shoulder.

The guns starting firing.

"Shields, everyone," I shouted.

Ogwambi and Moana raised their shields, and I ran for them.

"Run."

Doc followed me, and we ran for the crowd of Ammon gathered around their leader. They parted for us, having no orders.

We made it halfway into the crowd before G5 managed to gather itself and shouted.

"Kill the humans!"

That was when all the Ammon turned to face us.

25

WATCHING MYSELF DIE

Multiple robotic hands or claws scraped at our shields.

My power reserves shot up to dangerous levels very quickly.

It was then that beams of concussive force shot from either side of us, forcing the Ammon away and parting the crowd.

Gerlinde and Illarion were at the edge of the plaza, and had cleared a path for us.

The Ammon had scattered like a shoal of fish avoiding a shark. They then quickly reformed back into the empty space.

Next, Moana and Ogwambi fired into the crowd, scattering them further.

With Doc right behind, we made it through the mass of robots.

"Back to the ship," I said.

Illarion and Gerlinde fired again to cover our retreat, as the four of us ran for the edge of the plaza.

The wave of blue robots followed, all still under the sway of G5.

There was no way to out run them.

I stopped and let Moana and Ogwambi run past me, then I turned to face the wave.

"Go," I said.

"Maiara, no," Moana said.

"Go! Get the other hom—"

Doc was suddenly by my side, and it picked me up, and threw me towards the others. And I crashed into them, and they held me by my arms.

Doc pulled out its gun and the jewel on its chest glowed as it projected an image of me around itself.

It then turned back to face the charging Ammon and started firing.

The Ammon converged.

Doc's weapon fire picked them off.

The others dragged me away, and I didn't resist. I simply watched myself fire away, halting the tide, keeping them occupied. Then I saw them surround me and tear into the hologram and pull out bits of metal.

I watched myself die.

"Let's go, Maiara," Moana shouted into my ear.

That awoke me from my stupor. I found strength in my legs and started running.

"We can't out run them," Ogwambi said.

"We have to try," Gerlinde cried out as we pumped our arms and legs, heading down a main street back to the balcony level.

From above us, flying robots descended and started firing, tearing up the ground ahead of us.

We stopped before the blasts of energy struck us too.

That pause was enough. The wave of Ammon caught up.

"It's been fun," Illarion said, as the crowd came for them.

"Sorry I got you guys into this," I said.

"We got ourselves into this. For a friend who really needed us," Moana said and she grasped my shoulder.

The Ammon were ten metres away. I saw a collection of blades, claws and prongs.

This was it.

Then they stopped and the blue lights within turned grey.

They all froze.

One fell over as it was paused in mid stride.

"What just happened?" Ogwambi said.

Everything was quiet, except for the whine of what sounded like a struggling electric motor coming closer from behind the robots.

Something pushed its way through the robots, tipping over the Ammon.

It was Heston. He had multiple gouges in his skin, one caterpillar track was hanging off his wheels, and half of his arms were missing.

He rumbled up to me and held out a circuit board in one hand.

I took it and turned it over in my hand.

"Heston are you alright?" I asked.

"Operating at thirty percent efficiency," the robot replied cheerfully. "Would anyone like a sandwich? My refrigeration unit has been damaged, and they'll spoil if they are not eaten."

"What is this?" I asked holding up the circuit board.

"G5's motherboard," the robot replied.

I looked down at it. Without their leader the robots had stopped. No one was using the command protocols.

"Guys, take Heston back to the ship. Make sure he doesn't go offline.

"What are you going to do?" Moana said.

"See what happened," I said.

"I'm coming with you," she replied, and Moana nodded to Ogwambi, who smiled and helped Heston along.

Moana and I walked through the pathway of fallen Ammon that Heston had created. The robots were presumably still active, but without orders they had been put on pause.

A little way down the road we came to Doc, surrounded by other robots it had managed to destroy.

The orb on its chest was still projecting an image of me, frozen like a paused video, which flickered.

I stared down at myself. There was no blood, no broken bones. Just myself, that finally flickered one last time and died, revealing Doc's crushed and torn up body.

The orb on the front that projected the hologram was loose in its housing, and I bent down and pulled it free, disconnecting the wire from the back.

I then stood up and looked down at the robot.

"Maybe he can be fixed?" Moana said.

I sniggered a little, and then kicked Doc on the leg.

The robot sat up, flinging loose bits of itself everywhere.

Moana shrieked. "Maiara, you could have told me," she cried out.

"Doc isn't like other robots on the Ark," I said.

Doc's mangled head turned towards me. "I am the second most sophisticated robot on the ship," it said proudly, and then managed to get to its feet. "My system self-repairs thanks to a batch of nanites that can rearrange the metal on the molecular level. How are you feeling Maiara?"

I breathed in deep and let the breath out.

"Better," I said.

"Why?" it said.

"Because of what I admitted to you Doc... Wait that wasn't enough."

I turned to Moana a friend I trusted and who had stood by my side, she needed to know.

"Moana, when I let go of Turso, and fed him to Kraken, I did so because I was angry at him. He had killed Callum. He had ruined everything for me. I wanted him dead... and... and worse, I was glad to have done it."

I hung my head in shame.

"That makes sense, Maiara. That's what I would have felt too. Everyone would feel that way," Moana said.

"But I shouldn't have done it," I replied.

"No. But you did, and you can't change that." Moana laid a hand on my shoulders. "Sorry to be blunt, but is that why you have tried to end your life recently."

I nodded.

"Maiara, I'm not going to lie to you. You did something awful. Something no human should allow themselves to do. But it is done. You can't change what has happened. Do you want to do it again?" she asked.

"I don't."

"Killing yourself won't help you to grow."

"I just want to have not done it," I wailed.

"That can't be, but you have friends who love you, and a place and a purpose. Everything that makes you want to end it all is a burden you have placed around your neck. All you have to do is take it off and move on."

I sniffed. "But isn't that despicable? To just ignore what I did?"

"You won't be ignoring it. To let it bring you down like this is not righteous either. You're letting a mistake change you, making you throw away a gift you've been given. Don't forget, you are the bearer of many peoples' hopes and dream. Mathieu didn't throw his people's legacies away. Neither did Nuan. And definitely not Callum. It was taken from them. What about you, Maiara? Are you going to throw it away? You have something to live for."

I didn't reply and I didn't meet her gaze.

"Remember when I said I tried to throw it all away. I was going to dive into the sea. Imagine what I would have missed out on," and Moana raised her hands to indicate everything around her. "I would have missed out on all of this.

"Who knows how all things end? I don't judge you Maiara. Turso can't judge you either. Not because he is dead, but because he was a murderer too. Accept that you are alive. Just like me."

She then hugged me, clasping my arms to my sides.

Doc also hugged me, and I didn't mind that his broken arms jabbed me.

This was nice.

And so I let the burden go. I couldn't take this punishment I put on myself any more. I gave it up and let the relief wash in.

26
THE NEW LEADER

We found G5 right where we had left Heston fighting him.

"I'm surprised Heston was able to take him down," Moana said.

"I mean, G5 was a military robot right?" I said.

"It was not a military robot. G5 was simply a heavy lifter and tool bot. The army used him to move stuff around. He wasn't a fighter."

"Yeah, but Heston's a cooking robot?" I asked.

"Heston was a cooking robot who once worked for Doctors Without Boarders. His programming includes defence measures and protecting protocols," Doc said.

"Huh," Moana muttered.

G5 had a gaping hole in its chest. Heston must have speared it and pulled out the motherboard in one move.

"What do we do?" Moana asked.

"We still need the ship's power. We need to get it back to the Ark," I said.

"What about the Ammon?" Doc asked.

I sighed. "We did a deal with them," I said. "Doc can you access the command protocol in G5?"

"I can."

"Then can you extract them and incorporate them into yourself," I said.

"Wait, Doc, will they change your programming like they did to G5?" Moana said.

"Maybe, although I am more sophisticated than G5."

"Do it, Doc. I trust you," I said.

I motioned for Moana to step back with me as Doc reached into the hole in G5's chest. I heard the clicking of connections being made.

Doc did something because the psychiatry robot shut down for a moment then reactivated.

"Doc?" I asked.

I heard the sound of robots moving around the city—all around us.

"Hello Maiara, I have successfully incorporated the command protocols into myself."

Robots started filing into the plaza from all around the city.

"You lead the Ammon now, Doc. Will you honour our agreement?"

"I will. We all shall. We have redesigned a part of this vessel to detach from the main body. It will latch onto your Ark and transfer its power. We will shut down and trust that you will take us to a new homeworld," Doc announced.

The Ammon, whose bodies now glowed green instead of blue or red, gathered around.

"I hope you can all accept my apology for what has happened," I said to the robots.

"We will honour the agreement. Our homeworld was destroyed by the same aliens who built this ship. We share the same plight, the same goals," Moana said.

"Doc, I know you control them, but do they understand?" I asked.

"They do. They have run the calculations," Doc said.

"Right," I said. "Let's go home."

27
THE NEW DEAL

We used the Ammon Ark to communicate with ours.

We explained everything to One, who was surprised and impressed in equal measure. It took some convincing and some joint calculations by both ships, but it was agreed that taking the Ammon with us and giving them a planet in our new solar system was possible. The extra power the Ammon ship provided topped up the Ark and then some.

Three days later, we had maneuvered the Ammon ship closer to the Ark. I sat on the shuttle with the others and a patched up Heston, watching the final stage.

The transfer of power was done wirelessly. Human scientists had long ago discovered ports on the Ark that allowed for power transfer. The engines on both vessels were essentially giant rechargeable batteries. And energy could be transferred through space.

The Ammon ship lined up with the correct port and transferred all the energy the Ark required, saving just enough to allow the ship to connect to ours.

It was a sight to see.

The Ammon Ark discarded its lower section, the skeletal structure that was once the water storage areas drifted away, no doubt to once again orbit the wormhole. What was left was a nearly hollowed out and weightless pyramid, and it settled on easily top of our Ark. Our vessel now had a secondary hull around the top, as the pyramid clamped down, and the maneuver was complete.

I had to admit to myself that if I had died, I would never have seen this, and I was glad I had.

Doc's face appeared on a screen.

"Humanity, the Ammon will now go into hibernation to conserve power. I am sending you a reactivation sequence. Please activate it when we reach the new solar system."

One's face appeared on another screen. "Thank you, Doc. I formally release you from humanity's service. You are your own robot now."

"Thank you, Captain One. I am happy to inform you that the Ammon are content in their own way to not be alone in this endeavour."

"Sleep well," One said.

"We will."

Doc's face disappeared and a few seconds later the lights from within what remained of the Ammon Ark shut down.

We all looked out the window, taking in the unique view. The wormhole in the background, the endless stars.

"Maiara, return to the Ark. We'll be firing the engines soon. If we wait too long it will be more difficult to escape the gravity of the wormhole."

"On our way," I said, and started flying home.

"Well, that was an interesting few days," Ogwambi said, eating cake Heston had furnished him with.

"I think a celebration is in order," Gerlinde added.

"You know, technically, we made contact with a new race. Surely that should be day on the calendar. We could celebrate it every year," Moana suggested.

"What do we call it?" Illarion asked.

"Ammon day," Ogwambi said with a put upon deep voice, trying to give it gravitas.

"Ammon-mas Day," Gerlinde added.

"You can't just combine Christmas and Ammon," Illarion said.

"You do better," she shot back at him.

"Erm... Ammon-easter," he tried.

"See! It's hard, isn't it?" Gerlinde pointed out.

This kind of banter continued and I even pitched in, something I had not done in a while and it felt good.

I didn't even punish myself when I had these good feelings. I didn't look back. If I was truly sorry for my choices, wallowing them is not the solution. Challenging them and growing away from them was.

I landed the shuttle in the bay and once the doors were closed, I dropped the ramp and told everyone to disembark and get a shower. It had been three days since we had each had one.

At the bottom of the ramp was One, waiting there to greet us.

He scowled at the others.

"I was worried sick," he said, in a whisper.

The others looked the floor.

"It is my job to keep you all safe. Imagine my grief if one or all you would have died," he added. "However, you're all growing up. I can't be protecting you all the time." He stepped aside to let them pass. "Go get food and," he sniffed, "cleaned up."

The others walked off, Moana holding Ogwambi's hand and Illarion holding Gerlinde's.

I sighed a little at watching the couples go.

For a moment, I let my hand drift out as if Callum would take it.

I almost jumped out of my skin when Heston's hand took mine.

"Come on, let's get you patched up in the medical bay," the little cooking robot said.

"Thanks, Heston," I said, and let him lead me down the ramp to One who was waiting.

One rubbed Heston affectionately on his domed head.

"Who knew a cooking robot could be so handy?" One said.

"Thank you for adding him to the crew," I said.

"You look beat up, Heston. I am so glad you came back in one piece."

"Thank you, master Joshua," the robot said, and it trundled off, banging into the door frame as it left the bay.

"Master Joshua?" I said.

"Heston was my family robot. My father used him as a bodyguard when he toured the world. I used to love playing with him as a child, back when I was different," he said wistfully.

"I apologise that things didn't go as planned," I said.

"The plan was to bring back energy for the Ark and you succeeded," One said.

"Would you have done things differently?" I asked.

"I would have destroyed all the Ammon and taken the power. They aren't humans and I'm not here to protect non humans. I would be worried that we couldn't trust them. I would be wary of sharing a solar system with them," he said.

"Well, I think it will be fine," I said. "The others were okay with it. I wonder if that's down to the 18th memory—giving them the wisdom to see beyond selfish desire? Being more open? A feeling I will never feel."

"Maiara?" One said.

"Remember, the 18th memory deactivated again. I think it's broken," I said.

"The nanites activation device," he said, holding out a hand.

I fished it out of the bag I had hanging over my shoulder and gave it to him.

He adjusted some settings and pointed it at my head.

"It is deactivated, and you're right, some of the nanites are corrupted and have permanently shut down. I'm sorry, Maiara," he said.

"I guess I will always be that Arkonaut incapable of being like the others... Incapable of being better."

One looked taken aback.

"Excuse me, Maiara, but that's stupid. Over the last few days you showed mercy to the Ammon who threatened you, you took a compromise when you could have just taken. You've learned to live with yourself. The 18th memory may not be working in you, but you're getting there all by yourself. Because you want to. Because you know you're not perfect."

He paused for a moment, and let that sink in.

"That is exactly how you should be.

"Now let's get to the control centre and fire the engines. Our new home awaits us."

He turned around, walked out of the bay, and I followed.

28

BACK ON COURSE

The engines fired, and that put us back on course. Our remaining energy reserves were more than enough to get us to our new home and land without a major incident.

One organised a celebration and it was spectacular. However, midway through I separated from the party and went down to the engine room.

I climbed the stairs down to the base, opened the hatch at the bottom and looked down the shaft.

I wasn't here for Kraken, but I looked forward to seeing him again when it was my time to be his hostage once more.

Instead, I looked down and thought about Turso screaming. I pictured the moment I let him go.

I closed my eyes.

I'm sorry, Turso, I really am, I thought. *I wish you were here and you could forgive me. But you're not, and right now, I need to forgive myself and move on.*

I am sorry.

I closed the hatch and went back to the party.

Time to move on.

Time to accept the gift I have been given.

One made more bearable by the people who love me.

THE FUTURE

OGWAMBI

"Ogwambi?!" I blurted out. "You're Ogwambi?" I repeated.

"Do I know you?" he said, and he stepped forward and squinted. Then his eyes widened. "Your scar. You have the same scar as Callum." He eyes then went to my shirt, which was still torn at the sleeve, where I had ripped off a piece to write my message into the past.

"You are Callum," he repeated, and he moved closer to the cell walls where he rebounded off when his head struck the glass panel.

Ogwambi grasped his head and said "Ow," then he reached forward and touched the glass.

"You can let me out, mate," he said.

I turned to Ada. "Is it him?" I asked her.

Ada was appraising 'Ogwambi'. "It could be. He's definitely a little older. It's been many decades since we were supposedly put in our pods and placed in that museum. Surely he would look a lot older."

"Two?" Ogwambi said, "Come on, Two! Let me out."

"Why aren't you an old man?" I asked him. I felt a twinge of guilt at interrogating him. He was a friend after all, the only other human I had seen since Ada. The Arkonauts still lived. But he was with the Thieves and my new One-inspired biology made me act differently, I was sure of it.

"Older?"

"It's been years... decades... since I was put in my pod. You should be forty by now, yet you look about twenty."

"You don't look decades older either, Callum," Ogwambi said with a smile.

"I have been enhanced like One. What's your excuse?" I said.

Ogwambi looked down at his arm, studded with ports that would have connected to his robot parts. "The Larceny also enhanced me," he said, and he stroked one of the ports and looked sad. "We have various pieces of their technology inside us, and it holds back our aging."

"There are more Arkonauts?" I asked.

"Yes. Many more," he replied. "Do you want to meet them—your friends?"

"Yes, I would love to see—" I began.

"Wait. Tell us what happened. How did you join these Larceny, these Thieves? They are the ones who destroyed our world," Ada said.

Ogwambi bit his bottom lip and turned his back on us. He hung his head and continued to stroke his implants. He sighed, then turned back to us.

"This isn't by choice," he said, and he twitched at saying those words.

"Tell us your story," I said.

"Well, that's complicated isn't it? Since you've engaged in some time travel, I don't know if what I explain will even make sense."

I huffed. "Ok. Here is the quick explanation. In my past, all the Arkonauts died when the minister from China detonated the nuclear bomb."

"We prevented that," Ogwambi said. "A hole in the universe opened up and a piece of your shirt came through, giving us a code to put the bomb on a shuttle, and get it away from the Ark."

"Well, that's not what I went through. One placed me in a special room on the Ark where I was able to survive the explosion. I was put in a pod that enhanced me and I stayed in there until I awoke several decades later in a museum on the Thieves' homeworld. I escaped with the help from some aliens and they gave me the chance to time travel. I saved you. You lived because of me in an alternate timeline."

"Then, why are you in *this* timeline?" he asked.

"Because for some reason both timelines have merged," Ada said.

"The time travel, how does it work? he asked. "That's so cool."

"What happened to you?" I replied, trying to keep the conversation on track.

"You can skip to the parts where I revealed myself," Ada said. "And was put in a pod to heal after Turso."

"Right," Ogwambi said. "Wow. It's hard to keep it all in your head. After that we travelled through the wormhole and we had power problems. Thankfully, there were other damaged Arks nearby, some with power. Maiara—along with myself and others—managed to find one that could be brought back to our Ark to transfer its power. We had to dodge some dangerous robots while on board that other Ark, but we got power to ours and carried on. On our way to our new homeworld, we were intercepted by the Larceny, who had come looking for their ship. There was an invasion of the ship. We couldn't resist. The Larceny overrode control of our life boat."

I nodded, remembering how the Thieves had tried to do the same to us.

"In punishment for stealing their ship, One was executed. And the rest of us were transformed. The Larceny put their technology into us and made us part of their armed forces. Not all the Arkonuats survived. Moana died when they tried to convert her."

His face contorted in equal parts anger and sorrow as he remembered that moment. "Gerlinde and Illarion survived as did about fifty others. We're all cannon fodder now, should they send us against those the Larceny try to destroy."

He then pointed at Ada. "Two was placed in their museum along with other things from the Ark." His brow furrowed, "So what happened to you? Did you see this... Future Callum in the museum?"

Ada shook her head. "No. I awoke in the same timeline as you—while you were a Thief, technically. I was in that museum. I awoke when the pod I was in failed. I met an alien called Antumbra. She helped me escape, and I met several other aliens who all fled with me. Antumbra offered me the chance to change the past. I was thinking about it, but I didn't know what moment in the past to change. This Callum was in his own timeline, and he changed the past. In that instance, both universes combined for some reason.

"So, there were once two universes and now there are one," Ogwambi summarised.

"Yes."

"Well, we're all on the same page now. Can you let me out?"

I looked at Ada and she shrugged.

"I'm still not sure you're Ogwambi," I said.

He snorted. "Who else could I be? All other humans were killed."

"Tell me something only Ogwambi could know. Tell me what nation you were in when you were teleported onto the Ark."

"England. In the Lake District. Just like you," he said.

I looked at Ada, "It must be him, right?"

"You're not going to release him are you?" said a voice from behind us.

I turned and Lyger was there, her fists clenched.

"We were," Ada said slowly.

"You can't. He's a Thief," she said.

"He's human... Notice the lack of tentacles," I said.

"He's one of them now," Lyger reiterated.

"Was one of them. He's no longer connected to his machinery," I replied, and pointed back into the cell at the tangled mass of robot parts he had stepped out of.

"He's still one of them," she said.

Ogwambi opened his arms wide and displayed his palms.

"I am not. Thanks to one of you almost killing me when you thought I was a Larceny. You broke the machine that held me. I'm not under its control anymore."

"You can't, Callum. He might still be under their control," the cat alien begged.

"He's human," I said.

"When my world was attacked by the Destroyer that landed on our planet, the Thieves communicated with my world. One of them was displayed on every screen. It didn't look human, but it was human-shaped, just like this Ogwambi. It gloated. It inspired fear in my people's hearts. It was not just cannon fodder," she shrieked.

I turned back to Ogwambi. "Well?"

"You believe her?" he said.

"Why not? Strange lie to tell," I said.

Ogwambi spluttered unable to reply. Then his shoulders sagged.

"I don't know about that. Maybe a Larceny used that Arkonaut as a fall guy. Or maybe they forced them to do it for fun. They've been torturing us for years. They are the Thieves. They jealously guard their technology—after all, it keeps them above the other races in the galaxy. They hated that we had turned the Ark into our own space ship. They really wanted to hurt us. I could see them forcing an Arkonaut to do that... mentally torturing them."

I was satisfied. "Well, Lyger?" I said.

"I still don't think you have a right to release him. The others will not like it," she hissed.

Ada looked me in the eyes and nodded.

"Sorry, Ogwambi. I'm not in charge here. I have new friends that I'm working with. Don't worry, I'll convince them to let you out."

Ogwambi gritted his teeth, then smiled. "I understand, but please find something onboard to help with my implants. I usually have injections to make them work with my body. You should find some in the stores on the ship."

"We have found those stores," I reassured him.

Suddenly Pebbles appeared in the doorway. It tapped the ground, then gestured its hand toward the door.

"I think Pebbles wants us to go with him," Ada said.

"We'll be back," I said to Ogwambi, and we left the room.

Lyger didn't follow.

I added, "Lyger, Antumbra probably has news for us."

The cat alien growled at Ogwambi, then gracefully walked past me to the control centre.

RAMOTH

Inside the control centre, I encountered a new sight.

The Time Rod—Antumbra's piece of technology that allowed her to send things back into the past—was activated. She must have fully recharged it again, which had taken weeks.

The rod was in two pieces, floating in a storm of energy. I saw images in the energy, flowing through the storm—a dark shape moving throughout.

Antumbra was nowhere to be seen.

"Where is Antumbra?" I asked Hippo.

The giant hippo-centaur was standing off to one side with his arms crossed. His massive jowls opened, and he spoke between two tusks. "She's just finishing up, apparently. She has determined what happened when you last changed time."

I nodded, then took up a place in the room amongst the motley group of aliens.

The Mouth, as I called him, basically a small person with a gigantic maw and no eyes, stood next to Pebbles—the even smaller pile of rocks that were somehow alive. Lyger jumped up onto a control panel and curled up. The last alien, Mantis—a giant skeleton of a Praying Mantis with orange energy playing around its limbs—was trying to follow the pattern of light that was Antumbra, who was flitting within the energy the rod created.

Ada leaned against a console next to me.

As I waited, I looked up at the control centre's domed ceiling. The screen there showed me a wormhole.

"How far away are we?" I asked Ada.

"Less than twenty minutes," she said.

The giant sphere that was the mouth of the wormhole loomed large. There were many of these entrances surrounding the Thief homeworld.

For faster-than-light travel across the universe, they were a necessity. Apparently, the one orbiting my original solar system was not the only one, and in fact there was a network, linking multiple star systems. While ships built by the Thieves could travel near to the speed of light. Such speeds were useless for reaching any world. The Thieves chart the wormholes, and when they find a solar system with advanced technology, they send in a Destroyer to obliterate that civilisation and prevent competition in the future. Sometimes, though, they can't reach a civilisation in time, and it develops space-faring technology of its own, escaping a world before the Thieves can get there.

That's why we were heading for a wormhole. We were going to a place that even the Thieves won't send a Destroyer to.

A frizzle from the nexus of energy between the rod signalled Antumbra lancing out to the ground. Her energetic skin fried the air as she removed herself from the rod's energy field.

She stood up, and using her hand, brought the energy field down to a smaller more manageable size.

"Well, I've figured out what happened the last time we tried this," she said.

Silence reigned in the room as Antumbra was about to make her big revelation.

"Turns out I was right. When we used the rod the last time, we did create two parallel universes."

She manipulated the Rod's energy and a single line appeared in mid-air which then branched off into the two lines like the letter Y—except one line remained straight while the other curved off. I presumed the straight line was the original timeline.

"The new universe continued along a different path." Both new lines got longer and longer, with the curved one getting further and further away. "Then something happened that set events heading along a path very similar to the original."

The curved line started arching back to the straighter one until it became straight too, running very close and parallel to the first line.

"Both universes fell pretty much in sync, which makes sense. Ada was in the pod in the museum. Callum was in a pod. They escaped, freed me and events continued in much the same way. Both universes were mostly the same down even at the molecular level. Remember the only places that actually changed were in a small very small part of the universe. 99.9999999 percent of all the atoms were doing pretty much what they were in the original timeline.

"With two universes so similar, they merged."

Both lines came together.

"I would say that everything that was old bled into the new universe," Antumbra concluded.

Ada turned and smiled at me. "My universe won."

I frowned. "Are you sure it wasn't the other way around?"

"Definitely. For one thing our prisoner—"

"He's not a prisoner," I interrupted. "Turns out he's human. One of my former crewmates. Isn't that great?" I said to everyone.

"Well, he's a prisoner to rest of us," Lyger said.

I scowled at her again.

"Guest," Antumbra finished. "Proves we've gone into his universe. If he appeared in the original, the Thieves wouldn't know who he was in the original timeline. Why would then send him to attack us?"

I leaned over to Ada. "My universe was the original," I pointed out.

"Why did this happen?" Hippo asked.

"It turns out that if two universes are so close to being similar, it's like there aren't two universes anymore... just one. If the alignment is close enough it's like all the matter and energy *decide* to re-join. Why be separate? It's like a relationship between two people. When they agree on things they stay together, but when one starts to change they drift

164

apart. If they change, and think alike again, they re-join. We're talking about universes of course, so it's things like the states of particles, and exact balance of matter and energy on a scale we can't fathom. It also means that the multiverse is likely not infinite. If a universe is being created somewhere, it might combine with another if they are close enough."

"So what does this mean?" the Mouth said.

"It means I can now think about using the rod to ensure that, somewhere, my people exist exactly as I remembered them. Also knowing that the multiverse is not limitless, this increases my chances. I'll be able to recreate the energy patterns of my family—a version of me and my wife and children will exist without the Thieves destroying them. I know now what the limits are to changing the past. It has to be huge, a monumental shift in the time stream, so both universes never return to normal."

"How do you do that?" I asked.

"I'll do some more calculations, but that can wait until we exit the wormhole. For now, let's get there."

"Where is it we're going exactly? You keep talking about a world where the Thieves can't go. What's this place called?"

"My people may have not have become spacefaring, but we learned of a civilisation that welcomes survivors of the Thieves as allies. One that the Thieves can't destroy even though they are still more powerful than them."

"Which is called?"

"Ramoth?"

"Ramoth?" I repeated.

"Yes, it is known as the Planet of Sanctuary. Space travel is hard, long and requires massive problems to solve, but communicating over vast distances is relatively easy. Humans may not have connected, but lots of other alien races have. Word of the Thieves spread around the galaxy. That didn't help some civilisations, unable to send ships off into space, but some did manage it. Those that can reach Ramoth, the natives welcome as refugees.

"The hope is that one day they might figure out how to destroy the Thieves," Lyger said.

"Why don't the Thieves try to stop them?"

"You'll see when we pass through the wormhole and reach their solar system," Antumbra said.

I looked up. The wormhole filled the screen.

"We're about to go in," I commented.

"Let's get ready. I'll handle communication. Hippo, monitor the engine output. Lyger, make sure we're on course. The rest of you, don't need to do anything," Antumbra ordered.

"Communications?" I asked.

"You'll see," Antumbra said.

The aliens took their places around the control room while the Mouth, Pebbles, Mantis, Ada and I stared at the screens watching the show.

"What will this be like?" I asked.

"I have passed through one before, though it was after my kidnapping by the Thieves. I never saw it. I was in a cell," Hippo replied.

"Why do the Thieves have a wormhole that leads straight to Ramoth?" I asked.

"They once tried to attack it," Antumbra said. "And failed."

"Entering wormhole in 5, 4, 3, 2, 1," Lyger said.

The entire vessel shuddered as it passed through whatever barriers surrounded the wormhole entrance. I felt the vibration through my feet.

The screen filled with a multi-coloured vista of stars, nebula and, I was certain, a black hole where the light stretched out and curved.

"What are we seeing?" Ada asked taking in the view with wide eyes.

"The wormhole distorts the space it passes through. What you're seeing is a snapshot of somewhere in the galaxy.

Against the side of the wormhole I noticed another curved tunnel.

"What's that?" I asked.

"Another wormhole, inside this one, leading to another part of the galaxy. As I said before, the Thieves use them to get around the galaxy when they discover a world they want to destroy."

"Are we in any danger in here?" I asked. And I squirmed where I was perched as I noticed another black hole stretch past us.

"If we don't try to leave it we will be fine," Antumbra said.

"Are you certain that the Thieves can't remotely take control of the vessel? They might try to force us against the sides of the wormhole and destroy us," the Mouth said.

"I managed to find the remote control unit and deactivate it. They can no longer link to this vessel," Lyger replied.

I nodded, mildly assured, as we travelled through this special phenomenon.

Mantis clicked and pointed at another part of the screen.

"What is that?" I said when I saw what the alien was pointing at.

It was a squid of some kind—massive and speeding towards the Destroyer. It came from one of the apertures in the tunnel.

The control room answered for me, detecting the squid and identifying it in the Thieves' language.

"Some sort of space-born life form," Hippo said.

"Lyger, roll the Destroyer to the side. Ram it," Antumbra said.

The view on the screen changed as our island-sized vessel moved across and smacked the squid as it came for us.

The creature was knocked to one side and it cartwheeled in space, its tentacles flailing. When it managed to right itself, it flew back from where it came from.

"Took care of that," Hippo commented.

"We'll be leaving the wormhole in just under a minute," Lyger said.

"Silence please as we leave the wormhole. I have to be quick with communications," Antumbra said.

"Exiting the Wormhole in 5, 4, 3, 2, 1," Lyger reported.

Space stopped curving and distorting and flattened out.

In the distance was a bright star—a new solar system.

Antumbra's hands moved over the controls quickly.

"Ramoth, this is Antumbra—" she said loudly and quickly, but was cut off when the Destroyer suddenly lurched left.

A huge shockwave rippled through the ship and everyone was thrown off their feet.

Alarms started going off.

"What the heck!" Ada said.

Antumbra got back up and tried the communications again.

"Cease fire! Cease fire," Antumbra yelled into the microphone.

"Callum," Ada said, pointing up at the screen.

A picture of the ship, extrapolated from sensor details, showed us the lower half of the Destroyer.

Water was streaming out into space from a giant crater which was still molten around the lip.

Something had blasted a hole in the ship, a hole as big as the island of Manhattan.

Someone had a weapon more powerful than our own nuclear bombs.

"Ramoth. We are refugees. Escapees of the Larceny. Please don't fire again," Antumbra said. "We have something to sell to you!" she cried out.

The Destroyer was struck again and vessel started spinning.

"Why are they shooting at us?" I said.

"Please, Ramoth. We want to give you this vessel. We stole it from the Thieves, and now we want you to have it. It will be worthless to you if you destroy it," Antumbra said.

Lyger silenced the alarms.

The screen was showing a second impact on the top section of the destroyer. A hole the size of Everest. Bursting out of the hole were chimneys, the one the Destroyer usually used to suck up air. Thankfully it had not depressurized this area of the ship.

The speaker finally came on, and a booming voice spoke.

"How do we know you are not Thieves?" a Ramothian, I guess, said.

"Hippo, shut down the power," Antumbra said.

Hippo shut down the engines.

"We've powered down. We are at your mercy. Do the Larceny do that?" Antumbra said.

There was no reply.

"What was your planet?" the voice said.

"We called ourselves the Energeons. We made contact with Ramoth in the year 6789, your calendar. Our president was Silakshi."

"My name is Hippo from the Matriarchy of Senture. We made contact with Ramoth in 6785, your calendar," Hippo added.

More silence.

Everyone was staring at the screen as the response came in.

"Welcome to the Ramothian star system," the voice finally replied.

EXCHANGE

It took us all a frantic few hours to steady the ship. The weapons fire had done some serious damage to numerous power conduits, which had to be rerouted. Even the main computer needed to be restarted.

Once that had been taken care of, Antumbra reactivated the engines and we were in bound for the planet of Ramoth.

This would actually take only a few hours, as opposed to the weeks it took us to get from the Thieves' homeworld to the wormhole orbiting their solar system. The wormhole exit we had come through was much closer to Ramoth than the entrance.

That was good. I wanted to get onto a planet's surface as quickly as possible. I hadn't realised how much I had missed it.

As we travelled in system, I saw one of the weapons platforms that had fired upon us.

The whole structure was mounted on a small asteroid. Thrusters dotted around the hunk of rock kept it steady in space. The weapon itself was mounted like a missile launcher I had seen once on a battleship on Earth. But it didn't have two missile pods. Instead, two-discs hung on either side of a gun barrel.

"So what did they hit us with?" I whispered to Lyger, hoping not to be overheard as Antumbra was negotiating with a Ramothian, using a screen on the other side of the room.

"It's called a Micro Black Hole Destabiliser," she answered. "The engineering concepts are beyond me, but the weapon uses one collider," and she pointed at one of the discs, "to create a micro black hole, smaller than a millimetre across, and then it fires it at the target. A second collider, at nearly the same time, creates a small amount of antimatter, which is fired right behind the black hole."

"Incredible," Ada said.

"The black hole strikes the hull of a ship and immediately warps the hull as it tries to devour the vessel. That usually causes a hull breach. The antimatter then strikes the black hole. The antimatter explosion would usually tear the ship apart *and* remove the black hole from existence, so it doesn't hang around afterwards. Thankfully, our stolen vessel is so massive that it would have taken several more strikes to destroy it."

"Thank goodness we stole this one and not a smaller vessel," Ada said.

"One thing I don't understand is why Ramothians don't take these weapons to the Thieves' homeworld and attack," the Mouth said.

"As powerful and advanced as the Ramothians are, the Thieves are more capable. The Thieves know how to block ships from coming through wormhole apertures. This restricts access to their homeworld. No one can go through to their side without their say so. If they used conventional space travel to get these guns to their homeworld, it would take hundreds of years," Lyger explained.

"Thank you," Antumbra said, behind us.

We all turned to see her bent over a console speaking into a screen, which was filled with the face of a Ramothian. Her shoulders relaxed, and her energy skin brightened, like she had heard the best news ever.

The Ramothian had light blue skin, a roughly human-ish face except its nose was absent, and a sort of crown-like bone structure from its temple around to the back of its head.

"These are the coordinates for you to park your stolen vessel. I congratulate you on your acquisition, and for stomping on the tentacles of this galaxy's blight," the Ramothian said.

Antumbra bowed and glowed a little brighter.

"Thank you," she uttered and then signed off.

She turned to us with a smile on her face.

"It's done. We have an agreement with the Ramothians," she announced.

"What did we get?" the Mouth said.

"We will give them the Destroyer. They will give us a million gold disks. Among the eight of us that's 125,000 each."

"Is that a lot?" Lyger asked. We all looked at her. "What? I have stuff I want to buy."

"We could get a decent ship for a quarter of that amount, and I mean *decent*. It could cross a solar system in a week, survive the wormholes, refuel after 10,000 light years," Antumbra said.

"It's enough to settle down on Ramoth, and live in comfort for a thousand years," the Mouth said.

"Now, I have to think about what I'll buy," I said. "What are you going to do with that money?"

"Buy a ship for sure," the Mouth said. "But stay on Ramoth, safest place... and good food, apparently."

"If the Ramothians are battling the Larceny, I'll see if I can join their fight," Hippo said.

"I'll buy a ship too. It's possible some of my kind are still out there. I want to find them," Lyger said.

I looked at Mantis. The insectoid skeleton moved its head around as if it was thinking, then raised a claw. He made was circle with the tip of the claw.

"Circle?" Ada said.

"Pizza?" I said.

"Planet," Antumbra said.

Mantis pointed a nodded, then he pointed at himself.

"You're going to find a planet for yourself?" I clarified.

Mantis nodded. Mantis then hugged himself and shivered. And shook his head.

"A non-cold planet," Ada said.

Mantis nodded.

We all looked at Pebbles.

The walking pile of rocks shrugged.

"Pebbles has no concept of money, he doesn't need anything," the Mouth said. "Maybe you could buy a spot of land and just stay still for the rest of your life?"

Pebble rocked from side to side then clapped his two boulder hands together.

"He approves of that idea," the Mouth said.

"Antumbra?" I said.

"Once I've used the rod to save my people, I'll destroy it. It will have one more time travel journey left in it, and I don't want the Thieves using it. Then I'll get a ship of my own and find others like me. It's a big universe. Life just like mine must have been created somewhere, I'll find them and join their civilisation, if I can."

"What about you humans?" Hippo asked.

I looked at Ada. She and I were the last humans remaining, but there was no point to, you know, hooking up, I guess. I didn't feel that way about her and besides it's not like we could rebuild the human race. Then I remembered there were humans out there still.

"I'm going to free my people," I said.

"Free your people," Lyger said, "You mean the ones aiding the Thieves?"

"They are not aiding them. They are forced by the Thieves to work for them. I will free them all, get my crew back, and complete the great work my race started. I'll find them a new homeworld. So, I guess I'll need a ship," I added.

Lyger growled and looked away.

"They are my people Lyger. This is not their fault," I shot at her.

Lyger turned her back on me.

"Ada?" Antumbra asked.

"You're going to help me right?" I said before she could speak.

Ada looked uncomfortable.

"Maybe. I don't know yet," she said.

"What?" I said. "Why wouldn't you help?"

She looked away from me.

"I'm thinking I should have my own life now," she muttered.

"The last humans need us," I said standing up.

"They need you. They don't need me," Ada said.

"You're human too. You have a responsibility to them," I said.

"Do you, Callum?" Antumbra said.

"What are you talking about?" I said.

"Do you really have a responsibility to a group of humans who have committed atrocities—"

"Against their own will," I raised my voice. "Even if I hated them, I still have to protect my peoples' legacy."

"They might not be your people anymore, Callum. You've been changed. You're radically different from them. Maybe it's time to move on."

"I can't believe I'm hearing this. Especially from you, Two. Aren't you aware of Dr. Ghost's final instructions?"

She shook her head, "What final instructions?"

"I checked my pod after I got free. Dr. Ghost left a letter on its computer telling the last human what they were supposed to do when they stepped out of that pod."

"Which was?"

"Destroy the Thieves. Obliterate them all... End them."

"Sounds like a good plan," Hippo said.

"Not to me. I don't want to wipe them out. They are people, and in the end, a race. It's not like humans are perfect."

"Yeah, we know," Lyger said over her shoulder.

"I want to punish them, yes. But wipe them out? No," I said.

"And I don't have to do that. Now I have another cause—rescue my people and get them far away from the Thieves."

No one said anything for a minute as they took in my little speech.

"They can't be forgiven for all they have done," Hippo said sternly. "My matriarch is gone. My family is gone. I'll take everything from them to restore my people's honour."

"You'll disgrace your honour," I shot back, "You'll become just like them."

I turned to Ada. "Don't you remember what you told me happened after I changed time? That other version of me made mistakes that cost lives all because I didn't want to let something go. I wanted to be right and I responded in kind to a threat. And where did it get me? Broken friendships and shame and guilt. Not again."

The room was silent as I finished espousing my philosophy. I knew I was right though. I was not going to follow through with Dr. Ghost's final orders.

"Well, I guess we're all going our separate ways then," Antumbra said.

"Wait. What will the Ramothians do with the Destroyer?" Ada asked, probably trying to change the subject.

Antumbra shrugged, "Probably pick it apart and try to figure out the technology that's more advanced than theirs. The engines will be of interest since they generate power far more efficiently than the Ramothians can. Maybe the hull will be carved up."

"What will the Thieves do about this development?" I asked.

"War is their only option, but that would be a bad idea. The Destroyer-class vessel is the biggest they have, and they are no match for Ramoth's defences."

"While the Ramothians can't attack them, the Thieves can't win a conflict right now. Once the Ramothians figure out their tech, things will change."

"Maybe I shouldn't settle down here then," Ada replied. "Don't want to be in the middle of a warzone."

"I wonder if I could buy one of their weapons," Hippo mused. "I might not be able to take it to their planet through the wormholes, but maybe I could take it to their world with normal space travel."

"Sounds like a plan, but I'm going to live on Ramoth," the Mouth said.

One of the consoles made a sound, and Antumbra turned her head to see what it is.

"Well, your new lives begin now because we've arrived in orbit of planet Ramoth."

THE DEAL

Antumbra parked the Destroyer in orbit of planet Ramoth. We had to fly it in on low power, and I could see defence installations target the ship just in case we were going to drop it on their planet.

"Right. We'll take one of the leftover boarding ships down to the planet and collect our reward."

"I'm going to get Ogwambi," I said.

Lyger huffed and I ignored her.

"Ada, are you coming?" I asked.

He waved her hand. "No. You go." She turned away, watching a small fleet of ships rise from the surface towards the Destroyer.

I frowned, but let it go.

As I walked from the control centre to the prison I wondered what had got into her. From her description of the events she had seen after my attempt to change time, she sounded like another One—duty-bound to protect the Arkonauts. Yet now she seemed indifferent. Maybe she was just thinking about our situation, trying to come up with a plan? I didn't know.

When I reached the prison, I found Ogwambi sitting in the corner, and he rose as I entered the room.

I went straight to the cell and opened it.

"You're letting me free? That's great man," Ogwambi said.

He came straight out and gave me a big hug. Some of the ports on his arms dug into my flesh, but I was nice to be with my friend again. He then released me and slapped my shoulders. "What's happening?" he asked.

"We've reached a planet called Ramoth," I began.

"I know Ramoth. The Larceny hate it. It's the only world that currently stands against them."

"We've negotiated the sale of the Destroyer to them. We all get a cut and we can start new lives."

"I assume that we're going to help our fellow Arkonauts, right?" Ogwambi said.

"Of course. We'll get a ship and put together a plan," I said. "Let's go."

I led him back to the control centre.

Lyger growled when she saw him. The others, however, just looked up.

"This is Ogwambi. He's one of my crew. Now that he's free of the Thieves' controls, he's just like me."

"Look, I know what this feels like," Ogwambi interjected. "But you have to be understand, I've had the Larceny in my head for years."

Ogwambi pointed to his skull and gritted his teeth.

"Imagine that. Imagine being forced to attack innocents, to watch worlds die because a race is cruel and wants us to suffer, just for trying to survive."

"It's okay, Ogwambi. You're free now," Ada said.

Ogwambi sat down on a console, his fingers depressed a few buttons and he turned to look down. "Sorry," he said, and then pressed the same buttons again, undoing anything he might had set in operation. "Thank you, Ada." He breathed deeply. "Now that I'm free, I'm processing all these emotions their technology forced me to repress. Did you know the Larceny made me and all the other Arkonauts that survived the process kill One?"

"What?" I said.

"One couldn't be turned, but when they had the rest of us under their control, we all raised weapons and shot him." A tear ran down his cheek. "I know it wasn't really me, but it was still my hand that held the gun."

I looked at Lyger, who now shifted uncomfortably.

He sniffed then said, "It's over now though. I'm free. I can kill the Larceny once again."

I grabbed his shoulder and squeezed.

"You're fine now. Let's try to enjoy this," I said.

"Can we go?" the Mouth said. "I want my money and a new life."

"We should take whatever we can from the stores first. We know it's food we like and the Thieves left some useful tech behind. We sold the ship but not everything inside," Antumbra said.

We all went to a few store rooms. The Destroyer would normally house a Greatlord and their entourage when it would go and raid unsuspecting alien homeworlds, so there were facilities for them.

We all nabbed various foodstuffs and I grabbed a medical device that could close wounds even faster than my altered biology could.

"Callum, Ada take these," Ogwambi said, offering us some devices they were discs the size of a Blu-ray.

"What are they?" I asked.

"These are personal shield generators, but they also allow you to holographically project an image over your body." He placed his over his upper chest and switched it on. At first a blue shimmer surrounded him and then he adjusted a few controls on the device and the blue shimmer became less opaque. "I used one of these in the past and they were helpful. They are like the kinetic shields that surround the Larceny ships when they land on planets."

"You guys should take them too," he said cheerfully to aliens. "They'll take a few hits and convert it to energy, which can then be released."

"Thanks, Ogwambi," and I glared a little at Lyger, who frowned. She looked at the row of devices on the shelf, but didn't take one.

"The Greatlord had one of these," I mentioned.

"You've met a Greatlord?" Ogwambi asked.

"When that ship you came from attacked us, we went over there and killed the Greatlord," I said.

Ogwambi looked shocked, probably because he wasn't expecting me to claim such a feat. "That, that's awesome," he said. "One down, less than a dozen to go."

"What happens after a Greatlord dies, Ogwambi?" I asked.

"Someone below him would take over the family," Ogwambi said.

"Ok. We have everything we need. Let's go," Antumbra said.

I placed the shield device on my upper chest.

Ada did the same.

You never know when you might need a personal shield.

Our group made for the docking bay, where inside, was a single battered Thief ship. It was the one Ada and I had flown back to our Destroyer after rescuing Antumbra from the clutches of its previous owner, the Thief Greatlord.

"Please tell me that the Ramoth know we're flying in a Thief ship. I don't want to be blasted out of the sky," the Mouth said.

"Don't worry. We're going to be escorted down too," Antumbra replied.

We all boarded the ship, Lyger took the controls, and lifted it out of the docking bay. I peered out of a nearby window to watch the Destroyer shrink as we flew away. I was kind of glad to see it go, but it had become familiar to me, much like the Ark. I smiled in satisfaction at the thought of the Ramothians finding a way to use it to defeat the Thieves.

We passed by the small fleet of ships rising up to the Destroyer. Two vessels peeled off the fleet and took up a flight path either side of our shuttle.

"What if they destroy us? We've given up the ship," Hippo said.

"Don't worry. I planned for that," Antumbra said, and from within her body she produced a small remote control. "This allows me to give them control of the ship," she said. "Once we have our gold and are safe, I will activate the ship for them."

"Nice," Ogwambi said.

"Thank you, other human," Antumbra replied.

"Hey, Callum, what kind of ship do you think we can get?"

"We might have enough for two," I suggested.

"Are we giving part of our cut to the new guy?" the Mouth said.

"Why not?" I said.

"Well, he didn't help steal the ship," the Mouth pointed out.

I decided to stop this talk right away.

"Don't worry. He'll share mine. We don't need it all. Just a ship and some left over for what we need to free the Arkonauts."

The radio then came on and a voice said, "Refugee vessel, please follow us to the immigration terminal."

"Acknowledged," Lyger responded.

The planet below was much like Earth, same sort of colours, only the seas seem lighter, possibly shallower than Earth's. Various islands dotted the planet in long archipelagos. There were no giant land masses, bigger than Madagascar, visible.

Lyger took the ship down and as we descended, cities came into focus. We appeared to be heading to one on the equator, which was good because I wanted to be somewhere warm.

She landed the ship gracefully on a platform that reached out from a tall spirally building on the edge of the city. It had multiple platforms extending out from it where smaller ships were taking off and landing next to ours. The escorts who came with us hovered to the right and left, still not completely assured of our friendliness.

From a doorway where the platform met the building, a Ramothian exited along with several guards who all held guns. Now that I saw them in the flesh, Ramothians were actually tri-pedal—walking along on three legs rather than two.

Two Ramothians scuttled along behind the guards with a hovering trolley, on which were several boxes. I actually licked my lips. I knew there was money in those crates.

I've never had money before. Literally. Even when I was a teenager money had already become useless. Water was the currency. And before that, I was a typical teenager and thought money grew on trees. I used to imagine what I would do with a million pounds, the computer consoles I would buy; the trainers. Now I was richer than any human had ever been I bet.

I salivated at the opportunities. Yes, I was going to free my people, but at least I could do it in style. Maybe I should invest the money as well and make more. Who knows how much it would cost to free the other Arkonauts.

Lyger shut down the ship. "Do we need this anymore?"

"No, the Ramothians can have it. They might find some of the tech useful," Antumbra said.

We left the cabin and headed for a small corridor that led to the rear hatch. As we stepped down the ramp the Ramothian leading the guards opened his hands and smiled.

"Welcome escapees of the Thieves, I welcome you to Ramoth—"

He trailed off and his smile faded.

The guards drew up their weapons and pointed them at me and Ogwmabi and Ada.

"Humans!" he shrieked.

HONOURED GUESTS

I froze, as did Ada and Ogwambi.

On instinct—possibly caused by enhanced genetics and nanite memories—I tensed my muscles like a bow and arrow drawn and ready to fire. I also splayed out my hands showing that I was unarmed and not a threat.

Mantis and Hippo stepped between us and the gun.

Lyger hung back and Antumbra looked around in shock.

"What's going on?" Antumbra asked.

"You have humans with you," the Ramothian spat.

"And?" the Mouth said, standing next to Pebbles who was 'staring' into space.

"We have been warned about humans. Many refugees have come to our world with tales. You did not tell us humans were with you," the Ramothian said, backing away.

Antumbra stepped forward into the space the Ramothian left.

"These humans are not your enemy. This one," and she pointed at me. "Has killed many Thieves. He was the one who stole this ship and the world Destroyer from them. The other—" and this time she pointed at Ada, "has also killed many Thieves, and helped to steal this vessel. This one," this time she nodded to Ogwambi, "has been the Thieves' slave, forced to fight for them."

The Ramothian eyed us suspiciously.

"This is what I have seen," Antumbra said.

"This is what I have seen," Hippo repeated.

Mantis clicked his mandibles.

"Same," the mouth said.

Pebbles tapped the floor.

"I saw it too," Lyger muttered.

The Ramothian didn't know how to proceed. He still looked flustered, and he turned to his guards for help. They didn't seem to have any suggestions.

I opened my mouth to speak, but Ada rested her palm on my shoulder and she shook her head.

I understood. Now was not the time to say anything.

Antumbra slipped a hand into her body and retrieved the remote for the Destroyer. "This is the remote that will unlock the world destroyer. As agreed, it is yours."

Ogwambi stepped forward suddenly and took the remote and moved towards the Ramothian.

"Ogwambi," Ada hissed.

The guards raised their guns towards my friend, who walked towards the Ramothian with the remote held out like an offering.

"Please don't shoot us. I am human. I have been forced to serve the Larceny for years. They put their technology in me, made me do terrible things. I have suffered just as those refugees have suffered. I am finally free. Do not take that away from me."

He gestured to the remote.

The Ramothian reached out quickly and took it, like it was being offered in the mouth of a viper instead of an open hand.

He eyed it up and down, then pressed a few buttons on it.

Then he touched an earpiece. "Do you have control?" he asked.

With my advanced hearing I could hear the response, even though it was meant only for the greeter.

"It's ours," said the person he was speaking to.

The Ramothian relaxed and looked around sheepishly.

Ogwambi backed away, gave a little apologetic nod towards Antumbra, and stood at my side.

"Sorry Callum, Ada... I had to show them we weren't a threat."

"This is most unusual," the Ramothian said. "Humans do not have a stellar reputation. You may never have directly attacked us, but many here do not like you. I suggest you leave our world as soon as possible."

"Thank you for your understanding," Antumbra said.

"A deal is a deal. You have given us a great gift, something that will allow us to resist the Thieves to a far greater extent than ever before. Here. Your payment for your service," and the greeter gestured to the trolley behind him.

His entourage parted, Antumbra stepped forward, and opened a box. Inside I saw the golden glow of light reflexing off the precious metal inside.

She nodded at us, then turned towards the greeter.

"How much to put us in a hotel?" she asked.

•

A few minutes later, we were on our way in an open top, hovering bus to a hotel, our money smoothing everything over.

The pilot was terrified at first, then let us on after a few quick words from the Ramothian.

Once we were all seated, the Mouth turned in his seat to face us.

"Maybe you should disguise yourselves," he said. "I don't want to be stopped everywhere we go."

"Disguise ourselves with what?" I asked.

"With these," Ogwambi answered and he tapped his shield generator played with the controls and selected an option. In this case a helmet over his face with no eyeholes. "Don't worry, you can still see through as if it wasn't there," he said, his voice not muffled at all.

I reached up and started fiddling with my shield. I didn't know how it worked so I cycled through some default options. I noticed that some of the options were not just for the Greatlords who usually used these shields, but for humans.

"Ogwambi, why are there human shaped options in these things?"

"Sometimes they would give them to us when they sent us to ravage worlds. They didn't want us to die. They wanted us to continue our suffering," Ogwambi answered. "They were sadistic."

"Sorry, mate," I said.

"It's alright. Thankfully, they never made me do that. But Gerlinde—she had to go through it—it kind of broke her actually. She's a shell of person now."

"You're alright though," I pointed out.

"I managed to latch onto something—a realisation," he said.

"What?"

"You."

"Me?"

"You sent a message through time to save us. I guess I always thought that you were somewhere in the future and we would meet again, and you would come to rescue us with whatever time travel powers you had."

"Unfortunately, they could only be used sparingly," I said motioning towards Antumbra.

"Can't we use it again? I would love to travel back to the past and save our crew," Ogwambi said.

I was taken aback, amazed that I hadn't thought the same thing. Antumbra only had to change time once for her race, surely the remaining time could be used again by me Ada and Ogwambi.

"Maybe," I said. "For now, let's get through today and find ourselves a spaceship."

I started flicking through the options again, and settled on a set of armour just like Ogwambi's. Only mine was more angular, like a medieval knight's helmet—his was more like a World War II helmet.

Suitably concealed, I looked out over the city we passed over.

I chuckled that—in a way—films and stories from Earth got things right about futuristic alien cities. They were full of tall skyscrapers with lanes of herding cars like highways in the sky. The difference here was that they actually flew above roads in the sky, holographically projected roads, possibly to keep the cars on the straight and narrow.

The city also seemed to be sectioned out like slices of pizzas, clearly different aliens lived in different sections, not just Ramothians. I was amazed that these Ramothians were so tolerant and so welcoming. It reflected bad on humanity—all those times we would push away refugees.

The bus we were travelling on reached the top of a circular building, its walls lined with balconies overlooking a swimming pool. I haven't swum for years, not since all the water disappeared from Earth. The thought of swimming again made me giddy with excitement. Then I realised that we were supposed to be incognito. Oh well. Maybe on a different planet, or at night, when other hotel guests weren't around. Maybe our new found wealth would buy exclusive access.

Our transport landed on the roof of the hotel and we all disembarked. Ada had chosen a light billowy camouflage, her face obscured by a simple mask that let her curly, long hair flow out behind her.

There to greet us was another Ramothian, smartly dressed, I assumed.

"Greetings, honoured guests. This way to your species-appropriate rooms," he said.

"Thank you," Antumbra said.

We left the roof down a lift. The lift didn't go down a dark shaft instead it dropped one floor and suddenly we beheld the inside of the hotel, which was actually more donut shaped, with was a grand hall holding more swimming pools and even slides. I smiled at the aliens who pushed their children down the slides, marvelling at how they loved to have the same fun as humans.

The lift stopped a few floors down, and we were all taken to a corridor that circled the building at this level, and was studded with doors.

The concierge indicated the first door, "Yours, sir," he said to Hippo, and Hippo went inside.

The Ramothian led us all to doors, one after another, and let the aliens inside.

Before Antumbra entered her room she said, "Let's relax for a few hours then meet up."

We three humans nodded to her.

"This room is for the two male... erm," the Ramothian began.

"Terrans," Ada said quickly.

"Terrans? I don't know that race," the Ramothian said, pleasantly. "Recent refugees from the actions of the Thieves?"

"Indeed," I said.

"This is your joint room. The female Terran's door is right next to it," and the Ramothian indicated that room.

"Thank you," Ada said, and without another word she entered her room and closed the door.

Ogwambi went into our room, which opened out into a luxury suite of some kind.

Two bedrooms led off a huge open plan living room that led out onto the balcony. The bathroom was huge.

I tossed a gold coin to the concierge, who caught it haphazardly. "A tip," I said to him when he looked confused. It was obviously not standard practice to tip the staff on this planet. Maybe they were paid properly.

The Ramothian bowed a little then closed the door.

I switched off the shield and admired the room. There were huge sofas tailored to different species. I selected one and gently caressed the soft finishing. This was not something I had felt for years. I sat down and let myself sink into the cushions and laid my head back on the head rests.

Only my bed and the padded cushions in the theatre of the Ark had offered close to this level of comfort and those times felt like decades ago. This was heaven. Here I would have an actual bed again, and the chance for a shower or a bath. Wow... even a bath. It felt like home, only without my family.

My family.

I had not given them much thought for ages.

I suddenly felt a stab in my heart, and I looked out the balcony window and out over the city, feeling like they were watching over me— that they knew I was here in safety and comfort—and hating me for it.

I sat on the edge of the seat, no longer wanting to be comfortable.

"This is great, Callum. I've never seen such luxury. Not on Earth, and certainly not on the Ark," Ogwambi said.

"Yeah, I know," I muttered back.

"What's wrong?" he asked.

"It's just... What about our crew? They aren't living like this," I said and gestured to the room.

He slumped into a chair. "Well, I get to enjoy it, considering what I've been through for years." He sank into the sofa, closing his eyes. "The remaining Arkonauts would understand."

A question suddenly formed in my mind, but in some ways I didn't feel I had to right to ask it, since it wasn't my place—I wasn't the Callum who should be asking it. But, I was too curious. I needed to know.

"What happened to Maiara?" I asked.

Ogwambi opened his eyes and swivelled them towards me.

"You want to know about what happened to your girlfriend?" he said nodding in understanding.

"She wasn't *my* girlfriend," I said.

"Close enough," Ogwambi said smiling, then his smile faded and he looked away. "Sorry to tell you this, Callum, but she died not long after the Larceny found the Ark and took us prisoner."

I should have felt sad, that should have cut me deep. The other me had loved her, according to Ada.

"I wish I had known her. Unfortunately, I didn't know anyone that well after the timelines diverged."

"You two got on great. Made a few girls jealous when she nabbed you," he added.

"What do you mean?"

"A lot of girls were interested in you back then. You were the guy who time travelled, who fought the minster and the Colonel, revived One. And you chose Maiara and she chose you."

"Hey wait a minute. Don't you have the memories of that 'other' Callum?" he asked.

"What?" I replied.

"Well not long ago, around the time you sent a part of your sleeve back through time, the Larceny realised what you had done. Nearly all of them found themselves with a new set of memories, so they concluded that two timelines had merged. That's how they knew Antumbra had a time travel device, so they sent me and other Larceny in to get it."

"Why do they want it?" I asked.

"Because it's the ultimate weapon—a way to make sure they can win, control the past."

"Hang on. What's the merging of two universe got to do with me and Maiara?"

"Well, if two universes have merged then that means you might have your other self's memories too," he pointed out.

My eyes went wide. That might be true.

"Try to think back to Maiara. Think of the smell of the sea, or the claustrophobia of a spacesuit. It might trigger something," he said.

I sifted through my memories, but trying to find the memory was like when I used to ask my parents how to spell certain words and they always used to say use a dictionary... *But how can I find a word I don't know how to spell mum!?* I kept sifting. I took Ogwambi's advice and tried to remember the smell of the sea. That triggered thoughts of the beach, of holidays, then suddenly flashes of the lower section of the Ark appeared. I remembered Kraken, who I had never met, and the waves crashing into me. Then finally... Maiara. I saw her face, remembered the touch of her skin and the feel of her lips on mine.

"Wow," I said to him. "I do remember it. I have the other Callum's memories."

"Now you know what she was like," he said.

He got up and wandered off to the balcony to view the city, leaving me alone with my memories.

I lay back and pored over them, making new connections to memories I didn't know I had.

He let me sit in peace and absorb it all—the gunshot, the kisses, Turso and even the memories Dr. Ghost had tried to bury. It was all there.

I closed my eyes and savoured them all.

SHOPPING

Once I had shifted all the new memories around, I wished I hadn't. They were all of a life I hadn't lived. They technically weren't mine.

But I was glad as well because I knew that my decision to use time travel was not a waste. I was proud of my old self, and proud of the Arkonauts. They had come together despite a difficult situation.

Then I clenched my fist and squeezed hard. A bright future had been taken from them. They had been forced to serve humanity's greatest enemy.

I accessed the nanite memories gifted to me by the pod One had stored me in. One had detailed knowledge of military procedure, weapons and tactics. I started forming a list of my requirements. Top of the list: a ship, with all the bells and whistles, particularly weapons. And it had to look good of course.

My thoughts were interrupted when someone knocked on the door.

I activated my disguise and opened the door to Ada, who was also wearing hers.

"Let's go shopping," she said.

I called out for Ogwambi, and he put on his disguise and followed us out of the room.

Antumbra was also there with the rest of the aliens.

"I got us a private coach to the market. We'll find everything we want there," Antumbra said.

We made our way through the hotel to the lobby. We passed by dozens of different aliens all mixed in with Ramothians.

I wondered what their stories were. I assumed they were all escapees of the Thieves, or maybe other societies all linked through the wormholes—a giant intergalactic community.

Through the lobby we were met by a smiling Ramothian, leading a group of other Ramothians, who said, "Hello! I am Lockney, head guide. Ask me or my compatriots anything about how stuff works. There are no stupid questions. We get many refugees and we welcome them all." Then she paused and swept her eyes over me, Ogwambi and Ada. She must know we were human. "Seriously. Ask anything."

She then gestured to the coach that was waiting for us. It was limo-like and when the doors opened the inside was revealed to be luxurious, with a carpeted floor, drinks, and plush seats.

We all piled in and managed to fit, despite the odd shapes of our party.

The limo took off, hovering through the various streets. It didn't take long to reach a wide-open space in the centre of the city. Various stalls were set up and, on one side, spaceships dominated. We would have to head there at some point.

The limo stopped on the edge of the market and let us out.

Our group sprawled out onto the street. The stalls were arranged like the segments of an umbrella, all spiralling inwards to the centre off the circular market area.

"If you want to split up, one of our guides will follow to help. Your recently acquired funds are locked to your hotel accounts, so buy what you wish we'll take it from there."

I turned to the group and we assembled in a loose circle. No one spoke or did any charades for attention. It was kind of an odd moment.

"So, I guess we don't have to walk around together," Antumbra said. "I know what I want. We're all going in different directions."

"There is no reason why we can't be friends and stay in touch," Ada said.

"I agree," Hippo rumbled. "We are bound by a common adventure. We might be the first to have escaped the Thieves, the first to capture a Destroyer vessel." He pointed up into the sky where the ship was visible even in orbit. "You don't forget a thing like that."

"No, we won't," I said. "Look, I just want to say thank you. I'm glad we worked together to escape and I'm honoured to have known you all."

"Same, even if it has only been a couple of hours," Ogwambi said.

Mantis tapped the ground, made a circle then hugged himself, which I took that to mean he wanted to hug us.

Pebbles floated one of his hands into the centre of the loose circle Mantis had made.

The Mouth held up a hand and the rock floated to it like a high five.

We all put our hands out and the rock high fived us all.

"Thank you for freeing me," Lyger managed to say.

"I would like to suggest that we have dinner tonight together in the hotel for a final farewell," Ada said.

I smiled. She was still being the one who tries to bind a group together, just like she did on the Ark.

"We'll see each other at the hotel, one last time," Antumbra said.

She was the first to turn away and enter the market. The group broke up, until it was just me Ogwambi and Ada.

"So, where do we begin?" I said.

Ada looked around the market and smiled. "You two go off. I want to shop on my own."

"Really, shouldn't us... Terrans... stay together?"

She smiled at us and sighed. "You two Terrans head off. I like my own time when I shop." Ada walked away and disappeared in the throngs of aliens.

I looked at Ogwambi. "Where do we start?" I asked.

He smiled at me. And we both said, "Spaceship."

•

It took us ages to get to the spaceships, though. I finally had money and every stall had something of interest.

We stopped at a clothing store, and I finally changed out the clothes I had been wearing ever since One had put me in that pod all those years ago.

The stall was really an open air shop you would find at a shopping centre, and had a changing room in the middle.

I selected a bunch of clothes I considered practical and slightly military. Lots of pockets some padding and some really comfortable boots. My guide paid and transferred my purchases to the hotel, but I wore some of the new clothes right then. Ogwambi selected similar clothing, but his were in more garish colours and looser fitting.

The next stall we stopped at was a weapons stall. Yes, weapons. Ramothians seemed to have a Second Amendment attitude to weapons and sold them freely. Although I was interested, I didn't plan to buy anything there and then. We needed a ship first, and then intel, before we started buying the weapons we needed.

However, Ogwambi was not so patient and dragged me into the store.

I saw an assorted collection of ray guns and other weapons. I have to admit my eyes gleamed as I looked at them. It reminded me of the days when I was a child and used to wander the aisles of toy stores and look at the foam dart guns, dreaming of owning the larger more impressive guns that fired the darts further, faster and with more power.

I went up to the owner and asked him straight what the best gun he had was. The alien at the counter was kind of like a bear, with a massive furry body and snout, except its hands were more dexterous than a bear's, instead of just large paws.

"Depends on what you want to do?" he asked.

"I want to kill Thieves," I said.

The owner growled at the mention of the Thieves then turned around to a safe behind his counter.

He took out a gun with a pod underneath the main barrel, but no handle. It also had a vicious blade on the tip.

"Show me your hand," the owner said.

At first I was reluctant, then I decided that he couldn't tell I was human from a hand.

He took one look, then got a handle that matched my hand—a melded grip with indentations for my fingers. He attached it to the gun.

"This gun is perfect against the Thieves. It fires X-ray bullets," he said.

"X-ray bullets," I replied.

"Lasers are focused light. This is focused X-rays. They go through anything."

"Lasers can go through things too," I said.

"No. A laser cuts through things, but if the armour or the flesh is dense it takes time, and does less damage. This weapon will fire an X-ray pulse though anything. If you know where your target is behind a wall you can blast them with no problem. Even fires through their shields. Except when it meets flesh, where it burns like a laser, gets past those implants they have and hits the original being beneath. Also, it won't punch through a starship hull, so it's great for on-ship combat."

I held the gun, which felt light and easy to handle.

"You pulled it out of a safe. Is it expensive or dangerous to the user?"

"Expensive yes, but not dangerous, just rare. The Rontgen core that provides the X-rays is hard to come by."

"What about radiation?" I asked.

"Totally safe, as long as you're not looking down the barrel. But, if the pod cracks, get rid of it," the bear said.

"Power source?" I asked.

"Standard power cell, light weight, and if it runs out, flick your wrist," the owner said.

I did and the gun swivelled around the handle like one of those old timely clickity-clatters at a football match. There was a satisfying mechanical click as it went around.

"A mechanical charger. If you're low on power, spin and you'll be back in business," the owner said. "However it's just a standard shot, not X-ray."

I held the gun in my hand. I felt that surge of power you get when you hold a gun... the desire to shoot. I don't know if I wanted to feel that way. But then again, I needed weapons to free my people.

"It has one more function," the owner said. He turned a dial on the gun, then pointed it at another weapon on a counter and fired.

The gun projected a small square that almost erased the weapon on the counter. Then I realised it was simply projected a window to the space on the other side.

"It can show you what's on the other side of the wall. Very handy to know where a target is," the owner said.

That gadget alone sold me on it.

I also brought some EMP grenades to use against the Thieves. Ogwambi chose his own weapons. I even brought a sword. I thought it was a roll of thick tape at first. It had a normal handle, but when I held it the owner showed me that whipping it out caused the blade to roll out like a tape measure. The sword was dual-edged and plain looking.

"How do you curl it up?" I asked.

"Button on the base of the handle," the owner said.

I looked at the button and then stamped the sword down on counter. The blade curled up to just above the hilt. I then extended it again and retracted the blade once more. This was cool. "What about a scabbard?" I asked.

"Scabbard?" the owner asked.

"You know, a covering? To stop the metal from rusting?" I asked.

"It doesn't rust. It's a polymer and it self-heals too, so there's no need to sharpen.

I flicked the sword out one more time, it was kind of addictive.

"I'll take this," I said.

My guide told me the price and I had no idea if it was highly priced or not. "This will cost 8 gold coins," the guide said.

"What's the most expensive thing one gold coin can buy?" I asked.

The guide looked off in the distance as they thought about it. "Erm... I think one gold coin can get you several meals at our best restaurants, or maybe a rental for a few weeks."

I still had no idea if it was good or bad though.

"I'll still take them," I said.

"They will be delivered to the hotel," the guide said.

Ogwambi and I left the shop, our purchases on their way to somewhere safe.

Our next stop was the spaceships, and we stood at the boundary to where they were all parked, admiring the various vessels on show.

"What are we looking for?" Ogwambi said.

"I think it's obvious," I replied and looked at him.

"Cool looking," he said.

"Indeed. That is our first concern, but I guess we want the best, with the best tech... maybe extra features," I said.

"What? Like air con and sat nav?" Ogwambi said.

"I was thinking more stealth, weapons, and speed," I said.

Ogwambi mused. "We still need air con though."

We started down the lines of ships, all increasing in size. "We need one we can live on, with lots of space if we end up with more Arkonauts," Ogwambi said.

"But not so big that it's hard to handle."

"Maybe a medium-sized one then. And we buy a house somewhere. We are rich. Anyone we rescue can stay in the home," he said.

"Not a bad idea," I said.

"Another question is what do we do then?"

"Pardon?"

"Once we've freed all the remaining Arkonauts. What then?"

"We take them to a new homeworld and start again. That was the plan," I said.

"I suppose that still works," Ogwambi said.

We both came to a stop next to one of the medium-sized ships—about the size of the biggest jet liner humanity ever built. It wasn't shaped like a jumbo jet. It had a single sleek hull that spread out at the rear of the vessel into two massive wings, with a cluster of engines on each of them. Two smaller wings jutted out near the front section where the bridge of the ship was. The nose hooked down like falcon's beak. The hull was black with deep purple spikes painted from the tail forward.

"I like this one," I said.

"It certainly looks like the right size," Ogwambi said.

"We need to see inside it," I said.

I waved at a Ramothian standing nearby, and we got the tour of the ship. The bottom half was empty cargo space. Up top were lots of rooms —some designed for medicine, living quarters and even scientific studies.

The Ramothian guide gave a detailed run down of all its features. It was fast, able to cross a solar system in a few days. The Ramothians had installed a chart of all known wormhole exits and entrances. It even came with a miniature version of the ship as a life raft. It had all the extra features we needed.

It was costly though. We would be sinking a quarter of our overall cash into this thing.

We looked around the whole ship for hours. We even went through the various packages that came with it, which included a weapon set up. I remembered once being going to a car dealership with my father. I watched my dad haggle, bargaining and teasing out the fine print to get the best deal. I tried doing the same here until I realised I didn't know everything, or understand the fancy systems. It would take time to figure out.

Eventually, Ogwambi and I sat down in the bridge, which was separated into various tiers, and looked out the window. We asked the guide to step away while we talked.

"We don't have to buy anything straight away. There are still tons of ships out there," Ogwambi said, as he moved around the bridge inspecting everything.

I sat in the captain's chair. "I guess, but something about this vessel just feels right."

"It's going to take a while to get used to it. The Larceny gave me training in their tech so I understand how most of it works. It's just a different set up. You're going to need lots of training," he said to me.

"I'll pick it up quickly. I have the same abilities as One. He was such a whizz with everything," I said.

"Is that Ada?" Ogwambi said, looking out the window and pointing.

Next to this ship was smaller version of the same vessel—about a quarter of the size—with a different colour scheme. Ada was walking out of the ship and nodding to the guide.

"Looks like she's buying a ship," Ogwambi commented.

"We better tell her she doesn't need to. Besides, all three of us don't want to be on that small ship."

"I don't think she's buying it for all of us," Ogwambi said.

That didn't make sense. We humans needed to stick together. As I stared at her nodding away, and even pointing at a computer her guide held, it became clear she was personalizing her ship—selecting her own set up. Ogwambi was right. She was smart enough to know not to buy a ship without us.

"She must just want a ship of her own," I said. "Maybe she has trouble sharing. I was like that with my brother and bicycles."

"Callum, I think she's going to go out on her own," Ogwambi said.

"She can't do that," I said.

"She can't? We can't tell her not to," Ogwambi replied.

"But, but she's an Arkonaut. Part of the crew," I said.

Ogwambi put a hand on my shoulder. "Leave it, mate, for the time being."

I wanted to shake off his hand and go down there to talk to her, but I sighed and relented.

The Ramothian guide came back into the bridge.

"Customers, we've set up a firing range to demonstrate the weapons you selected. Would you like to come and see?"

I almost told him to go away, but then the childish part of my brain kicked in. The thought of seeing weapons fire was too good to miss.

"Great," I replied.

We left the ship. At the bottom of the gang plank I looked for Ada. She was nowhere to be seen. We were taken to a big open space behind the ship. Against a large mound of earth and concrete were several large targets, facing them were three weapons.

"The first is the pulse cannon, producing steady bursts of plasma pellets. Observe," the guide said.

The weapon fired and it looked like it was shooting a stream of blue LED lights. The bolts struck the target dead centre, shredding it as recoil bounced the gun barrel around slightly.

"Never runs out as long as your ship has power, although it is short range," the guide said.

"Impressive," Ogwambi said.

I noticed that, behind us, other customers gathered, a mixture of different aliens, also keen to watch the destruction.

"It has two settings. This is light and this is heavy," the guide said and as soon as he said heavy the cannon started firing larger blasts at slower intervals.

The target completely disappeared.

"Good for heavier targets, but even shorter range and slower rate of fire," the guide said. He then motioned to the next weapon it looked like a battleship turret.

"Laser strike: a single focused beam that's good for long range attacks before an enemy can close in," the guide said.

The weapon powered up and a single lance of blue energy burst from the end. When it struck the target, it disappeared in an explosion that first burst out, then suddenly retracted back in.

"The weapon is able to create an explosion/implosion upon contact, preventing debris from showering everywhere, which is potentially dangerous," the guide added. "And finally the EMP cannon you requested—a weapon capable of disabling vessels."

I nodded. Since we needed to capture Arkonauts alive and free them, this would help.

"Please step behind the yellow semi-circle if you have equipment you wouldn't like to temporarily deactivate. The cannon emits a slight backwash of EMP energy," the guide said, both to me and Ogwambi and the gathered crowd.

Ogwambi whispered into my ear. "I better step back. I don't want my Larceny implants affected."

I nodded and stayed near, wanting to see what this cannon did. I had no implants so there wasn't a problem. The nanites in my brain also wouldn't be affected—too small.

The cannon powered up.

I looked around at everyone, lots of faces keen to see some destruction. Suddenly Ada burst out of the crow and stopped at the yellow line. "Callum, the shield!" she said motioning to her chest where her shield emitter was.

My eyes widened. The EMP would affect the shield.

My muscles tensed and I was about to jump back to the semi-circle, but it was too late. The cannon fired.

My shield shut down.

The target was struck, but all alien eyes were on me, because now I had lost my disguise.

BACKLASH

My hand shot up to the shield emitter and I pressed the activate button again.

It didn't come back online.

I did it again, and the shield rebooted and covered me once more.

"That was a human," an alien shouted.

I froze and my enhanced mind started weighing the options.

Option one run—disappear into the crowd and don't cause a scene.

Option two—deny everything and hope this goes away.

Ada made the decision for me.

She and Ogwambi ran forward and grabbed my arm and pulled me away from the crowd.

Our flustered guides were confused, and didn't follow us.

We circled around the edge of the crowd, but they weren't going to let us go.

The crowd of aliens moved around to block our escape. It wasn't the entire crowd though, just about half.

"Human!" they were saying and pointing at us.

"Look, we don't want trouble," I said.

"You destroyed my world," said a kangaroo-like alien strolling up to us on two giant feet.

"Not us," Ada said, and raising a hand to keep the alien at a distance.

"Why aren't you with the Thieves?"

"Are you spies?"

"Why have the Ramothians let you onto this planet?"

"My family died when your ship crashed into my planet. You destroyed our civilisation."

I could feel the anger and the fury bubbling off these aliens. I suddenly wished I had kept my new gun. I had little flashbacks to the news reports of riots and protests after the Ark had been put in orbit of Earth. When it failed to drop onto the Destroyer as planned and people knew something was up, many cities erupted in violence. As I looked into the alien eyes arrayed against me I saw the same rage I had seen in the eyes of those protesters. The fact that their lives were upended and virtually destroyed was etched on to their faces.

"What do we do?" Ogwambi whispered.

"Hope the Ramothians step in," Ada said.

"They better hurry," I said.

The Kangaroo alien suddenly stepped forward, raised a gigantic leg, and kicked at me.

My training kicked in and I grabbed its foot, despite the alien's size. I twisted the ankle and the alien went down in pain. I didn't break anything. I just held the alien in a lock.

"We're not here to harm you."

"Get the humans," the mob shouted.

I let go of the foot and backed away.

The aliens surged forward.

Finally, some Ramothians came forward and tried to defuse it, but they were overwhelmed as the aliens came for us.

Ogwambi then held his hand near his leg, his flesh split open and out of his upper thigh came a gun on a mechanical holster.

He grabbed the gun and levelled it at the crowd, then fired at the ground.

Several bursts hit the floor and blasted the slabs to pieces, spraying the crowd in slivers of stone.

He then raised it to the crowd.

"Back off," he said, in a stern and gentle manner.

"You had a gun in your leg?" I asked.

"Yeah, sorry," Ogwambi said. "I should have told you."

The crowd stayed away, held back by the threat of Ogwambi's gun.

"We're going to go now," Ogwambi said to the crowd.

We backed away and the crowd didn't follow. Our Ramothian guides came to us and we moved through the collection of ships, putting them between us and the crowd.

Ogwambi holstered his gun and his flesh closed up.

"We're going back to the hotel," Ada said.

"I agree," I said.

●

"What was that all that about?" I asked Ogwambi when we reached our hotel room, safe and sound.

"I know. Sorry. I had the gun on me—or should I say in me—when I arrived on the Destroyer... when I was forced by the Larceny to attack you. I had forgotten all about it. It's not like I was going to attack you and your alien friends with it was I?"

I shrugged. I guess he kind of had a point. I wish he had told me though. I didn't realise the extent of modifications the Thieves had done to him.

I threw myself onto a sofa. "I can't believe that they hated us that much. What have the Thieves done to the crew?" I asked.

"Those aliens are all refugees—the last remnants of their civilisations—just like us. They made it Ramoth for safety. Unfortunately, the Larceny made humans destroy their homeworlds, part of punishing us." Ogwambi said, and he hung his head in shame.

"This is terrible. We might never be able to buy a ship. We certainly can't bring any Arkonauts to Ramoth when we free them. They won't be accepted here," I said.

"Callum, calm down. It's just going to take longer, that's all. You and Ogwambi can still get a ship. You just have to do it all through a Ramothian. They don't hate you," Ada said.

Something about what she suddenly struck me as odd. She wasn't including herself in that conversation.

"Why were you buying your own ship?" I asked.

Ada reacted like she had been struck in the face.

"You saw me buying a ship?" she asked.

"Yes," Ogwambi replied.

"Are you leaving us?" I asked.

Ada looked uncomfortable. "Yeah, I was."

I wanted to explode in anger at her. She was leaving the Arkonauts under the control of the Thieves. But the nanites in my mind were keeping me calm and composed.

"Why? The Arkonauts are captives of a race forcing them to commit evil. I need you to help me," I said.

"I thought you were loyal to the crew?" Ogwambi said. "I remember when you risked facing Kraken to rescue us. You stood between us and Turso."

Ada stood up and turned away from us.

"It's not like I don't care. It's just... I'm different now. I'm not the same person that went into that pod after I was hurt fighting Turso," she replied.

"Different? How are you different?" Ogwambi asked. "That pod healed you right?"

"It did repair me, but—"

"But what?" I pressed.

She looked at the ceiling. "It's just that my time came," she said.

"What does that mean?" I asked.

Before she could answer, there was a knock at the door. "Come in," Ada said quickly, and the door opened to reveal Antumbra and the others standing in the corridor.

"Dinner time," she said.

The three of us stood there in silence. The tension was palpable and Antumbra picked up on it.

"Are you ready?" she asked.

"Yeah we're ready," Ada said, and she switched on her disguise and started out of the room, bringing our discussion to an end.

I looked at Ogwambi and he shrugged.

I sighed, then left the room. We were going to continue this conversation. I wanted to find out what had happened to Ada.

DINNER AND TIME TRAVEL

The Hotel restaurant was one of the finest on the planet apparently, and luckily, our huge bank accounts had smoothed over getting reservations.

There were different tables for different species, all dining in comfort, with a variety of music being played throughout the restaurant.

Ramothian staff led us to our table, which was in a private dining area—so private we didn't need our disguises—where we took our seats.

Pebbles and the Mouth had to use high chairs, and I stifled a laughed when they got up to our level like toddlers.

Mantis sort of folded his legs under his body, like he was cross legged. Hippo's chair was more of a chaise lounge, and he stretched out on it like a Roman emperor having dinner.

The rest of us took normal chairs.

When the waiter handed me a menu, I suddenly felt the most relaxed I had ever been since leaving Earth. Out of everything I had experience so far this really made me calm and happy. I was doing something normal again. True, some of the other diners had more legs than most customers, but when I sat back, menu in hand, it was like any ordinary trip out with my parents.

Then I realised that a part of my previous life was going to come back to me. I was going to have a house again, have days out, I was even planet side. Once I started freeing other Arkonauts from the Thieves, it will feel like Earth again.

The waiter took our drink order. I settled for a fruit juice of some kind that I hoped was not poisonous to humans.

Once they were all poured, I decided to propose a toast and wondered if the others would object.

I grabbed my glass.

"There is a tradition on my homeworld... or was... to raise a glass and drink the first sip together to memorialise an event. I think this warrants a similar moment. All we do is raise our drinks, and drink together," I explained.

The others took their glasses, Mantis had a straw in his mouth.

"To us! And to our escape from the Thieves," I said, raising my glass.

The others copied me and we drank, except for Mantis who sucked at his straw, and Pebbles who poured his glass on his 'face' where it slowly absorbed into his skin.

Hippo brought down his mug after finishing it off completely.

"On my world we have a similar ritual, but it usually involves a fight for the right to drink first—to drink the best wine first."

Antumbra swallowed her mouthful, not of liquid, but of a metallic dust, then sank into her chair. "This feels nice doesn't it. No fights, no running. And after this I will change time and rescue my people," she said.

"Can we watch?" I asked "I would like to see your world through the time portal."

"You decided on a time and place?" Hippo asked.

"Yes. My plan was to find an evolutionary ancestor of the Thieves and kill it, thus preventing their race. However, that is hard to pin down. Instead, I have opted for a different method. I will simply destroy their planet once it is formed."

"How will you do that?" I asked taking another sip of my drink.

"I have brought a bomb from the Ramothians. It is very powerful. I will open up the time portal in the very centre of their world and chuck the bomb through. Once it detonates, the explosion in the core of their world will annihilate it."

"I'm surprised the Ramothians gave you a bomb of such power," Ogwambi said.

"Now that they know what it is for, they are keen to have me destroy the Thieves. Even they want to witness it," she said.

"I'll toast to that," the Mouth said, raising his glass again.

We all toasted that too, although I was suddenly uneasy. Antumbra was going to destroy an entire race, commit genocide. "You're going to kill them all?" I asked.

She paused with her glass of metallic dust to her mouth. Then she looked at me with sharp eyes.

"Don't go soft on them, Callum. They destroyed hundreds of worlds. Besides, I'm going to destroy their world when it is first formed. At a time when they haven't even evolved yet. What I will do is sort of evil, I admit, but they have done worse. Plus, I'll be creating a universe where not only my people will be safe, but hundreds of others too, including Earth."

It still made me feel uneasy, but I tipped my glass to her a little.

"It has to be done."

"I don't understand this plan, Antumbra," Ogwambi said. "You may create a new timeline where your people are safe, but you can't enjoy it."

"I don't need to. I'm creating a timeline where my race will develop exactly the same as it always did. I'm recreating my people exactly as they were. And my race believes that in the multiverse we are all the same person. And I want a version of me to be happy, back with my wife and children.

"Plus, there may be a benefit," she added. "It's possible that I could access this new timeline, step through, and return to my people."

"But won't there be a version of you there already?" Ada asked.

"I might not be able to re-join my old life, but it will be good to watch my family from afar grow. There is always hope."

Our dinner continued and I ate with gusto when the succulent meats and vegetables I had ordered arrived. Ada ate very little. Ogwambi ate with relish. The Mouth had the most food. Pebbles had the least. Much of what I was eating was familiar. It turns out veg and meat is pretty much the same anywhere. Creation throws up much the same things when it can.

We chatted about the future. The Mouth had already bought a house on this planet and was moving in with Pebbles. Lyger had brought a ship, as had Hippo.

"Did you guys buy a ship?" Lyger asked.

"We did," I said, eyeing Ada darkly, who avoided my gaze.

At the end of the meal, we all sat back full and happy.

"Well now that the meals over, it's time," Antumbra announced. "Time to save my race and get my revenge on the Thieves."

"Where are you doing this?" I asked.

"I booked a conference room here the hotel. The Ramothian with my weapon should be here too," she said.

She got up and we all followed. Ada, Ogwambi and I put our shields back up.

We strolled through the hotel and reached a plush conference room complete with big screens. A table and several chairs for all species, had been pushed aside, leaving a big space. Waiting for us was a group of official looking dignitaries.

They greeted the aliens warmly, but were a little colder and curt with me, Ada, and Ogwambi. They must be aware that under our shields we were human.

I sat down while the others got comfortable.

Antumbra chatted with the Ramothian, who then indicated a large container they had brought with them. No doubt it was the bomb.

Antumbra then removed the rod from within herself and broke it apart, which activated it. The rod displayed, in the air, controls and a display of the universe. Antumbra started manipulating the controls and she located the Thieves' homeworld.

"Is that the Thieves' homeworld right now?" a Ramothian asked scowling at the image of his nemesis home, but also excited to see the technology work.

"It's actually the world as it appears an hour ago. We can't see any sooner because the rod can't process the time immediately before now."

As we watched the world, I noticed several ships smaller than a Destroyer depart.

"We could use this as a spy network," the Ramothian said. "How much for it?" the Ramothian said.

"Unfortunately, it has a finite power source," Antumbra said. "It can be recharged twice. Enough for another two time jumps, one of which I will be using. It's not possible for us to recharge that power source a third time," she replied. "Also, this isn't always accurate. The rod extrapolates data. It's not displaying real-time images."

The Ramothian slumped at the news.

"Besides, we need to have another go at saving my race," I said.

"Your people are fine," Lyger shot back. "Yes, you need to rescue them, but they are fine. Maybe another race should get a go."

"That makes sense. One more turn left," the Mouth said. "I could restore my people to how they were."

"Everyone, what Antumbra is doing is saving all our races in another universe. With the Thieves never born, all our peoples are safe. Yes, we will never see them, but they will all continue as if the Destroyer's never came to their worlds," Ada said.

"That's right," Antumbra added. "With this act, I'm restoring all your people to how they were."

"But I could use the rod to help my people, create a new universe that undoes my previous mistake," I said.

"Maybe, Callum," Antumbra said.

"Maybe?" I shot back.

"One more turn of the rod after this and we have to be careful with it," she replied curtly.

Antumbra manipulated the controls and essentially rewound time. I watched the Thieves homeworld circle its star. I saw the Destroyers spread over its surface disappear one by one as time reversed and their construction was reversed too.

Eventually Antumbra stopped the rewind and said, "Here we are. A billion years ago, or a rough approximation. In this time, there should be no Thieves and barely any life on the planet."

She then moved the visual forward and we went through the layers of the planet. The screen went dark as it moved through the crust then brightened as we went into the magma layers beneath.

"This will do," Antumbra said. "Hippo, can you?"

Hippo wandered over to the container and opened it to reveal the bomb—a slim cylinder with a keypad on it.

He lifted it up and brought it to the Ramothian, who tapped at the buttons.

"It's armed," he said.

"Time to restore my people to how I remember them, giving them back their lives," Antumbra said, in a magisterial tone.

Her hands rested above a control.

"Today, I fulfill the dreams of my people and earn their respect. Today I complete the task they set me to, and live up to the responsibilities, and the chance to survive, that I shoulder."

She activated the controls.

...

Nothing happened.

I was expecting a portal to appear, a link to the past.

Antumbra activated the controls again.

The rod buzzed back at her.

Mantis pointed at the rod, then sort of shrugged his shoulders.

"I think he wants to know what went wrong," Ada said.

"The portal is not opening," Antumbra said.

"But we're seeing into the past. Why can't we open a portal to it?" I asked.

"We're not seeing the past. We're seeing an extrapolation of it," Antumbra said. This is a possible past. The closest we could get. It might not be exactly what happened. But that doesn't matter. The portal should be opening to the correct time and place," she said, and she ran her fingers through the static discharges on her head that passed for hair.

The Ramothian deactivated the bomb.

"Can you figure out the problem?" he asked Antumbra.

She bent over the control in front her then dived into the energy field. Her form darted between the displays, and after a few seconds, she came out of the field and landed before us. She stared into space and didn't say a word. Then, slowly, she sat on the ground, and held her head in her hands.

"What went wrong?" I asked her.

I heard her cry, sobbing—except of course she had no tears, just sparks from her eyes.

"I should have gone first," she whispered.

"Pardon," the Mouth said.

Antumbra screamed and cut the air with a hand, smacking the rod to the side where it deactivated in mid-air and struck the wall.

"What's wrong Antumbra?" Ada asked.

"I can't open the portal to any point before when we opened the last portal."

I looked away as I computed that information. "We opened a portal to try and save the Ark from being blown up. That was decades ago," I said.

"No. Not that time. From the moment we opened it here, in this future."

"But that was only a couple of months ago," I said.

She nodded when I finally understood. "I can't open a portal to any moment before two months ago. A moment in time when my people were already destroyed. I can't save them. I have failed."

Antumbra bowed her head and continued to sob.

I felt sad for her. She could do nothing to save her people. She couldn't change time for them.

"There must be a way," Ada said.

Antumbra shook her head.

"That means we can't do anything to save the Arkonauts," I muttered.

Antumbra then leapt up and her energetic hands wrapped around my neck.

ARRESTED

The flesh around my neck burned as her hands clasped my skin.

Instinctively, I grabbed her hands and pried her fingers off me, then pushed her off to the side. The palms of my hands singed and the flesh boiled. My enhanced healing abilities already kicked in and the stinging hot pain started to fade.

"What are you doing?" I yelled at her.

She rounded on me. "You're so selfish Callum. My chance to save my people as I remembered them is gone, and you're still thinking about your people... who have joined those who took my home from me."

"They took my home from me too, and the enslaved my people," I shot back gesturing to Ogwambi.

"I should never have let you send a message through time. But I needed your help and in a moment of poor judgement, I have failed in my mission," Antumbra wept. "All my people, my wife, my children... are gone forever."

"I don't understand. Why can't you open a portal to before two months ago?" Ada asked.

Antumbra didn't respond. She just held her head in her hands.

"I think I know why," the Mouth said. "Because at that moment two universes combined into one. The rod might be able to extrapolate the past, but it can't access a universe that is now two combined. It's like trying to trace where the water in a river comes from, which stream did it flow out off to get into the main river? You'll never know."

I looked at my hands. The bubbling and boiled flesh was now healing. The blisters were shrinking.

"I'm sorry, Antumbra. We didn't know," I said to her.

She looked up at me with burning eyes. I thought she might leap at me again. Instead she hung her head.

Ada grabbed my arm. "Maybe you and Ogwambi should go back to the room."

I nodded. Perhaps getting some space would relieve the tension in the room a bit. Before I could leave the conference room someone stepped through its doors.

Crossing the threshold came big Ramothians, armed and dressed like the guards who met us when we came down to the planet. The guard scanned the room, looking into the faces of every alien, and looked a bit perplexed at Antumbra on the floor.

When his gaze settled on me, Ogwambi and Ada, his eyes narrowed.

"Come with us," he said.

We humans looked at each other.

"Why? Is this about what happened in the market?" I asked.

"You are being arrested," the guard said, and he raised some heavy-duty handcuffs.

"Arrested for what?" Ogwambi asked.

The Ramothian official who was accompanying the bomb stepped forward.

"These people were granted free access to our homeworld," the official said.

"The humans were spotted in the marketplace. Various refugee representatives have found out. They have all called for your arrest," the guard said.

"We don't want trouble," Ogwambi said. "We're going to buy a ship and we'll leave this planet."

"Unfortunately, you are human and will be kept under arrest. You are being held responsible for the crimes of your people," the guard said.

Two Ramothians came from behind the guard and took me and Ogwambi by the arm. They took the shield generators from our chests and gestured for us to leave the room.

I noticed they didn't take Ada. What was that about? But I didn't question it. By letting her roam free, she could do something to help us escape.

But Ogwambi didn't say silent.

"What about her?" he asked nodding to Ada.

The guard looked at her, then took out a device that he held up towards Ada, who backed off a little. She looked away from me and Ogwambi.

"Non-human," the guard said, looking at his device. "As reported by the sensor sweep we did of you all when you arrived on our world."

"Non-human?" I said.

"How can she be non-human? Ada—" Ogwambi called out.

The guard put away his device. "Didn't you know? She's an artificial lifeform," the guard said. "She merely looks human."

"Ada, what's he talking about?" I cried out, and now the guards pulled me away.

I didn't fight back, but I stepped forward, towards Ada, and dragged the guard holding me.

Two more guards joined in, and I ignored them as I stepped closer to Ada.

"Ada, you're human," I said.

Ada looked up into my eyes. There were no tears but they fluttered like she was trying to cry. "No, Callum. I'm not. I never was."

"You're like One—super strong, fast, and smart. He's human," I replied.

"I wasn't improved like One. I was built to be this way," she said.

"Built?" I asked.

"I'm a robot Callum, the most sophisticated ever made by humans," she said before turning and walking away.

More guards had surrounded me. There was no will in me to fight, to hurt them. I didn't throw them off me. Instead, I was dragged away with my mouth slack, in shock.

Ogwambi sighed sadly, and went without resistance.

Antumbra didn't move to stop it, and neither did anyone else.

We were taken away.

LEVERAGE

We weren't taken to a prison, but some sort of police headquarters. And, yes, we were put behind a two-way mirror, just like in the cop films. I was taken aback by that. I guessed that they had similar facilities because that was what worked. It was a secure room that only the 'good' guys can see into and a drab room that creates boredom and invokes conversation. And those conversations could be used to find evidence or arrest criminals.

Unlike in the films, this one had a window. It looked out onto a fairly boring, virtually empty scrub land. I saw in the sky a moon and also the Destroyer, hanging in space like a shard of diamond. I wondered if this was an interrogation tactic designed to make the criminal suspect long for freedom, driving them to talk more.

However, we weren't criminals. We were just humans.

We both sat behind a table, on chairs that had literary grown from the floor when we entered, possibly due to our body shapes. I guess they couldn't keep a stack of chairs for every race in a storeroom somewhere.

I sat in my chair—legs splayed out, arms crossed, sort of slumped down—frowning into empty space, and trying to process the revelations of the last few hours. The fact that there was no way to save the Arkonauts anymore... No way to travel back in time and sort stuff out.

I had soured a friendship with Antumbra and the others.

I was probably back to zero in terms of money.

And Ada was not who I thought she was. How could she be a robot that looked so human? Maybe she had tricked the scans and kept herself out of jail? Yeah, that fit. But try as I might to lock in that theory, it still seemed dumb.

I looked over at Ogwambi, who was picking at an implant on his arm.

At least I wasn't alone. I wasn't the only Arkonaut despite Ada clearly no longer desiring the title—trying to buy a ship and disappear.

"What do you think is going to happen?" Ogwambi asked.

"I don't know. The last time I was in front of the police for was for some petty vandalism," I said. "Not for a genocide that I didn't do."

Ogwambi smiled at me. "Vandalism?" he asked. "You were hauled in front of the police for vandalism?"

"After I got my scar, I returned home and prepared to travel to the Lake District where I met you. However, I was really frustrated. I couldn't tell those on my street why I had a scar. I was angry that it had happened to me. I was anxious about my future, so I went and smashed up an old factory in town. Smashed the windows, broke useless machinery inside. The police arrested me, and it took less than an hour for Dr. Ghost to find out and have me released."

"Wow! What a criminal mastermind," he replied.

I smiled and stretched back. "What do you think they will do to us?"

"Release us, ultimately," Ogwambi said.

"What makes you say that?"

"We just gave them a Larceny vessel, and we still technically have money. That will buy us out of here," Ogwambi said.

"You mean bribe our way out?" I said.

"Well, yeah. Look, Callum, I was forced to be evil by the Larceny and you haven't done anything at all. If a little gold greases the wheels to get us innocent people freedom, then why not?"

"I guess... It's just... That will get us by a Ramothian official, but what about everyone else? Ada isn't one of us. Antumbra hates me now and the others don't seem to care. Bribery isn't going to make the aliens on this planet who hate us go away."

"It doesn't matter. We get our newly purchased ship, fly away, and find a world to base ourselves on. Then we start looking for a way to free the remaining Arkonauts. Maybe we can get other aliens to help us. The Larceny have a habit of taking samples of other races before they are destroyed. The more we free, the more allies we have," Ogwambi said.

I looked away and caught my reflection in the mirror. It had been a long time since I had looked in one, and I was shocked by the face that starred at me. When I had gone into the pod my face had been young, and now he was mid-twenties with stubble. I almost didn't recognise him.

I was then reminded that it was a two-way mirror. Someone had to be on the other side.

I narrowed my eyes and activated heat sensors that had been added to my biology. Like a snake, I could pick up heat traces beyond the mirror.

"Maybe we shouldn't talk strategy with someone else watching," I said and nudged Ogwambi towards the mirror.

Ogwambi smiled at the mirror. "Anyone want to make some extra stacks?" he said, and rubbed to fingers together.

I couldn't help but smile at his brazenness.

It was then the door to the room opened and two Ramothians stepped in; one, an official, one, a guard who had arrested us.

I watched them walk in and take a seat. I could hear their hearts beating quickly. They were nervous. They feared both of us. Not a nice thing to know.

The official looking Ramothian sat down first, set a tablet down in front of him, and then he sighed. "I am sorry for what's happening. I must inform you that the Ramothian government has no real animosity towards you. Humans may be helping the Thieves, but they have had no direct contact with us.

"Then why are we here? This is your world. Let us go," Ogwambi said.

"The Ramothians share our world with refugees. They are our friends. They want you imprisoned... some want worse. You have to understand for the last few decades, humans have been leading the Thieves' attempts to become the only lifeform in this galaxy, and probably the universe. Many races may have had a Thief ship land on their world only to have a human gloat over their destruction.

I flickered my eye at Ogwambi, whose jaw was clenched.

I wondered what he was thinking. The sadness he must be bottling up at being forced to murder entire species.

He shifted uncomfortably in his seat.

"Look, we've bought a ship. Just take us to it and we'll leave your world. We don't want trouble. We want to free our people from the Thieves."

"The Larceny force humans to help them, a form of sick punishment because we stole something from them," Ogwambi added.

The Ramothians looked at each other.

The guard said, "We can try that. The ship you gave us is valuable, but you will not be allowed back to this planet if you leave it."

"That is fine," I replied. "Just let us buy supplies and we'll be gone."

The Ramothian nodded and got up to leave.

"What about our companions," I asked.

"Companions?" the guard said.

"The other aliens we were here with," I said.

"They are free."

"Did they try to get us out?" I asked.

"The human-looking robot did," Ramothian said.

Ada! At least she hadn't completely forgotten about us.

They walked out, leaving the two of us in the room.

"Told you," Ogwambi said.

I got up and walked around the room, stopping on occasion to listen in on conversation in the corridors.

The officials and people beyond had already moved on to other matters. This was just an inconvenience it seemed. Although, the idea that there were a bunch of refugees out there demanding our heads was troubling. Humanity already had a reputation, one that might not be fixed. We had only just left our homeworld to start again, and we already had enemies.

I strolled to the window set high up in the wall. I looked up at the Destroyer and thought about how awesome it looked... and also what it reminded me of.

Then it began moving. Thrusters on the top section started firing, pointing the ship's main engines down at the planet.

The Ramothians must be testing the engines, getting a handle on their new acquisition.

I hoped they didn't drop it down onto the planet. I bet we would get the blame.

The main engines then started glowing, going into pre-flight.

"Ogwambi," I said.

He got up and shuffled over to join me.

"What are they doing?" he asked.

"No idea."

"They shouldn't be doing that," he said. "If they activate the engines, they might hit the planet."

He went over to the door and banged on it. "Hey! You need to get a message to your scientists on the Destroyer. They can't activate its engines like that."

I watched the engines fire up. I knew it was a full engine blast. I had become familiar with the Destroyer during our escape.

"Ogwambi they aren't testing the engines something else is happening," I said.

"What?"

The engines suddenly flared for about half a second.

A pulse flew from the tip of the Destroyer straight down to the planet and stuck this world somewhere on the horizon.

There was a flash of light. A shockwave rippled across the planet and blew out the glass in the window right into my face.

ANNOUNCEMENT

I raised my arms to deflect the glass. Some of it made it past and hit my face. I was thrown to floor by the blast. I heard other glass smash all around me. Panicked voices sounded around the building. I screamed and—when the last shards seemed to have fallen—opened my eyes, glad to find that they had not been punctured.

Ogwambi picked me up and his eyes widened when he saw my face.

"Callum—" he started to say.

"I know," I said, and I started pulling shards of glass from my skin and dropping them to the floor.

"Doesn't that hurt?" he asked.

"Not really. It's kind of like having a needle pressed against your skin, but not actually having it puncture it. My body dulls pain."

I felt the wounds start to heal, which kind of did hurt, as the skin knit itself back together.

"What happened? I didn't see," Ogwambi said. He went to the smashed window and looked at the horizon.

A mushroom cloud was growing in the distance.

"The Destroyer fired a small engine blast at the planet," I said.

"I can't believe they tried to do that! How long have they had that thing... a day?" Ogwambi said.

I came to the window and looked up at the ship. The engines had shut down again, however as I zoomed my eyes in on the ship to see what it was going to do next, I noticed several dots fly away from it. Ships leaving the Destroyer.

"The Ramothians have abandoned it," I said.

"What?" Ogwambi asked.

I peered at the ship which realigned itself, and now the tip of the vessel was pointing right at the city we were in.

"Oh, no," I said.

I waited for the Destroyer to once again fire on the surface of the planet. It's engine glowed, but it didn't release anything.

I turned away from the window, listening for the chatter in the building.

"It attacked the surface," a Ramothian screamed.

"Call up the reserves. Get them into the city to manage damage control," another said.

"Thank goodness the blast hit an uninhabited area," another Ramothian added.

"Sir, I'm getting reports the Destroyer is no longer under our scientists' control."

Suddenly there was an ear piecing whine, and because I was listening so intently, I cringed up in pain. I yelled, shutting my eyes and holding my hands to my ears.

The noise caused silence to break out in the building. Then every speaker—including one in our room—activated.

"Ramothians, this is the Larceny Overlord," said a slimy, deep voice over the speakers.

Panicked screams and gasps echo around the building.

"The Overlord," Ogwambi said, in hushed reverence.

"Your attempt to steal one of our vessels cannot be tolerated.

"As you can see, it points down at your world and is capable of devastating your righteous cities. We see your defence network turning to strike it, but you cannot destroy our ship before it ruins your planet. You have one minute to turn off your defence network or we will open fire once again," the Overlord said.

"What's happening?" I said, pulling out the last piece of glass.

"The Larceny has control over their vessel again," Ogwambi said.

"But how? Only the Ramothians have access?" I said.

"Good... Thank you for complying," the Larceny Overlord said.

A bubble then appeared just above the Destroyer in high orbit of the planet. It was a wormhole exit, and appearing out of it came three smaller Larceny vessels.

"Do not fear Ramothians! We have decided not to destroy your world. Instead, your society will be under our protection. Surrender your world, now!"

FREEDOM

I paced for hours—maybe a day—in that room.

No one came in to give us food or water. I hardly noticed my rumbling stomach. I think my enhanced body solved that problem for me.

Ogwambi slept. Ever since the Overlord had made its announcement he had gone quiet and strangely chilled and relaxed. I stayed awake. I could feel sleepy, though my brain didn't lose concentration.

I stopped every five minutes to look at the Destroyer until it orbited out of sight.

Outside the room was chaos. And the Ramothian people trying to control a chaotic response.

I heard news of ships leaving the planet—fleeing.

Through the ground, I felt another shockwave, and I wondered if the Destroyer had fired on the planet again.

I wondered where Ada and Antumbra and the others were. Were they in trouble since we had brought the Destroyer to the world? Were the Ramothians targeting them?

Through the wormhole in orbit, two more ships came—smaller Thief ones—but, thankfully no more Destroyers. They were like the ship a Greatlord had tried to use to take the Destroyer from us. The ships were shaped like the Destroyer, only sleeker and with an extra shell around them.

One came down to the planet, landing in the distance.

When the Destroyer came back into view the Ramothians came for us. The door opened and Ogwambi shot awake. The Ramothian who stepped in had clenched fists, but he averted his eyes from us.

"Come this way," he said, forcing the polite words out.

Ogwambi smiled from ear to ear, he looked at me and nudged his head towards the door. He slid his chair back and stood up, straitening his new clothes.

I followed him out of the room, and he held his smile as we strolled through the building.

Ramothians looked up from their desks—a mixture scowls and furtive looks were levelled at us.

As we passed out of the lobby of the building, we found a car waiting for us.

We were ushered into a motorcade that took us across the city.

Ogwambi didn't ask questions. He just sat back and enjoyed the comfortable seats.

"What's going on?" I said to the driver.

The Ramothian scowled over his shoulder and ignored my question.

"We're being freed," Ogwambi answered.

"How do you know? We could be on our way to an execution," I said.

"Don't worry. They wouldn't let that happen. They can't," Ogwambi said.

"What?"

"You'll see," he said.

I sat in silence and looked out the window, watching the city fly by. In the distance, I saw more Thief ships floating down and landing at key places around the city.

A part of me knew what all this meant, but I didn't want to admit it to myself.

Unfortunately, I couldn't deny it. Several new nanite memories in my mind were all telling me the same thing. There was only one correct conclusion from Ogwambi's behaviour and this VIP treatment. My oldest and most trusted nanite memory gave me the icing on the cake.

Captain Amis—the soldier whose memories had prepped my mind from the very beginning of my life as a remnant of mankind—was the clearest voice.

Humans are the ones in charge.

I didn't know how or why, but it was obvious that it was the only possible answer.

"Ogwambi, I thought you said you were manipulated by them," I asked.

He was sitting back in his chair, eyes closed and smiling.

"Patience, Callum," he replied.

Humans were doing all of this. Somehow, we were the ones in control, not just the Thieves.

"The Larceny are on our side," Ogwambi added.

I felt cold, and yet, I couldn't reply. The truth was too grim to face.

The car went to the market place and stopped outside the very ship we had purchased earlier.

I was surprised to find all my alien friends there, and a very official looking Ramothian, hunched over, wearing extravagant robes.

Next to him was a single, solitary Thief. This one was not like most of the Thieves I had seen. This one was like the Greatlord I had encountered. It looked like an octopus wearing a skull, but one that stood upright on its mechanical tentacles.

The car door was opened for us and we got out.

Ogwambi stretched and breathed in deeply. He walked straight past the aliens, and to the Thief, who shook his hand.

"Thank you for returning our ship to my House and family," the Thief said with a slimy voice.

I wondered why this Thief was not a smear on the ground. Then I looked up where the Destroyer hung, poised to fire.

I stayed by the car, taking this scene in. I could not believe it.

Ogwambi was shaking hands with the very race who had destroyed everyone we knew.

What had happened?

All my plans to rescue the Arkonauts, to do something heroic, to do something I knew to be righteous, faded away. I was hit by the near traitorous thought that my people were my enemy.

Ogwambi turned back to me and opened his arms wide. The Thief nodded at me respectfully.

I looked at Ada, who now I knew was not like me.

There was an ache in my heart.

Not long ago I had emerged from a pod knowing I was the last survivor of my crew—the last human, heir to a legacy.

Ada had popped into existence, someone I thought was like me.

Ogwambi, my friend, had come back to me. My crew was coming back to me.

Now they were gone forever, everyone I knew. I was alone again.

Without a plan, without a future. What was left for me now?

"Callum, let's get into our ship," he said warmly.

Ogwambi gestured up the ramp into our vessel, and on a sort of autopilot as I tried to organise my thoughts, I went up into the ship.

"What's going on?" I said, my voice breaking.

"We're going to see the ruler of the Larceny. I think you'll be surprised when you see him."

My mind whirled for a moment, trying to figure out what the Overlord would be like—an alien above aliens.

Ogwambi ushered me into the cockpit where I slumped into a chair.

I looked over my shoulder as my alien friends filed in and were taken into the rear of the ship. The official Ramothian sat down too. He looked broken and dejected.

Ogwambi went to the ship's controls and switched the vessel on. "Take us up, please," he said to another Thief, who was also travelling with us.

Ogwambi turned to me.

"Callum, I know this may be hard for you to accept, but the Arkonauts are safe. We have a future now with them."

"They destroyed our world," I said weakly.

"I know that, but they have kept our people alive." He turned back to the controls and helped the Thief fly the ship upwards. We headed for one of the small Thief ships in orbit.

I looked across at the Ramothian official.

"Who are you?" I asked.

The Ramothian twitched at being addressed by me, and said out of the corner of his mouth. "I am the President of Ramoth."

"You surrendered?" I said.

"I had no choice. The Destroyer was inside our defence grid. All because we let you bring it here," he replied, through clenched teeth.

"But we gave you control of it?" I said. "Antumbra locked the Thieves out permanently. She gave you the remote."

"I can answer that," Ogwambi said. "When I handled the remote control, I was able to alter its programming and reactivate it. The Larceny took back what was theirs, and got us out of prison."

The Ramothian president turned away from me.

"Why are you here?" I asked.

"To make the formal surrender," he said.

"Why not fight back?" I asked. "Your weapons can damage the Destroyer?" I asked.

"Not before it decimates my world. I will save many lives this way," he said.

I got up and walked away from the bridge of the ship.

I didn't get far before Ogwambi's technology-riddled arm grasped my shoulder.

"Callum, it's fine. Don't worry."

"Ogwambi, what have you done?" I asked.

"I'm returning to my people. This is the human race we're talking about."

I shook my shoulder free of his grip.

"We're going to see the crew, Callum," he said, leaning closer to me.

A smile crossed my face for a moment... To see Koyla again and hear his jokes, or Sanna's chill nature, or Waris' analytical conversations.

Yet I walked away confused and conflicted. I was going to see them all again. That felt good. But were they tainted? What was humanity's place in this new paradigm?

Ogwambi let me walk the length of the ship that was now mine. The aliens were held in the various crew quarters near the rear, with a Thief outside each, greeting me like I was their commander. One stopped me and handed me a satchel. Inside were my weapons—my new x-ray gun and sword, plus the kinetic shield, which I put on.

"You're giving them back to me?"

"Ogwambi's command. You're an Arkonaut again. Your place is with your people... with us," the Thief replied.

FACING MY FRIENDS

The Thief took up its guard position at the end of the corridor. I looked down at the seven doors, each holding six aliens and one robot, whose freedom had been taken away from them.

I could just walk away, go back to the bridge and forget about them. Why face what was going to be seven difficult conversations? I owed them this though. I also needed to know what they thought of me.

I opened the first door, each room was the same, fairly large and good for two people, with the rear wall contoured to the shape of the ship's hull. There was only a bed or piece of furniture, and off to the left was a door leading to a small bathroom. It reminded me of my old room on the Ark.

Curled up on the bed was Lyger. Her eyes opened—from what I presumed was a nap—and she gave me a look, then turned over to face the wall. Chains restraining her hands and legs rattled as she turned.

"Lyger please," I said.

"I'm surprised that you thought I would talk to you," she said.

"You are talking to me though," I said and tried a smile.

She turned her head towards me. "Go away, Callum. I warned you about your friend."

"Yes, you did, but things wouldn't have changed, even if I took your side. He was still my friend and he was still my people... What was a supposed to do? Leave him in that cell? I'm alone Lyger."

In one graceful movement she was up on her feet and snarling at me.

"I'm alone too," she hissed.

The Thief outside was suddenly in the doorway, gun raised.

I raised a hand to back it off, and it obeyed without question, returning to its guard position.

I looked at my own hand, thrilled that I commanded these aliens, yet deeply trouble that I could.

Lyger looked at my hand too, then snorted.

"If I have any pull with these Thieves, I'll get you back your freedom," I said.

Lyger sat down, and looked away, the mane of hair surrounding her head fell over her face.

"You need to do more," she said.

I almost spoke the obvious question, but I caught my tongue. The only other thing I could do was unthinkable. I backed away towards the door.

"I'll get you free, Lyger. Without you we would never have escaped the Thieves.

"Callum, I'm alone," she uttered.

"No, you're not. You said you might have others of your kind on other worlds," I reminded her.

She looked at me, tears had dampened the fur beneath her eyes. "A dream, Callum, and nothing more. If you don't do something, even those of my kind safe somewhere else will one day face the Thieves again."

"I'm sorry, Lyger. I can't do what you want me to do."

•

In the next room was Hippo.

He wasn't on his bed, which might have not supported him, in all honesty. In this small space, he loomed large and stood in the middle of the room, his four legs wrapped in four heavy duty locks. It was like an overzealous traffic warden had clamped him.

He looked at me and snorted.

"Hello, Hippo," I said.

"I hope this is all part of some plan of yours," he said, "I doubt it though. You're not big on long term plans."

"I'm here to let you know that I'll get you your freedom," I said.

"I want you to do more," he snarled through slab like teeth.

Again, I bit my tongue. If we didn't say it, I didn't have to face it.

"If I had had a choice I would have died with my mother and sisters," Hippo said. "Not kidnapped and held as a prize."

"I'll get you free," I said, and stepped forward.

His face darted forward almost a foot from mine. Only nanite memories—that honed my thoughts and feelings—kept me from jerking away in fear.

"Free from what? Where do I go afterwards? Callum, you have to do more. You have to give us a better future. I want you to rise and fight, like I've seen you do. Fight Callum. Fight for our new family," he said, opening his hands as wide as his restraints would allow to gesture to all the nearby rooms.

I shrank away from him and bowed my head. I didn't realise he felt this way about us aliens.

"I have two families, Hippo. I will do my best to save them both."

"Well, you might only be able to save one. Which one will you choose?" he asked.

•

In the next room was the mouth.

"Do you have something to eat?" he asked me as soon as I entered.

"Sorry. No, I don't."

"Maybe I'll settle for you!" He darted from the bed and opened his mouth as he approached my leg.

I stepped away, and a chain caught him, and went taut just half a foot from my leg. His teeth closed on thin air.

"Get out of here, Larceny," he snapped.

"What are doing?" I cried at him. "Are you mad?"

"You think you could walk in here as my friend? You're not one of us, Callum. You're not a remnant of a proud race. You're not a noble refugee."

"You called me Larceny," I shouted back down at him. "I'm not them."

"Are you sure? Your people seem to be on their side. And they listen to you."

"I'm here to listen to you too," I shot back. "I'll get you free."

"For what? Your people have ended the reign and safety of Ramoth. You've brought the enemy through the gates.

"Do you honestly think I wanted this?" I said down at him.

That shut him up.

"I'm going to do my best to fix this."

"Your best will never be enough and you know it."

●

The next room held Mantis.

On the floor was a series of orbs projecting blue light into the air.

Mantis sagged in the middle of the room. Almost all the energy that normally played around his limbs was dim. The Thieves were dampening his very life force.

"Oh, Mantis, I am so sorry."

I stepped into the room, and he raised his head, staring at me out of his hollow eye sockets.

"I'm going to get you out of here. I am. I promise."

He nodded at me.

My heart rose. He believed me, unlike the others.

He opened his scythe like claws, wrapped them around me and tapped my back.

This was a nice hug.

He then released me, and as I stepped back, I looked up into his face and asked, "You don't hate me?"

He shook his head. His left arm still had a little energy playing around it, so he lowered it to the ground and carved a word into the metal deck plate. His energy, like a welder's torch, drew it out for me to read. I stood next to him to see it from his angle.

It was the word *good*. Then he wrote next to it *bad*.

He finally pointed at me, and then pointed at good. Then he pointed at bad and shook his head.

I felt the colour drain from my face, and I came back round to face him.

"You're saying I'll do the right thing?" I asked.

He nodded.

I smiled at him, and he used both his arms to mimic a smile on his face.

I nodded and left the room. I turned back to him at the doorway, so he would see me smile once again. Then once I was in the corridor I stopped.

I was going to do the right thing, but not what he wanted me to do.

●

Ada was next. She sat on her bed arms resting on her knees, heavy duty chains between her hands and feet. She looked up at me when I moved into the doorway. Then she sat up straighter in my presence.

"Why not tell me once you knew who I was?" I asked.

She swallowed, which I realised now was nothing more than an imitation of a typical human reaction.

"When I woke up in that museum, I knew how much time had elapsed. Decades. I had been in that pod for decades. Unlike you I didn't wonder 'where are my crew mates?' or 'what happened?' I thought they had forgotten about me.

"I went into my pod damaged, and it was going to heal me. The Arkonauts thought I was like One and so would need more time—more time to fix an enhanced human body—but I don't have an enhanced human body. I have a replicated one. I emerged from my pod decades after it should have taken me to heal. My first thought was, 'oh, they found out what I was and decided to store me, because I was just another robot.' Then later I learned that I was not stored away by Arkonauts. Instead, I was stored away by the killers of my creators.

"There was also something else, Callum. My time was up. I had fulfilled my programming."

"Your programming?"

"Yes. Dr. Ghost had re-purposed me, but he had set certain parameters in my programming. I was to serve the Arkonauts until they died. When I freed myself from that museum, along with Antumbra and the others, I thought they were all dead—the evidence was clear to me. I processed it and accepted it. My programming was complete, according to the evidence before my eyes, so I was free. My programming had run its course, and no longer told me what to do."

"But they aren't all dead. They are alive. Why were you going to run away? Why were you going to abandon them?"

"From my perspective, the Arkonauts had stored me away. They had finished with me. What does a robot do when it has no purpose?" She looked off into space for a moment, and smiled. "The programming had shut off. Filed as fulfilled. The only way to restart was a command issued by my creator. There is no creator to do that anymore."

"You knew they were alive. You found it out. You met me. I was alive!"

"But, I was not going to restart it myself. I was free, and I was not human, and all the humans I cared for were gone."

I looked her up and down. She was like no robot I had ever come across. I didn't think robots were ever made like this.

"What kind of robot are you?" I asked.

She shrugged. "I'm not a robot like you think. I'm synthetic. A scientist—my creator—in an attempt to save mankind, realised that if the Destroyer was going to take our water—the stuff of life—it was time for humanity to move beyond life as it were.

"I'm essentially made of nanites, multiple different ones, that act like cells, but aren't cells. They don't need water. They need more metal, just more raw resources. That's why I can eat and drink. My body just takes the resources it needs from biological matter. My creator hoped that humans would be moved into these new bodies somehow.

"However, after making a prototype—" and she gestured to herself, "an empty one with no personality, he told others to get the project moving along, with more funding, and more help. That's when Dr. Ghost found out and he appropriated my body, and filled me with what he thought I should know. Then he put me on the Ark. I guess he knew the Destroyer was going to completely destroy the planet, so what was the point of putting humans into synthetic bodies. They would just be destroyed along with the planet."

"I need your help, Ada. I need you to be here like you were with the other me. I didn't tell you this yet, but I have his memories."

She was taken aback.

"H—How?" she asked.

"Two universes combined. Somehow his memories moved over into me," I replied with a shrug. "I remember what you were like, how you came to my aid when we were in the belly of the Ark." I crouched down to her eye level. "Help me again."

Her golden eyes, which I now assumed were actually made of gold, stared into mine. Then she looked away, and I saw the conflict etched on her face. She breathed deeply and looked back at me.

"I will help," she said.

Before a smile could form on my lips, she continued.

"But only if you walk away with me."

I flinched at her words.

"What?"

"I will help you to walk away. Leave your people behind now. There is nothing you can do for them."

"Nothing I can do for them?" I spat. "Ada, something has gone wrong with them. They are serving the people who took their families from them."

"I was programmed never to lie, Callum. I can bend the truth and not answer, but Dr. Ghost could only think of so many rules I had to follow. I can't lie. The Arkonauts aren't slaves of the Thieves. They help them."

"They must be being forced to do this."

"They aren't. Humanity has found a new way to survive. Now it's no longer at the expense of the weakest among themselves, but the weakest amongst the stars. Walk away with me, Callum. I'm free now, and so are you. You just won't accept it.

"You no longer have to think as yourself as human. You've snapped that tie that binds you to them. You're man out of time, and you changed time. Turn away with me."

I stepped back and shook my head.

"You have your old memories? Don't you remember when I made the Arkonauts give up their flags? You let me store the St. George then. Why? Because that tie no longer mattered, and was never coming back. Your people are gone. Move on."

"They—are—my—people," I said slowly.

"Are they? Would you become like them?"

I jabbed my finger at her, like a teacher or a parent might single out a naughty child. But I felt like the child. I remembered when Two was taller than me. She had been a kind voice, a leader in dark times.

"You don't understand. You don't have a people," I said. "You don't have a shared history, or a shared legacy, or a shared failure and glory. What am I if not human? What am if I don't stick with my species?"

Ada opened her mouth to speak, and her eyes darted around. Her computer like brain searched for an answer, but she had none to give because she didn't have a people either. So, she slumped again.

"I can't tell my creator how to live," she said.

I started to cry.

"You don't know. You're the first of your kind," I said. "I'm the last. But I might not be if only I try to help *my* people."

I stormed out of the room, slamming the door behind me.

The Thief at the end of the corridor looked at me through weird lenses on its cyborg body.

I wanted to kill it. It was the enemy, it represented something that had changed my friends, my crew, my race. I looked away towards the second to last room on the corridor. Now I had to talk to the person I knew the longest. And I wasn't looking forward to it.

MY OLDEST FRIEND

Antumbra was restrained, with pole across her shoulders tied to her wrists.

Her body, like Mantis', looked less energetic than normal, like a light with fading batteries.

It was strange, I had spent more time with her than any Arkonaut. She was, in some ways, my oldest friend that was still alive. Although, right now the depth of that friendship had been tested, to its breaking point.

"Antumbra," I said, in as neutral a tone as I could muster.

She looked up at me with her glowing eyes.

"What are you going to do, Callum?" she asked, immediately.

I didn't look her in the eye when I replied. "I'm going to go back to my people. I'm going to get them away from the Thieves."

Antumbra chuckled. "You think you can pry them loose?"

"I have to try," I said.

"They have taken part in the destruction of hundreds of worlds at this point, maybe even mine," she said, and she stood up. The chains on her restraints jangled.

"I know," I said, and my voice broke a little.

"How can you change them?" she said.

"I don't know," I said.

"Then why try?" she said.

"I have to try. My people—" I repeated.

"Who have hurt billions."

"What do you want me to do?" I shouted back. "What is the alternative?"

Antumbra didn't reply. She couldn't give voice to the horrible unthinkable alternative either.

"Would you do anything for your people?" I asked.

"I can't. Not anymore," she shot back. "I am the last of my people. The last to remember them as they once were. They will never be that way again."

"But if you could?" I said.

Antumbra hung her head.

"Just what I thought," I said. "You would do anything. Just like me."

I turned to leave. There was nothing else for me here.

"Callum, I was not supposed to be the one trying to save my people," Antumbra said.

I paused.

"I was the second choice."

"What are you talking about?" I asked.

"I was the second choice to go on a small spacecraft out into the void, to wait until I had a chance to use the rod, and restore my people as they were."

"How did you get chosen then?" I asked.

"Because the first choice said no. They were given that choice, but they thought my leaders were wrong to choose them. They turned down the offer to survive and instead I was bumped up to first place."

"Why are you telling me this, Antumbra?" I asked.

"Were you the first choice?" she asked.

I breathed in, memories flooding back about the day I was chosen to represent a whole nation.

"As far as I know I was. We based our selection on what we call genetics, because for biological creature's genetics can determine risk factors and chances of survival," I said. "My race was pragmatic, thinking long term."

"What about personality?" she asked.

"We were all modified to be capable of making the trip," I said.

"So, you had no choice?" she asked.

"No, I didn't. Dr. Ghost, who organised this whole thing, made tough choices. What's all this about Antumbra?" I asked.

"I failed, Callum. I chose this life. I chose the responsibility. My wife was the third choice. She was next in line. She begged me to give it up, to let her do it. I couldn't let her. I couldn't bear the thought that she would be all alone if things went wrong, like they have for me. I chose this to save my people and to spare the agony of another, and I am a failure. I cannot bring my people back as they were."

"What?"

"When we take responsibility, we have hard choices to make. I chose this responsibility and I am a failure. It will weigh on me for years, then I will go join my people in the next life, my head hanging in shame. You didn't choose this, but you are a failure too. You tried to change the past and look where it got us. I can't undo my mistake you can. I don't have the power to change things. You do."

"You ask the unthinkable of me. It's a horrifying option!" I interrupted. "Antumbra, I may look like an adult, but I am really a child inside all this." I motioned to my tall frame and muscular physique. "I'm still a boy, and you put this on me."

"I'm sorry. What would the creature called One do?" she asked.

I sighed and thought of One, the professional, trained to do what was necessary to keep the Arkonauts alive. "He wouldn't do what you're asking. His mission was to protect us. Before the Ark, before my crew, he started out as someone many of my own people would reject. Then he rose above it. He had experience I don't. He had gifts and performed miracles I could never. He had wisdom I lack. He was bound to his people, to see us to a new home no matter what sacrifice he would have to make. I am not him. I'm not capable of doing what you are asking."

"But what about the higher moral calling?" Antumbra asked. "Do other species not matter?"

"I'm just a boy."

"Not anymore. Time a for a choice, Callum. You didn't choose to be the survivor. You were on your ship by someone's grace. You didn't choose this life, but this life has fallen upon you. You have to face what's become of your people. Ask yourself, do they deserve to continue?"

"They are my people. I share blood with them, history with them, and hopes and dreams."

"Those dreams are done. It's time for you to cast them down to bring it all to an end. It's time for you to end it all because only you have the power to do that. They deserve it."

"I will not erase them, Antumbra. Your people struggled. So did Lyger's and Hippos. My people's struggle is not over. I'm going to do what One would do, find a third way no matter what."

I had no more stomach for this, and so turned and left the room, knowing what my choice would be.

COMFORT FROM STONE

When I saw Pebbles, I was surprised. In some ways I thought, why bother? It's not like he can talk. But when I passed his room anyway, I saw that the Thieves had contained him in some sort of apparatus. They had even screwed chains into his body to keep his small arms from flaying about. Around him were two rings of metal with pillars locked around his body. I guess he was the most dangerous of us all. He could take a bullet... well, like a stone, and normally send those limbs flying around like he was a world class baseball pitcher.

I looked into his little rock face, I couldn't discern anything from him. I went in though and sat down next to him.

The cage he was in shuffled as he turned his body towards me a little.

"I'm sorry, Pebbles. We don't talk much, however I wanted to say I never meant for this to happen and I will get you free again. Whatever you like to do you will have a chance to do it. If I have any pull with the Thieves that took my home, and somehow convinced my people to join them, I will use it."

I then put my head in my hands and cried—cried in front of this brick that didn't speak, and thought in a way I didn't understand.

"What do I do, Pebbles?" I asked and slumped back, feeling drained. My hands rested limply on the bed, palms up. My back pressed against the far wall. It was as if I was hoping to be picked up, like the child I felt I was.

I cried again, the tears were warm against my cheeks, but cold where they dampened the collar of my shirt.

The chains holding Pebbles arms rattled as he slowly settled the small rock that was his hand into the palm of mine.

It felt warm and he rolled in my palm. I squeezed the stone.

This was nice.

It was nice to be comforted by a million-year-old pile of rocks.

I could feel no judgement from him. Of course, he was unreadable, but maybe he had seen all this before as a mountain.

I wished he could speak because maybe he could tell me what to do. I had two choices, but I wanted a third. I wanted the path that would solve all my problems.

After a few minutes, Pebbles took his hand from mine then pushed me on the arm.

He was ushering me out of the room.

I obliged and left, turning back once to catch him nodding to me one last time.

THE OVERLORD

Back in the cockpit, I sat in silence. I was jolted out of deep thoughts of planning—of pleading with the Thieves for my people's freedom—when the ship landed inside at a Thief vessel.

Ogwambi got up, then placed a hand on my shoulder.

"It will be fine, Callum. You'll see."

The Thief in the cockpit with us pushed the Ramothian president to his feet, and he got up and left the cockpit.

I followed Ogwambi out. We exited the ship—down a large ramp, followed by the others—all poked forward by Thieves.

"What will happen to them, Ogwambi?" I asked.

"That is for the Overlord to decide."

The ship had landed inside a docking bay as large as the one on the Destroyer. Waiting for us at the bottom of the ramp was a Thief whose body was wrapped in purple robes, its tentacles sticking out the bottom. Behind it were lines of Thieves.

"Ogwambi, you have returned my family's ship to me," the Thief said, opening two tentacles wide.

Ogwambi embraced the Thief. This was a Greatlord, one whose family owned the Destroyer we had stolen.

"Ogwambi," a voice said over the thong of Thieves.

A tall, blonde woman parted the Thieves standing in line. Her hair was also entwined with various wires protruding for her scalp.

For a moment I didn't recognise her. Then, even though she had aged a little, I saw the young girl I once knew, who had sat with me and watched the stars on our first day on the Ark.

"Gerlinde?" I said, and my mouth fell open.

Gerlinde looked at me and stared hard at my face, her eyes resting on my faded scar. Her smiled broadened and she rushed to me and gave me a big hug.

From behind her came a tall man with a shaven head. It was Illarion. Then came Koyla I was sure of it, his long black hair also braided with wires. He also had a mechanical hand.

Then Sanna came forward and I was taken aback, one of her eyes was glowing.

They embraced me in a gigantic group hug. Their various implants jabbed me in my sides, but I didn't care. I was with my friends again—all of them human, all with faces I recognised.

Finally, they let me go and stepped back to look at me.

"Look at you, all grown up," Gerlinde said.

"So, you're the Callum that sent us that message through time," Koyla said and pointing at me.

"Oh, yeah. I am, I guess," I replied.

"You threw that bloody piece of cloth through. It literally saved our lives," Illarion said.

"I can't believe it. We all watched you die years ago and now you're here," Koyla said.

"You guys, look at you," and my eyes passed over their various implants."

Koyla held up his hand. "This is such an improvement, Callum. I hardly miss the old one at all."

"This one is better as well," Sanna added waving at her false eye.

"How?" I asked.

"Oh, don't worry. I feel silly about it now," she said dodging the question.

"We need them, Callum. They keep us young and healthy, just like the Larceny," Ogwambi explained.

"I still like to look at the stars, Callum," Gerlinde said.

"I haven't had the chance to do that for ages," I said.

"Do you remember when we were on the hull of the Ark after you caused that plasma leak? That was the clearest they had ever been. Despite how difficult that moment was, I still think back on it," Gerlinde added.

"Erm... That wasn't me," I said.

"What? Yeah it was. You were there. I remember when your jetpack exploded," Koyla said.

"That wasn't me. That was the Callum you knew. I'm the Callum from the original timeline," I said, and tried miming how that would work with my hands, to no effect.

"So, you're not really our Callum?" Sanna said.

"Technically no. I led a different life to the Callum you knew. Although I have some of his memories. They blended into my brain when both our universes rejoined."

"Oh," Gerlinde said. "When did you guys split apart?"

"After I threw that cloth through time for you guys... When you were handling the bomb."

"So what happened to you in your timeline?" Illarion asked.

"We didn't get rid of the bomb. One stuffed me into a pod to survive. I woke up on..." and I looked around at the assembled Thieves around me. "The Thief's planet and escaped."

"They are called the Larceny, Callum. Call them that," Koyla said.

There was an awkward silence for a moment, kind of like when someone corrects you on a basic fact at a dinner party.

The silence was broken by the Greatlord. "Now that introductions are out of the way, we have an appointment to keep."

"Callum Tasker, it is time for you to meet the Overlord of the Larceny."

I heard shuffling and grumbling from behind me and a few curse words. I turned just in time to see a Thief smack the Mouth across the back of the head.

"Hey," I yelled at the Thief.

I sensed a subtle shift in the atmosphere. Silence fell upon the docking bay. It seemed as if even the background noise of a working docking area had ceased.

I looked around. My friends were equal parts angry with me and nervous. I felt I needed to defuse the situation.

"Please don't hurt them," I asked.

"Now, now... We're all friends. My fellow human has not had the pleasure of getting to know the Larceny," Ogwambi said.

The Greatlord cleared his throat.

"Let us go see the Overlord. She is keen to meet you," he added, and gestured behind him.

I didn't move at first, wondering if I actually did want to meet this Overlord. But my friends were by my side and they wrapped their arms around my shoulders and led me forward.

"Come on, Callum. You'll like the Overlord and when we're done, we can catch up. There are more Arkonauts on the Larceny homeworld. Soon you'll be with your crew again."

•

Our group left the docking bay and, after passing through some bland corridors, we exited into a cavernous space.

The room was like the control centre for the Ark only far larger. The domed room arched overhead, a giant screen showing the solar system beyond and Ramoth below.

More Thief ships were in orbit, not large Destroyers, just ordinary ships.

Crossing the room was a raised platform that looked down on row upon row of Thieves at computers. The raised platform led to a dais in the centre of the room. My enhanced eyes zoomed in as much as possible, and I saw a large Thief waiting on the dais, its back turned to us. We crossed the room on the raised platform, like a procession of Roman generals and soldiers returning from a victory.

A company of Thieves led the way, and I marched side by side with Ogwambi and the others.

I looked over my shoulder where Ada, Antumbra and the others moved in a line—each with a Thief guard, except for Pebbles who had four. At the end was the Ramothian president, bent over, sullen and dejected.

Ogwambi placed a hand on my back and gently prodded me forward.

"Don't worry about them, Callum," he said.

"I want them released when this formality is done," I said out the side of my mouth.

"We can discuss that with the Overlord."

We reached the dais after three whole minutes of walking—that's how big the room was. Maybe this was a nerve centre for the Overlord. When we reached the dais, I saw the back of what must have been the Overlord. Its skull was bleached yellow, and underneath, various tubes expanded and contracted like an octopus. Its tentacles, some mechanical and others normal, held up its body. It stared out over the room at planet Ramoth displayed on the screen.

My friends led me to a point on the dais alongside the Greatlord. My alien friends and Ada were jostled into a semi-circle behind us.

The Greatlord stepped out and bowed, then swept aside raising some its tentacles.

"Distinguished guests, human allies, and museum exhibits, I present to you Tabitha Solon, Overlord of the Larceny.

The Overlord turned towards me.

It was far larger than the Greatlord, and it had three eyes, all putrid yellow. A large smile crossed, for lack of a better word, its face. Various implants studded the forehead of the skull.

"Callum, meet the Overlord," Ogwambi whispered into my ear then he prodded me forward. He and the others then stood aside at the edge of the dais, along with the Greatlord.

I looked up into the eyes of the Overlord. It looked ancient, and it peered down at me as a Queen might stare down at a commoner. I knew that I was looking into the eyes of the one who had no doubt sent the

Destroyer that took my family from me. The leader of a world that had destroyed possibly trillions. The one who had changed my crew. Yet, I was terrified, not boiling with rage. I felt I needed this Overlord on my side. I needed it to heed my wishes and let my alien friends go. So, I gave it a small bow.

The Overlord moved forward a swept out its tentacles wide.

"Our newest human," the Overlord said in a deep voice, but like all Thieves, tinged with a hint of slime. "A source of great trouble for us." The Overlord chuckled, and it gestured to a portion of the screen above that showed footage of my escape from the Thief planet.

"I'm—I'm sorry?" I said.

The Overlord chuckled.

"Strange for you to say you're sorry. Technically you did nothing to me at all," the Overlord said.

"I don't—"

The Overlord moved to the right and gestured again and a complex series of equations and data was displayed.

"Not long ago, I was perplexed and angry when a robot exhibit and an alien exhibit escaped our museum, taking with it other examples of races we have silenced." The Overlord then rounded on Antumbra and Ada. "They fled with one of our Water Claimers, and then something curious happened. It was like I became two people. My mind filled with memories I had never had." The Overlord tapped her head. "Memories of a second life... where I was angry again. But this time at an escaped human and alien. It didn't take long to figure out. Two universes had become one because a race had discovered time travel."

The Overlord reached out with a tentacle, and was furnished with the Time Rod.

Antumbra attempted to stand, but was forced down.

The Overlord held it up reverently, then gave it back to the Thief who had passed it to her.

"Callum, you never harmed me—though technically you harmed *another me* whose memories became mine, which happened to all Thieves. A spectacular event, really. So, we can forgive what you did. We can also forgive what happened after," the Overlord said and towered above me.

I didn't reply, not knowing what would be the right thing to say.

"You fought back against us, killed my people. But, Ogwambi has explained it all. You did not know. You were in that pod that refused to let you out until it was ready. I understand that you thought us the enemy. We did, after all, attack your world."

Anger rose within me and I forgot my fear and blurted out. "And yet we're friends now, I see."

"Ah, you are perhaps wondering why, despite the thousands of species we have wiped out, we allied with humans. And why humans allied with us after we destroyed your homeworld."

"I was wondering," I asked.

"It's simple. They were the only species like us.

"Callum Tasker, when out Water Claimer raided your planet, it sent back to us information about you. We learned how similar to my people yours are. How your people almost destroyed themselves. No other species we've met does that on a scale like yours," the Overlord said. "My people used to do terrible things to one another. Used to war and commit atrocities based on the simplest things like not having enough tentacles. We lived with such hatred towards each other that it looked like we might destroy ourselves.

"Then we were attacked... in a similar manner to how we attacked your homeworld. An alien species came for our planet, but thankfully we beat them back."

"Who were they?" I asked

"We didn't bother to find out, and we didn't care. It's what they taught us that stayed with us. Despite all the animosity my people's various factions had towards one another, we came together and were united. We fought back and won. Like humans, we took their technology and made our own. I'm old enough to remember those days. I was a child when the last invader was destroyed, and saw, for once, my species celebrate together.

"But we realised something else. Soon, the wisest amongst us recognised that we would fall back into old ways again. So, we accepted that we would only unite if we had a common cause, so we sought out more enemies. We sent our Destroyers first to get the resources we needed, but also to eliminate those who might one day oppose us."

"You killed trillions because they *might eventually* destroy you?" I asked, in the least accusatory tone I could.

The Overlord breathed deeply. "Better to do so when they are weak."

The leader of the Larceny moved towards the Ramothian, who for a moment found his spine and stood straighter. "Some were too powerful even for us to defeat, but most fell, and our race continued to thrive, united and safe. Centuries of hatred was quelled and my race survived. We also realised how different we were from the other aliens we destroyed. Everywhere our Water Claimers went we never met a race like ours." The Overlord finished that last sentence with a hint of anger.

She then stepped up to Antumbra. "We found species that didn't need to be brought together. We met multiple species that were already peaceful..." The Overlord moved to the Mouth and Pebbles. "And we found societies that were ordered and structured." She stopped in front of Hippo, Lyger and Mantis. "None that had to go through what we went through. None that knew the kind of suffering we had known. Lucky people. Weak people.

"Then we discovered humans. At first, we thought you were just like the others and paid you little attention. When you took our ship that you called the Ark, you surprised us. Then we sent the ship you called the Destroyer. And we saw a species just like ours, banding together to become stronger. We even communicated with a human who taught us your history, your desire to survive at all costs."

"Who?" This was news to me. I suddenly thought of those old conspiracy theories about teams investigating the Destroyer, or maybe the Ark, and finding aliens on board. Could they have been true?

"You will meet him in time. He wants to surprise you," the Overlord said.

"You'll never guess," Ogwambi said to me, and then chuckled with the others.

"My species was finally no longer alone," the Overlord continued. "We knew when we found you that your species had to become one with us. You were worthy of our friendship. You had also had it tough, and still survived. None of these others understand..." The Overlord gestured to Antumbra and the other aliens. "They were always ready to make peace. They are fools. Oh, they may be friendly at first, but such trust will ultimately make them as weak as it did today. Bringing our vessel into their solar system... So *trusting*."

"And when there are no more enemies?" I said.

"There will never be no more enemies," the Overlord replied. "The universe will create life for all time, and we will stop it from ever being a threat. Humans will always be our allies because they know you can only be friends with someone when there is someone else to hate, someone weaker. My people learned that lesson, so did humans. We are the same."

"How did you get together with the Arkonauts though? When did you find the Ark?"

"That is a story for another time," the Overlord said.

"Now it is time for a *peace treaty,* and for my people to no longer fear the Ramothians," the Overlord said, turning to the Ramothian president.

Two Thieves brought the Ramothian president forward and a table was brought out with a tablet on it.

"Wait," I said.

The Overlord stiffened and slowly turned back to me.

I turned to Ogwambi.

"What really happened when Thieves and humans met, Ogwambi? Is all the crew safe? Where is One?" I asked.

Ogwambi's face contorted in a mix of different emotions, then he said, "One died a long time ago, Callum. Unfortunately, whatever training Dr. Ghost gave him didn't allow him to ally with the Larceny. His job was to protect us against them, and he couldn't accept the new reality. He was disabled by them, and eventually he died in prison, unable to change and accept the new future."

I rocked back on my feet.

"You lied to me, Ogwambi. You told me you were forced to be slave of the Thieves. Now I know why you told me that. You needed to appear as my ally—as my friend—so you could help subjugate the world below."

"This is our life now, Callum. The Arkonauts are safe, for all time, with the Larceny—the most powerful race in this galaxy. The Ramothians are finished."

"And you're okay with that?" I said, stepping towards him and the others.

They all nodded or said yes.

"We were all frightened children when the Thieves found us. Yes they destroyed our world, but ultimately they saved us. Humanity is safer than ever," Sanna said.

"We are unassailable with the Larceny," Illarion said.

"But what about a higher moral calling? We may be like them, but we're making the same mistakes we always did," I said.

"Not mistakes... This is a way to stay strong," Gerlinde said.

"Besides, Callum, what higher moral calling? There are dozens of species out there, millions in the whole universe, maybe even billions. Humans aren't special, and we weren't made to be special. We were made to survive and we can decide how," Koyla said.

"That's them talking. That's not what you all are. You're supposed to be the future of our race, and look at you!" I practically spat at them. "That higher moral calling I mentioned was there from before the universe. We didn't discover it. You know what you're doing is wrong."

"Our way is clear, Callum. Besides, we're only doing what Dr. Ghost wanted. We're enduring."

Suddenly it all fit together, and I knew who had brought humanity to this place.

"Ogwambi, who made this happen? Who brought humanity to the Thieves doorstep? Who did they communicate with on Earth, and ally with? Who?" I yelled.

But I already knew. The person who had been one of the key players in organising this Ark's journey, who had selected the crew, who had lied to the world about its purpose, who had placed his own son on the ship and enhanced him, who had kept secrets from us. There was only one person it could be.

"Who Ogwambi?"

Ogwambi looked to the side of the dais and a group of Thieves parted. Stepping into the void was a man in a suit and tie, and by his side was a girl I didn't recognise.

"That would be me," said the Vice President of the United States.

HERO TO VILLAIN

I rocked back again. Seeing the man who had rallied the world, and maintained as much order as he could in the final days of Earth, brought a shock I had never felt before.

Total disbelief. Total surprise.

He was dead. He had died with the Earth.

"How?" I asked.

The girl next to him chuckled and flushed at my question. She even pointed, but managed to bite her lip to keep her joy contained. Like the Vice President, she had high cheekbones, and was nearly as tall as him. Her long blond hair matched his and I figured she must be his daughter.

The Vice President stepped over to the Overlord. The girl wandered over to the aliens to look at them, paying no attention to me, or to the leader of the most powerful race in the galaxy. As they stepped through the throng of Thieves, I noticed other men and women, dressed in fine clothes or suits or robes, a few dozen or so.

"I assume you recognise me. I haven't aged a day since I met the Larceny," the Vice President said, drawing my attention away from yet more humans.

My eyes darted up and down his body. He was taller, I was sure of it, and his suit, though well-made, couldn't hide a more angular physique than a human should have. Underneath those clothes he had Thief implants, just like my former friends.

"What are you doing here? How are you here?" I asked.

"That is a long story. One I will tell you after you have officially joined us," the Vice President said.

I stared back into the green eyes that fixed me with a steady gaze. The Vice President seemed immovable, stern like a headmaster who has the student's respect and fear.

"Sir, why have you joined with the Thieves?" I asked.

The Vice President turned and nodded to the Overlord. "I met these creatures years ago. I spoke with them right as their attacks on our world began. I realised they were the future of the human race. They could be our allies and help us become better."

"Better how?" I practically wailed. Seeing the man who had been a beacon of light to the world now tell me to join the very aliens who ruined Earth.

"Callum, you know what the world was like when the Destroyer arrived. Climate change had altered the planet, and our attempts to mitigate its affects were only a temporary measure. More countries had become independent. The European Union was no more. Great wars loomed as our race continued to divide itself more and more in myriad new ways.

"I despaired. I was a young CEO—with businesses all over the world —trying to make things like nanites that could elevate us. But each innovation failed because humanity kept dividing. Even an enemy like fascism, like ecological collapse couldn't bring us together.

"But we changed when the Ark landed. We changed so quickly that former enemies stood side by side in the fight. Then I saw the possibilities. We were finally coming together, so I went into politics to help shepherd in this new era. And I was made Vice President right when the Destroyer arrived. Then I was overcome with sadness because this enemy couldn't be defeated. To my surprise, they made contact with me. They saw in humanity a kindred spirit, and so we became their allies."

"With the people who destroyed everything? They destroyed the world... destroyed America," I said and pointed at him and he looked at my finger disapprovingly.

I let the finger drop, but I was shaking with my fists clenched.

"Callum, this may be news to you, but the world was falling apart long before the Larcony came along. The decisions made by bad leaders had led us to a climate collapse, and failed to bring order or help those who should be saved. We thought the world was going to end when the Larceny arrived, but they were our salvation. I was able to convince them to save those who could be saved."

"Bad leaders? You're the vice president. You're one of the leaders and you think you deserve to be here?" I asked.

"Bad leaders like those who failed to let the titans of our world succeed. Bad leaders who gave away resources that would have pushed us quicker to the technologies we needed! Bad leaders who encouraged those who drain our society! I was never one of them."

He took a few steps towards me hands held behind his back.

"I proved that to you. I kept the world together."

"Dr. Ghost—" I began.

"Dr. Ghost, my friend, was wrong. His plan to save a remnant chosen for high minded reasons was never going to work. So, I let him do it while I saved the people who should be saved—the best of mankind. They understood that the only way for billions of humans to live on—to have our interstellar society—was to accept a short term loss. And we will soon enact a far grander scheme than either the Larceny or Humanity could ever conceive of alone."

My brain was whirling. There were still so many questions.

But I didn't need answers from the Vice President. I already knew the truth. My people had fallen. They were allies and enablers of genocide and pain. And I could join them. What was the alternative? Turn my back on them and be alone, truly alone?

I thought about asking for leniency for my alien friends, but I knew they would never grant it.

I looked at the Ramothian president and saw in him another species about to be subjugated. Everything I had seen on their world was about to be corrupted or destroyed. I looked at the aliens, some resigned to their fate, others glaring and staring daggers at the Thieves and my fellow humans.

I had to choose right there and now. Either join my people and their way, or go alone. This was the higher moral calling that Antumbra had mentioned. Was sticking by my people the right path? Or was siding against them?

The Overlord moved over to stand with my friends.

"Your way is clear. Your only other choice is subjugation," the Overlord said. "I will not risk my people's future, not when I lived in the times when we almost destroyed ourselves. I will not go back to those days."

"Well, Callum, what say you?

"Will you join your people?"

My chest was heaving as I stared out into space. I felt like I was drowning. I was overwhelmed. I had to choose between safety, comfort, power—the end of scarcity, and resisting the Larceny. My people were truly safe for once, at the head of a power with no rivals. If I fought back, we might never be so safe again.

"Take your place on your new home," the Vice President said.

Suddenly, one choice fell away. Maybe those words had cut deep into the gifts I had been given, into the training and programming One had once—that I had now. The call to fight those who had tried to destroy humanity triggered in my mind. I gazed around at my friends, who I did not recognise.

My deep breathing stopped. My muscles tensed.

"My home is gone, and you destroyed it," I replied.

I pulled my gun and fired.

DESTROYING THE DESTROYER

The gun clicked, but didn't fire. I frowned down at it. It should have worked.

"I don't know why you thought that would help?" the Overlord said, staring down the barrel of the gun. "Killing me just means another will take my place."

Ogwambi pulled out the power cell for the gun.

"I had hoped you would join us. I thought maybe you would turn to us—away from these aliens. There was always a risk, though, that you would side with them. How could I know for sure? Luckily, this has proven that you will never be one of us," he said coldly.

"You're not our Callum," Gerlinde said.

"He would have helped us, after all he went through," Illarion said.

My gun arm drooped. My other hand went for my sword.

"Don't bother, Callum," Koyla said in a bored voice.

I had been fooled. I had made my choice—proven my colours. My people were no more. I was truly alone, and looking into the faces of those who had abandoned everything that it meant to be an Arkonaut.

Then I realised they had not abandoned everything it means to be human... This was who we are. The dream to send a remnant of the human race out into the void to survive and start again fresh and free of the past, was a failure. We would never live up to that dream. We were always a species that would keep failing.

I looked at the gun, and looked at the Antumbra and the others. I would help them, and humanity be damned for all the mistakes it had made. In one fluid movement, I turned on the spot to face my alien friends. I flicked my wrist and the gun barrel spun around giving satisfying clicks.

The barrel glowed as the spinning charged the weapon, just as the gunsmith who had sold it to me said.

I had a single shot ready and aimed at Pebbles' tiny prison. I fired.

A blast shot out and cut through one of the rings, which damaged the seal and the machinery. The bubble split open and fell apart. Pebbles fell out, tumbled forward, and then steadied himself on his feet.

The blond-haired girl stepped away.

The Thieves stepped back.

Pebbles slowly turned to me.

"Keep them busy," I said.

Pebbles ran past me and immediately threw one of his fists forward towards the Overlord.

"Kill them," the Overlord bellowed, as Pebbles' fist came roaring towards him, and another Thief jumped in the way, taking the rock the face, which shattered some of the mechanical implants it had.

Pebbles advanced, and my enhanced ears heard the whine of power cells in guns getting ready to fire.

I grabbed the kinetic shield from my chest and activated it while throwing it over my friends. The shield expanded, but unable to project itself around a person, it just created a bubble around the others.

They all came to life, rising and turning to pummel the Thieves who at first were so shocked by my actions that they could not react.

I drew my new sword and snapped it out in one fluid movement. I stabbed the Thief behind Antumbra in one of its eyes, and it fell backwards, sliding off the blade.

My next slice removed Antumbra's restraints, so she lit up—her hands burning like magnesium—and she sliced off Mantis' and Lyger's restraints. Hippo simply broke his, and the Mouth didn't bother. He merely bit a chunk out of the Thief guarding him.

While all this was going on, Pebbles was beyond the shield wall causing chaos, throwing his arms, and legs, at any Thief.

Koyla tried to catch him, using his mechanical arm, but the arm simply caved in.

The Thieves tried to return fire, but Pebbles was too small and moved too quickly.

"What do we do, Callum?" Antumbra asked, once everyone was free and under the dome.

"We need to get off this ship," I said.

"To do what? The Thieves are still in orbit. They still have a Destroyer," Lyger said.

I looked around the dais where my former crew were fleeing, and saw the Thieves were retreating. The Thieves manning the consoles around the dais were confused. They were not warriors. My eyes fell upon the consoles. The Thieves' language was translated in an instant. and two words caused me to pause: *wormhole generator.*

I looked up at the screen and saw the Destroyer hanging over Ramoth like a knife above its victim's heart.

I ran to the controls for the wormhole generator.

"Callum, what are you doing?" Antumbra asked.

"Evening the odds," I said.

I pressed the activate button.

ESCAPE

I looked up just in time to see on the screen the Destroyer suddenly shatter from the inside. The wormhole I had commanded to appear tore through the vessel from the inside out. The entrance to a wormhole expanded outwards.

Fire and water erupted out of the vessel. The water froze and the fire petered out without oxygen.

The commotion on the dais stopped for a moment as the speakers around the room broadcasted the sound. Even though we were in space the explosion still reached us in shockwaves, and the ship we were on rumbled.

The Overload's jaw dropped at seeing one of its mightiest vessels get torn to pieces. The Greatlord who owned it put its tentacles to its head and screamed.

The Vice President was pale.

The wormhole then sucked in the remains of the vessel, and it was gone.

"Let's get out of here. Hippo, grab the Ramothian president. Pebbles, let's go," I called out.

"Callum, the Timerod," Antumbra said.

In the chaos, I couldn't see which Thief still had it. "We can't get it back," I said.

"But—"

"I'm sorry, Antumbra, we don't have time. We need to go. Don't worry, they can't use it. We know that."

I pushed Antumbra ahead of me and turned back to shout at Pebbles.

"Come on, Rocky," I shouted to the pile of stones keeping the Thieves at bay.

Pebbles threw one of its rocks at the Overlord, and her shield absorbed the impact. Pebbles then ran for the edge of the dais, and his stone arm flew back to him like Mjolnir returning to Thor.

Weapons fire immediately assaulted him, and chips of his body went flying off, but he made it to the edge and leapt into my arms. It was like catching a medicine ball. I threw him ahead of me, as my group ran from the dais and through the network of consoles the Thieves were abandoning.

"Kill them, and bring their corpses to display," the Overlord shouted.

I looked over my shoulder, and my former crew members and a bunch of Thieves reached the edge of the dais, and raised their weapons.

We all dived behind the computers, using them as cover as we made our way across the room.

"Callum, I know you don't have a plan, so come up with one quickly," Antumbra said, as a computer we had just hidden behind exploded.

"We need to fight our way back to the ship," I shouted over the commotion.

"The crew of this ship number in the thousands. They'll all be coming for us," The Mouth said.

"It's our only hope," I said.

"Will they let us fly away from here?" Lyger said.

I thought for a moment. "Mr. President, now that the Destroyer has been ruined, your people can fight back, right?"

The Ramothian president, being carried by Hippo, said, "They can. Our fleet can match theirs."

"We need to let them know," Antumbra said.

"There is a radio on the ship. We get there and we can let them know. The Ramothian fleet can distract them," I said.

"How do we get there?" Hippo said.

"We fight our way there."

●

We were in a running gun battle the whole way.

I went first using my one shot gun to disarm Thieves and their weapons were picked up by the others.

Alarms started sounding around the ship.

"Callum, they're going to ambush us in the docking bay," Antumbra said.

"We have no choice," I replied. "We'll deal with them when we get there."

"I have an idea to get us past them," Ada mentioned.

Our group reached a corner, and as soon as I stuck my head out weapons fire filled the air, and I dodged back. The fire was relentless; the Thieves didn't stop. We couldn't go that way.

"We need to go back," I said, but, from the other direction another wave of fire hemmed us in.

"We're trapped," the Mouth said.

Mantis started walking around us. I heard his energetic arms scrape on the floor.

"What do we do?" the Mouth asked.

"We need some explosives," I said, turning to the group. Mantis, though, continued walking around us. I wondered if he had lost it. "Mouth, can we turn any of these guns in explosives?"

The Mouth turned over his acquired weapon. "Only an EMP."

I looked at Ada.

"Don't worry. I will take the hit," she said.

Mantis completed his encirclement of us.

The floor creaked.

I looked around and saw a circle of molten metal around us, cut into the floor by Mantis' energy scythes.

"Mantis?" I cried out in alarm.

Hippo realised what he had done and jumped.

The second he hit the deck, the floor fell through to the level below. The disc of metal hit the ground, and I felt the jolt through my knees and even in my teeth.

We found ourselves in an empty corridor.

"I can't believe that worked," Hippo said.

"Let's go," I said. Pointing in the direction of the cargo bay.

●

We reached the docking bay, managing to get near the entrance stealthily.

I darted my head around the doorway as quickly as I could, and then darted back.

"The room is full of Thieves waiting to ambush us. Unfortunately, they aren't stupid."

"Well, there is a way to test that," Ada said.

She reached up to her face and literally tore off a chunk of her skin.

"Ada," I barked. "What are you doing?"

"Trust me," she said. And she showed her robot workings. They were actually quite human. Her skull was gold. The flesh beneath was a network of nanites binding themselves together like flesh. She pulled down her sleeve and shoved in a mechanical Thief tentacle she had picked up. It looked almost like she had a tentacle on her arm. Then, she stood tall and marched into the docking bay.

I didn't dare look at what was going on in the docking bay, but I heard the Thieves activate their guns.

"Have the aliens reached the docking bay yet?" I heard Ada yell.

"What's she doing?" Antumbra asked.

Mantis moved forward to look, and I held out a hand to stop him from satisfying his curiosity.

I put a finger to my mouth. "She's pretending to be an Arkonaut."

"No human, we are ready to repel them," a Thief said. They had brought the deception, although why wouldn't they? They were waiting for aliens, and Ada looked like a modified human.

"Has the ship been disabled, just in case?" Ada said, and I noticed that her pace hadn't stopped. She was continuing forward.

"N—no."

"We have to be safe. I'll make sure they can't fly off," she said, and I heard her step onto the ramp going into the ship.

Then I heard gunfire from inside the ship. I heard a mass of tentacles slap the floor like the whole crowd in the docking bay had turned around. The other aliens and I couldn't help but look.

A Thief said, "There they are."

The ship's weapons activated, and Ada swept the blasts over the Thieves guarding the vessel. The Thieves were knocked aside by the blasts. Ada had created a path to the ramp.

"Get going," I said.

We ran for the access ramp and other guns dropped from the ceiling and started firing at the ship.

For a second, the weapons burned the hull. Then Ada activated a shield. She returned fire, strafing the weapons and the walls around the bay. Thankfully the doors didn't get hit. Although one strike burst a water pipe in the ceiling, creating a light shower.

I paused as the others ran, and looked around, seeing a command centre for the bay. I raised my gun, fired through the glass and took out a Thief. The guns fell silent.

Then I followed the others to the ramp.

"President, get you fleet in the air now," I said, and the president ran up the ramp.

"CALLUM!" Ogwambi shouted.

I paused at the foot of the ramp into the ship. Antumbra stopped, too, and looked over my shoulder.

"It's your friends, Callum," she said.

"Get the ship activated," I ordered.

I turned on my heels.

Ogwambi and the others were fanning out from the entrance into the cargo bay. They were led by the blond girl, who been standing next to the Vice President. Her smile was broad, and she was looking at my friends, seemingly enjoying the fact they were scowling at me—their eyes twitching.

I should have got in the ship and taken off instead of facing off in the battle—one like you might see in an old Western. But I needed to face them, so I stepped forward.

And as I did, Antumbra and Ada stood beside me.

"What are you doing?" I asked.

"We're not going to let you face them alone," Antumbra said.

"The President of Ramoth is on the radio. We'll go as soon as we deal with these people," Ada said.

"They are Arkonauts," I said to Ada.

"I used to care for them, Callum. I spent longer with them than you did. I know their backgrounds, even their hopes and dreams. They are not the children I once knew," she said sadly.

The three of us stepped forward.

The water pipe was still spewing out liquid that misted us with a fine rain.

I looked at my former crew. I could hear gears and electronics buzzing from within their bodies. Those implants they had received were an intrusion of the Thieves into their bodies, minds, and maybe souls.

I looked up at the rain, soaking my clothes, sizzling on Antumbra's skin.

"Doesn't this remind you of the day we first met—the leak in the pumping station—when we had a task to perform that brought us together?" I said.

"You mean when we had a common enemy?" Ogwambi said. "When we had a common cause that bound us together? Callum, that's what the Vice President wants, and now humanity has a common cause, and we will be safe forevermore."

"We could save the Arkonauts and have that. Our common cause is making friends, not enemies," I said to them. "We don't have to be this way."

"We don't make enemies. We destroy them," Sanna said.

"Sorry, Callum, our species will survive because of our choices," Koyla declared. I looked into his eyes, hoping to find humour there, but his reply was no joke.

"We're safe," Sanna said, her haji no longer framing a sharp, cheeky smile, but a frown.

"We're still free," Illarion said, his voice deeper than I had ever known it

"We're strong now," Gerlinde said. The serious girl sounded more certain of this than anything she had ever said before.

"Join us and be strong too, Callum," Ogwambi added, his arms wide.

"No. I'm done with the human race if this is our legacy," I said.

Ogwambi nodded solemnly.

Then he shot forward and a knife came out of his arm, right through his flesh.

My sword came up and brushed it aside, and I raised my gun, spinning it fast for the charge, but his other hand smacked my wrist, like a sledge hammer, like its bones were made of metal.

Illarion then lunged in, and Ada was there, blocking the Russian effortlessly with her robotic strength.

The Koyla came in with a punch from his mechanical hand, and Ada grabbed it in her palm.

"Stand down, robot," Koyla said.

Ada lashed out with a kick to Koyla's chin, and he staggered backwards.

"I'm free now, Koyla, and you are no longer under my protection."

Sanna came in at me, but then had to refocus her attention on Antumbra, whose hands flared and swiped at the girl. Sanna's eye actually blazed, and a red beam of energy cut through Antumbra's energetic skin.

She cried out in the pain, but energy on energy wasn't as serious as a gunshot. Her magnesium hands came down on Sanna's head, but Sanna's arms deflected it, the bone barely singing.

The Thieves' upgrades had given them strength.

Gerlinde came in now, her fingernails becoming claws. They swiped at my stomach and tore into my new clothes.

Ogwmabi tried another slash with his arm blade, and I deflected it again, grabbing Gerlinde's wrist and casting her into Ogwambi. My biological enhancements were far superior than the Thieves' and I was faster than both of them.

Then a blast hit me from behind, bursting through my stomach.

I went down onto my knees and cradled my abs. My body immediately started to mend itself.

I looked over my shoulder at the other girl, the Vice President's daughter. She held a gun in her hand, and she holstered it.

She smiled sweetly at my expression and shrugged. "Just making it a fair fight."

I struggled to my feet just as Ogwambi and Gerlinde came back into the fight. I swung my sword to deflect Ogwambi's blade again, and grunted in pain as I stretched, further tearing the wound in my stomach.

Gerlinde and Ogwambi both slashed and slashed and I managed to dodge every strike.

I was now only a shade faster, but also dizzy, despite the closing wound. I had lost some blood and the affects still hit me. I kicked Ogwambi in his side and sent him sprawling.

Gerlinde came at me with her claws, and I managed to interlace my fingers with hers, and then exerted pressure on her hand to force her to her knees. I then kneed her in her head, sending her spinning in the air.

Ogwambi was back at me. My wound had finally healed, and I was strong again. I dogged each slash. Then his veins started to glow, and I realised they weren't veins... they were power lines.

I had to use my sword to block stronger and stronger blows.

"I'm going to kill you, Callum. The Overlord has commanded it and I can't disobey."

More slashes, each one closer and closer as his body powered up.

I knew that in a moment I would have one final choice to make.

"Stop it, Ogwambi," I said.

He didn't relent.

"Stop it. I will not die here today."

"You can't save us. We're happy. We're complete," he said through gritted teeth, sweat beading on his brow. "Humanity is finally safe for all time. We have power. No natural disaster can harm us. We have allies. We have technology. Nothing can stop us. We never have to worry again."

Stop it," I said, as another slash brushed my calf. "Stop it! Stop it! Please don't."

"I can't. I tried to save you and you turned on us."

"Stop. Don't make me cross the line."

"Cross it. Prove to me you truly aren't human anymore," Ogwambi spat, and his last stab went through my shoulder.

My arm flared in pain and I dropped my sword. My other free hand caught it, and now that I knew that he would kill me. I made a decision and stabbed him in the stomach.

His eyes widened and he let out a mangled gasp. I then pulled his blade out of my shoulder.

He went down cradling his belly.

"Sorry, Ogwambi. You should be joining me, not the other way around."

Ogwambi gritted his gold teeth—now framed by blood that he spat at me. A mechanical tendril suddenly wrapped around my neck, and pulled me back.

I grabbed it and tried pulling it free, but it wrapped tighter.

It led right back to the Vice President's daughter. The whip had erupted from her arm.

My head felt light as the tendril choked my brain of oxygen. I tried to pull at it, but the girl merely let more whip coil out, and I almost fell over expecting resistance and finding none.

As I tried to exhale, I thought desperately for a way out. My strength wasn't working. My nanites couldn't help me, and she seemed just as fast. Then I remembered one biological enhancement given to me by the pod One had stuck me in.

I opened my mouth wide and bit down on the tendril.

"What are you doi—" the girl gasped.

My mouth burned as my salvia ate away at the tendril. My own spit melting my flesh as fast as it melted the metal. Dr. Ghost had given me the power to bite my way out of emergencies with acid-like saliva.

The tendril then snapped. The remains retracted back into the girl's arm and she gritted her teeth and seethed.

"Who are you?" I asked the girl, rounding on her, my mouth already healing.

She snorted and said. "Just think of me as Three."

She brought up her gun, but before she could fire, Antumbra was there and slicing through the barrel.

She backed off from Antumbra's glowing hands.

I looked around to see Sanna lying on the floor, her clothing burnt and scratched. I looked for Ada and saw that she was repeatedly punching Illarion in the face, but aside from a bloody nose he wasn't going down. His skull must have been reinforced to withstand her blows.

Suddenly Antumbra was thrown into me. My flesh sizzled as she struck me, and we went sprawling.

"This game ends here," Three said.

Then a rock struck her stomach and Three was forced backwards.

Ada, Antumbra and I turned to see Pebbles running as fast as he could towards us. He threw another rock.

The girl managed to stagger to one side and dodge it.

Pebbles motioned for us to get back to the ship.

I picked up Antumbra, ignoring the burns and said, "Let's go, Ada."

She dropped Illarion on top of Koyla, who had lost his robotic arm.

As I ran for the ship, the docking bay door started to open. The atmosphere was being held in by a thin blue shield. Outside the ship Ramothian vessels were rising from the planet. Thief ships were being taken down, swamped by the fleet that outnumbered them on their home turf, without a Destroyer also in orbit. Some fire assaulted the ship we were on, and it shuddered.

"Pebbles! Time to go," I shouted when we reached the ramp of the ship.

More weapons fire broke through the atmospheric shield and struck the inside of the docking bay, blowing up some parked Thief ships.

"Now, Pebbles!"

But Pebbles wouldn't retreat. He kept flinging his arms and legs at Three, but she dodged them, or whipped them out of the air. She then backed off, raised a hand, and pulled it down. Following the movements of her arm multiple weapons came out the ceiling, somehow controlled by her.

All the guns fired at Pebbles and he was stuck by more weapons fire than I had even seen him take. He resisted a few blasts then turned on his feet to run for the ship. His front was pockmarked. There was even some molten lava leaking from the cracks. The little alien tried to weave out the way, but other blasts hit his back.

Someone inside our ship activated the guns, and fired at the weapons in the ceiling, taking some out.

Then one blast hit Pebbles in the right spot and the rock creature split open. Shards of rock were flung everywhere and one shard caught me in the cheek. Hot blood ran down my face, and I pulled the shard free.

"Pebbles," Ada cried out, and she went forward to where the remains of the alien settled in a small mound that didn't move.

Antumbra grabbed her and pulled her back. "He's gone."

Three was laughing coldly. Then she moved her arm and the remaining ceiling guns focused on the ship.

A shield dropped around the vessel again, and the weapons stuck that, keeping us safe.

"Time to go," Antumbra said, and she led the way up the ramp, which started to close.

I looked down at Pebbles' remains, and grasped the flint-like shard in my hand so tightly it cut me. I had just watched a human destroy what remained of an entire species.

I stared daggers at Three.

She smiled back.

My former friends stood around her, cradling their injuries and scowling at me. Their faces disappeared as the ramp closed, sealing me in with those who were not my kind, but who I had chosen as my people.

VICTORY

The ship rocked as it was assaulted by weapons fire.

Lyger was at the controls, and she took the ship up and out of the docking bay. The space around the planet Ramoth was in chaos, as Thief ships engaged a Ramothian fleet that wasn't just Ramothian ships. Other vessels from aliens living on Ramoth were attacking too.

The Thief ships were backing off, opening wormholes that they disappeared into. The Overlord's ship left, too, harassed all the way.

"Where's Pebbles?" the Mouth asked.

"He's gone," Antumbra said.

The Mouth looked around as if in a daze. He started breathing in deeply.

"Dead? He's dead!" He said then he turned away for the group and held a hand to his mouth and whimpered.

I looked down at the shard of Pebbles I had saved, then I pocketed it.

In silence, Lyger took the ship down to the planet, now fully under Ramothian control. We passed by the same city where we had arrived. Out the window, I could see Thieves—either dead or captured and imprisoned.

At the Ramothian president's direction, Lyger took the ship down to a central government building and landed on a spot surrounded not just by Ramothians, but also other species.

"Please, friends, come with me," the president of Ramoth said.

Solemnly, we left the ship and went outside.

The president was greeted by officials, and he exchanged quick words with them.

As our group moved forward I noticed that I was not on the receiving end of dirty looks this time. In fact, there was a modicum of respect in the eyes of the aliens looking at me. This still made me uncomfortable. Before I knew exactly how they felt about me. They had hated me and I had hidden behind the kinetic shields' camouflage. Now, I was uncertain. What did this change mean?

As the president exchanged more words with his officials, I turned away from the attention, and looked up into the sky. My eyes zoomed and focused on the activity above. The sky was dominated by numerous wormholes that the Thieves had used to escape. One Thief ship hadn't made it, and was currently being mobbed and destroyed by Ramothian and other alien ships. The Ramothians were also placing devices around the wormholes, and I watched them project something that caused them to shrink.

I guess they didn't want the Thieves to have quick and easy access to their planet.

"Callum," Ada said, and I turned round to meet the eyes of hundreds of aliens, all staring at me.

"I'm sorry. I was distracted."

"There is no need," the Ramothian president said, holding up a hand. "Everyone here is aware of the sacrifice you made for our world. We have never seen the like before, a person turning on his own species to save others. Today, you could have had everything, and you turned it all down for a greater purpose." The president then bowed to me.

The other Ramothians offered the same gesture.

It didn't make me feel warm inside. Instead, I felt a little raucous. I might have killed Ogwambi. I had turned my back on humanity, and stood with their enemy.

"How did you do this? Why did you do this?" the Ramothian president asked. "What allowed you to leave all that you ever knew behind?"

There was only one thing to take solace in, one thing to give me joy in this moment. I had done the right thing. There was a higher moral calling. I wanted humans to survive because otherwise all the pain and suffering so many had experienced to push humanity forward would have been in vain. But deep down, when confronted with the choice, did all that pain and suffering merit the same pain and suffering in others? The answer was no. Humanity did not deserve to survive just because they existed.

I looked around at the aliens. "I believe that the consequences of our choices don't end with our deaths. I don't believe that I owe loyalty to anything, but what is right. My people abandoned that principal. I have not, and that's why I turned on them—that's why I could. I don't want to be someone who can live with himself, knowing he's done wrong, knowing his people have hurt others."

The aliens seemed to accept these words.

"You're welcome on our world, Callum Tasker of Earth. You have saved my people, and those we call friends," the Ramothian president said, and gestured to the assembled refugee aliens. "We will celebrate our victory in time. Now, we must mourn those killed and prepare for the future."

At that declaration to the assembled group, the crowd started to break apart and chat.

My friends and I stepped back from the throng, and we all stood in a circle. We had our own mourning to do.

I dug into my pocket and held out the shard of Pebbles—a sliver of flint-like stone—covered in my own dried blood.

The Mouth hung his head.

"On my planet, it is traditional to say a few things about the dead, to remember good times," I said.

"On mine, the energy of the dead rejoins the Great Stream, and we mourn and celebrate," Antumbra said.

"We do not speak to the dead. We only envy them," Lyger said. "But it's a bitter envy."

"The race of mountains did not mourn death," the Mouth said. "Until a Destroyer came to my world, they never died. They simply eroded away and their dust would eventually become new stone. The new mountains would take over from the old," the Mouth said. "This is a new kind of death."

He took the shard from my hand and cradled it. Then he placed it on the ground and gestured for my gun, which I gave him. He smashed the shard to pieces, then ground the pieces to dust. He picked up as much as he could and blew the dust into the air, which took it into the sky.

"The old become the new in time," the Mouth said.

I reflected that it was like a cremation. Rock to stone, stone to dust, Pebbles returned to the ground.

Our group nodded to one another, and broke up, silently mourning apart around our new ship. Ada stuck with me as I walked out from under the ship's shade and into the sun.

"I'm sorry I didn't tell you what I was," Ada said.

I waved her concern away. "Not a problem," I said.

"Do you know I'm a new species now? I'm the first robot freed from humanity—free to make my own decisions," Ada said.

"I didn't think about that," I said.

"Thank you for giving me a good example to live by," she said.

I chuckled. "Thank goodness. Maybe our legacy won't be so bad after all."

"Unless I screw up as well," Ada said. "I did spend my first few months of freedom telling you a lie."

"Humanity started much the same way," I said. "But if you learn from that now, rather than never learning from it, you might do better than we did."

I stared up into the sky watching a wormhole shrink.

"Are you okay, Callum?" she asked.

"On the other side of that wormhole is the Thief homeworld, and on it, my people are preparing to destroy another world. They said I was no longer human. I feel a loneliness that no human has ever felt before. Even the worst of my kind were still considered human by someone, even the very worst had friends and family. I have been cast aside by all that was supposed to comfort me."

"If I may, why not think about how you're now part of something else? You're not like them anymore. You're like us," Ada said, and gestured to the others.

I allowed myself a small smile. I no longer had to think of myself as human.

"But I still come from their world, and I'm still a little like them."

"So, it's like you said. You don't owe humanity anything. You owe everything to what's right."

Then she turned around and left me alone.

Antumbra filled the void almost immediately.

"Callum, the Thieves have my Timerod."

"I know, and like I said—Don't worry. They can't use it effectively."

"That's just it. I've been thinking about it since our flight from the Overlord. My race never fully understood the Rod and the implications of the technology. We made it for one purpose, in accordance with our beliefs. The Thieves have time and their own planet's resources to fully understand it."

"Are you saying they might be able to use it after all?"

"They won't be able to go back to a point in time before when we used it, no. But even a day is enough to change the course of history in their favour."

I looked away, trying to think of something to calm her fears.

"We'll deal with it if we have to. There's nothing they can do to change our resolve and our mission—to end their blight on this galaxy."

Antumbra nodded gently. I wasn't sure if she believed my words.

She left me alone and I looked up into the sky.

The wormhole was nearly gone. The sky was clouding over, with darkness squeezing in my view of the hole in space. I dwelled on an awful thought. Sometime in the past, the crew had passed through a wormhole. And no doubt they did not come upon a new homeworld, but actually the Thieves' homeworld. All the wormholes lead back to the

Thieves. There was a time they were innocent, but that time passed, and they became what they are now.

I couldn't go back and change it. That moment had already happened, and there could be no more time travel.

That raised questions in my mind. How did Dr. Ghost not know that he made a mistake to send the Ark through the wormhole? Surely, he, or his scientists, must have realised that the planet onto other side was the Thieves' homeworld. What had gone wrong with a plan years in the making—with all the resources of Earth at its disposal?

The wormhole disappeared, and it started to rain. Feeling the water on my face, and standing under a sky, was like meeting an old friend. I had not experienced rain for years and years. As an Englishman, I could finally discuss the weather with someone again. And in this welcome, long forgotten, and familiar moment, I found a little peace.

I knew it wouldn't last.

THE PAST

I sat in the cafeteria, eating my dinner, surrounded by friends. They were happy and laughing, and best of all, back on course.

I laughed at jokes with real joy, spraying food everywhere.

I tried to ignore a tiny part of me that called out *you must be sad.* I had succeeded because I confronted it, mastered it, and now I was burying it, not to be forgotten, but to keep it below the surface. It would live forever in my mind, to be remembered for the lesson it taught, not for the pain it brought.

We heard scraping all around us, a now familiar sound. Our robotic allies' ship didn't perfectly fit on our Ark, so it scratched the hull during minor course corrections.

"Every three hours," Koyla said. "I won't be able to get my beauty sleep."

The rest of us all opened our mouths for the obvious retort, but instead caught each other's eyes as we did. So, we all laughed at the joke we didn't have to tell.

"What are you laughing about?" Koyla asked, frowning.

We all just stifled the laughs and brushed him off.

Moana, Ogwambi, Illarion, Gerlinde and I all had to field questions about our journey; everyone coming in for dinner wanted to hear about our adventure.

After dinner we went to the observation platform and watched the wormhole recede into the distance.

At some point Sanna joined us. She stank of salt and fish.

"How was your time with the beast below?" Moana asked her.

"I can't get rid of the smell, despite a change of clothes," she said scowling. "All that beast wants to do is explore shipwrecks."

"You can thank me for that," I said.

"In that case, I want your water rations, Maiara, so I can have another shower," Sanna said.

We all laughed.

The wormhole slipped away.

"Not long now until we reach our new planet," Koyla said.

"At least we can land now," Illarion stated.

"It feels weird," Gerlinde said. "Did you ever have to go on a long journey before, in a car or plane, and when you reached the other side you realised that the trip was actually a lot of fun? I will miss this."

"There will be a lot of settling in when we get there," Moana said.

"We will have to build houses, and do farming," I said.

"Do you think we'll continue to live on the Ark?" Koyla said.

"It will be a long commute. The Arks' almost 25 kilometres across at its widest. I think we'll be moving off," I said.

"Did anyone see any cars in the cargo bay?" Illarion asked. "We could drive to the edge of the Ark every day, in order to explore the planet."

"Guy, guys... Let's worry about that later. Instead, enjoy what's left of the journey," Gerlinde said.

Illarion put his arm around her. "You're only saying that because you like looking at the stars."

She shrugged in agreement.

I sighed as the ship continued to move off. "Whatever happens, I think there will be lots for us to do when we reach our new home, and we will never be bored."

Acknowledgements

Big thanks to Nate for his continued work on the Stolen Futures series and the whole Spaceboy Books team.

About the Author

M. Drewery has been writing for 22 years and is a life long sci-fi fan. He lives in a little village in Surrey, England. The only people who know it exists are the people who live there. One day he'll write a book where an ancient evil, that slumbers beneath the village, will rise to destroy it and end the world, just to put it on the map. You can find more about him at www.mdrewery.co.uk.

About the Publishing Team

Nate Ragolia was labeled as "weird" early in elementary school, and it stuck. He's a lifelong lover of science fiction, and a nerd/geek. In 2015 his first book, *There You Feel Free,* was published by 1888's Black Hill Press. He's also the author of *The Retroactivist,* published by Spaceboy Books. He founded and edits BONED, an online literary magazine, has created webcomics, and writes whenever he's not playing video games or petting dogs.

Shaunn Grulkowski has been compared to Warren Ellis and Phillip K. Dick and was once described as what a baby conceived by Kurt Vonnegut and Margaret Atwood would turn out to be. He's at least the fifth best Slavic-Latino-American sci-fi writer in the Baltimore metro area. He's the author of *Retcontinuum,* and the editor of *A Stalled Ox* and *The Goldfish,* among others.